SERENITY

E. G. KEITH

GREMLYN PRODUCTIONS

DEDICATION

For the most generous person I know: my father.

PRONUNCIATION GUIDE

Ruri [**ru**-ree]

Merrik [**meh**-rik]

Veridet [**vehr**-a-det]

Soigner [**swen**-ye]

Combatants [**kom**-ba-tants]

Pugnatores [**pug**-nah-tor-eez]

Solis [**soh**-lis]

SERENITY

E. G. KEITH

PROLOGUE

FINN

When I wake, my head is pounding. My eyes water as I glance around at my dark surroundings. There's an eerie feeling in Room 106, a feeling I do not wish to mess with.

Despite my not wanting it to, a high-pitched sound of cowardice escapes my throat. There's a deep, rhythmic pounding in my ears, like the spirits that possess the room are laughing at me, at how pathetic I must look.

I reach up and touch my flaming cheeks. My fingers are coated in blood and grime and dirt, and my face is wet with white-hot tears. I swallow roughly, wishing I was anywhere but here, awaiting my death.

Through the window, I see dirt mixing with creeks, forming wet clumps of mud that well in the dry ground. I try to find comfort in that, but there's really nothing comforting about a basic cycle.

"You will die today, Finn Brocker," says a voice from above, taunting me. Its words float through my ears and I shiver as hot breath runs down my spine. "It is inevitable. You came into our home, disrupted our slumber. We have seen your cruel actions, and you will die for them."

I sniff. It's really the most unmanly thing I could do at this time, but I don't care. Not when I'm about to be killed.

I lost Ashlyn, the only girl I have ever loved, and I lost her friends, my enemies. I lost my guards and my home and my kingdom and my prisoner and my revenge, and I am about to lose my life. It's not a happy thought, but a humbling one, one that gets me to my senses.

I peer around the room, squinting to see the fuzzier objects in the dark. I feel around with my calloused hands for my sword, but it's nowhere I can reach. I take in the smell of smoke and blood and death and my nose wrinkles in disgust. With a start, I realize that the body of the girl I killed is below me, below my hands, and I draw them back quickly, resisting the urge to gag.

"Any last words?" the voice hisses in my ear, a final, fatal question.

I struggle to find my strength. "Y-you are h-horrible," I manage, and then my voice fails.

The spirit laughs. "Maybe," it says with amusement, "but you are much worse. And that is why I will make your death slow, as slow as possible. So, you can feel every last bit of it."

Something hard hits my back, launching me forward, onto my stomach. My clothes are shredded, and my hands can't stop the fall quickly enough, so I get splinters and a gash in the middle of my forehead. I groan in pain, but the spirit is back at it again, whacking at my back with incredible force.

The spirits continue to hit me until I can feel the blood spilling onto my clothes, until the dampness and gore of it registers with the situation, until my mind catches up with my body. *I'm dying,* is one of my thoughts. Another, bitter one breathes, *And it's all because of that girl.*

Anger consumes me. The pain fades into a dull throb as I focus all my energy on this anger. Then, just as before, everything goes dark.

* * *

When I open my eyes for the second time, there is no more pain. In fact, there's no more Room 106. All I see is white, blinding light. I reach up and touch my forehead, and I am surprised when no blood comes back on my fingers. The spirits and their horrid whispers are gone, left back in Room 106. I stand and almost fall over again, but then a door appears out of nowhere, and I use the doorknob to stabilize myself.

The dark color of the door helps me adjust my eyes, and I blink a few times. The door is so random that I want to laugh, but my throat has closed and I don't have the strength to. I do the only thing I can: I walk through the door.

Immediately, I am hit with the absurdity of what's inside. A crackling fire sits to one side of the dimly lit room. Carpets below my soles drown my feet, and the wallpaper is a flattering shade of red. It looks like the room was decorated by Eve, the goddess of holidays.

I stand there for a bit, my mouth open. Then a loud, booming voice comes from the other side of the red wall. "You finally came!" it declares. "I was hoping I'd see you."

I freeze. I recognize that voice.

Then, Ashlyn's mother steps into the room, carrying a plate of cookies.

She smiles warmly at me, but I can't do anything. This woman…she's dead. Ashlyn killed her. She's *dead.* How in the gods' names is this possible?

"W-wha—?" I trail off. This *can't* be possible.

"Hello, dear," says Eliana Kave, the corners of her mouth tilting upwards. "I have missed you. Desperately."

Her strange pause sends chills down my spine. "What do you mean, you missed me? I—I have failed you, have I not? Your daughter—s-she got away from me."

"Perhaps." Eliana's smile never fades. "You have kept her alive, and that is all I wanted. Trust me, Merrik has a plan for my daughter. He will take care of her." Her sincere smile turns into a smirk. "And, if you wish, my daughter will be your wife. I give you my permission." She laughs, like there's nothing wrong with the current situation.

Meanwhile, I stare at her. Millions of questions run through my mind, but mostly, the one that's screaming at me the loudest is: "Who is Merrik?"

Eliana smiles again. "You will find out soon enough, Finn. You have done well. You are not dead. You have made room for him. He will reward you for that."

"Eliana—" I start, but I am cut off when she turns around, her floor-length black silk dress almost hitting me.

"Come," she orders, and I follow after her through another door that has randomly appeared, into a different room.

In this room, the tones are more neutral. There's a white counter with black accents on it, and the kitchen tiles are the traditional black and white. Eliana surveys the room, then glances back at me proudly, beaming. "You could have all you ever wanted with him, Finn. He will give you everything. All you have to do is—"

Before she can tell me what I have to do, two children with bright smiles that match Eliana's and hair the color of a raven's feathers come bounding toward her, wrapping their skinny arms around her waist. They have come from another room in this house, somewhere I do not want to imagine. Eliana hugs them back, her smile growing larger still, though I don't know how it's possible.

"Hello, my darlings," she greets, talking to the boys. They stand protectively next to her after hugging her, like she means a lot to them.

"Who are they?" I ask, glancing from the children to Eliana.

"My children, Finn," she says, but after she says it, I don't want to listen. "Aren't they adorable?"

"*Ashlyn* is your child, Eliana," I say. "What do you mean?"

Eliana sighs. "After Ashlyn killed me, which I did not appreciate, I wandered a bit. Finally, once you took her in, Merrik appeared. He promised me all I could ever want, just for the price of selling my soul to him. I agreed, of course, because it was a good deal. I got a new husband, and I got these children—seven years old now. This is Erik, named after Merrik, and this is Geoff, named after…Geoff." She flashes a smile. "Oh and guess who my husband is. Guess, guess, guess!"

Eliana has changed. She is no longer the mother I wished I had. She is no longer the strong, independent woman who told me she had just the plan to destroy Magics. She is someone unrecognizable, yet familiar at the same time. She is like my own mother. The one who abandoned me.

"Sold your soul?" I ask, aghast. "How could you do that?"

"Is that your guess?" Eliana says. "Well, that's not it. I married *Merrik*! Oh, I was so surprised. Especially since otherworldly powers don't normally tend to stay around too long, considering the upcoming war, and the fact that I am basically forever in his debt. I guess it was just...meant to be."

"Otherworldly powers? War? Forever in his debt? Marriage?" I shake my head, bile creeping up my throat. The pain is coming back, though slowly, and I can feel my time here with her running out. "Eliana, what *happened* to you?"

"*Merrik* happened!" she says cheerfully. "Isn't it great? You should join him, if you want to win. That's what he told me to tell you. He said he will be on the winning side of the war. He will help you get revenge. He will help you marry Ashlyn and kill her friends. All you have to do is sell your soul to him. Easy."

I glance at Eliana, then down at her children. Her *new* children. They have no idea what she has done, what she will do to get wherever she needs to. They are not ready.

But, at the same time, am I?

Am I ready to give up my freedom, my *soul,* just for revenge and marrying Ashlyn, the two things I have craved ever since I saw her looking for refuge at my doorstep?

No, a small voice says in my mind. It is quiet but powerful. *You are stronger than this, Finn Brocker. You can do great things. Do not listen to him.*

Yes, says another one. *Give in to me, and you will never have to think about consequences again. You will have whatever you desire. Doesn't that sound nice?*

Yes, I think.

Another door opens, and I walk through it.

CHAPTER 1

SELENA

I come face to face with a Healer as soon as my eyes open. She has an old but strong face, intimidating, wise eyes, and is wearing a nurse's uniform. I can tell she's a Healer because of her clothes—and the fact that as she works, a tingling sensation buzzes through my senses like something's about to explode.

I cough, and blood splatters onto my clothes. The Healer's eyes widen slightly, but she just goes right back to work.

"Who—who are you?" I ask, my throat aching.

"It's best if you don't talk right now, sweetie," the Healer tells me, and there's pity in those dark eyes of hers. "You were in severe condition when they brought you in. We want to reduce the bleeding and heal you quickly, so try not to talk or move too much."

I shake my head, confused. It sends pain ricocheting through me like a bullet. "They brought me in? Who is 'they'?"

"The spirits."

I study her, expecting to see a tiny bit of joking manner, but her expression is the same as before. She's completely serious.

That makes me chuckle, despite the pain it causes. "What do you mean, the *spirits*? *What* spirits? Is this all a big joke? I thought I was dead. I—I *hoped* I was dead. Then I wouldn't have to fight anymore. I'd get to see my brother again. I wouldn't have to see my kingdom go to ruins. I—I *wanted* to die." I'm talking quickly, frantically reaching for something to hold on to.

The Healer says nothing. Instead, she insists on cleaning my wounds. She dabs at my eyebrow with a wet cloth, and my blood comes back, soaking the rag, staining it.

"What is your name?" she finally asks.

"Selena," I respond, though with the pain I'm experiencing and the fuzziness that has become my memory, I'm sure my name is all I can say right now. "S-Selena Torsney."

My name, especially my surname, reminds me of my brother, and the fact that he's dead. It's a sobering thought, and it makes my memory not so fuzzy. I glance around the room I'm in, which is a stark contrast from Room 106, where Finn stabbed me in the stomach with a sword. The walls are white and I'm sitting on what seems to be a hospital bed, and the concoctions and medicines beside me on a dark wood side table prove my theory. The Healer looks kind enough, but her clothes are splattered with blood—most likely mine.

Then, once I can regain my senses long enough to answer more than one of her questions, the Healer senses it. She says, "My name is Lillian. I'm sixty-seven. How old are you, Selena?"

"Twenty-three," I respond. "I'm twenty-three."

"Good, good. Do you have any family, Selena? A spouse? Mother, father? Siblings?"

"I used to," I reply as her cloth moves down to my stomach, where the main wound is. I'm wearing a hospital gown, I notice. "Before…before they killed him."

Lillian hesitates. "Who killed who?"

"My brother," I try. "Dead. Guards."

A look of pity flashes on Lillian's face. "Do you have any parents?"

"My dad left. Drinking. And my mom—she's crazy."

"Any friends?"

"Elysian and Sage." I pause. "And Ash. Milo…I don't know what he is."

Lillian smiles faintly. "That's good, dear. Your wound is almost cleaned, and then we'll give you some *soigner* as soon as you're ready."

"Heal," I say, "in French." The translation pops into my mind quickly, and it's gone just as quickly, replaced by the constant pounding.

Her smile doesn't fade, even as she throws the rag to the side and stands from the bed, filing through the different medicines on the side table. "That's right."

Finally, she must find what she's looking for, because she opens a bottle, pours two pills into her hand, and puts them into mine.

After she's done with that, she gives me a plastic cup of water and I gulp down the pills, eager to be rid of this pain.

Lillian studies my blood-soaked hospital gown. "I'll get you a new outfit. You stay here, okay? And no exploring."

She leaves the room, and I'm honestly grateful, for it gives me an opportunity to look around. The room is pretty big, and there's a curtain separating me from the other side of the room. On my left, there's a window letting bright light stream in. The hospital is cheery, I think, but as a man missing fingers and screaming while blood spills from a gash across his chest passes by my door, those thoughts disappear pretty quickly.

I swallow and force my eyes away from the sight as nausea sets in. I glance down at my bloody hospital gown. Most of the blood is in random splatters, but there's one spot of blood that's in a straight line, right where Finn stabbed me. The memory makes my blood roar in my ears, makes anger stir up inside of me. *How* dare *he stab me,* says a voice in the back of my mind, one I want to listen to. However, a bigger, louder voice says, *Don't you deserve it?*

It doesn't sound like mine, even when I can't really hear it. Then I realize I *can* hear it. It's not in my head at all.

I raise my gaze and lock eyes with a tall, cloaked figure. The cloak's head restricts his face from view, but I can tell we are having an intense staring contest. I glare, and he does not look away. He simply lowers his cloak, and he takes my breath away.

His skin is the color of sand, his hair a tone not too different. His eyes are a surprisingly blue color, the color of a clear day's sky. He has a taunting, cocky smirk on his face, and though he has a slight resemblance to my brother, there is some sort of power that radiates from him.

"Well?" asks the man. He looks about my age, if not older, but there are centuries trapped in his stance, in his smirk, in his eyes. "Don't you?"

I register what he's talking about, and then my jaw clenches. "Don't I," I reply snarkily, and the man raises an eyebrow. "If *he* deserves to stab *me,* then it's a twisted world we're living in."

"Please, Selena, it already is." The man sits on the edge of the bed. He holds out a hand. "Merrik. I've heard much about you, Selena. You're powerful, and you know how to fight."

I ignore his hand. "And you think *I* am going to fight for *you,* a charming man with a wretched view of life?"

"Yours is just as messed up as mine," he muses, dropping his hand. "Thanks for calling me charming, though, dear. Do you know who I am?"

When I send him a questioning look, he says, "Let me rephrase. Do you know *what* I am?"

"A god," I answer immediately. "That's obvious. But I'm not sure which one."

He laughs, a low, deep, intimidating sound. "I am much more than a simple *god,* dear. Guess again."

My mouth dries. "You can't be serious."

Merrik smirks when he notices I've figured it out. "As that stab wound." He glances down at the line of blood, and I'm suddenly very glad that my hospital gown is covering it.

"You're an entity?"

His smirk grows. Merrik stands from the bed, still maintaining eye contact. "So you know why I'm here, then?"

"No," I breathe. "No, I don't."

"Well, it's simple. Take a guess."

"You want me to join you." My voice shakes as I respond. "To destroy what? Kill where? Fight when?"

"Do you agree?" Merrik asks. "That's what I really want you to think about. I can give you everything you've ever wanted. You'll have every person you've ever hated dead at your feet. All your hard work will be avenged. You, my warrior, will be victorious."

Then, he looks away, breaking some sort of spell. I consider it. I consider what he's asking of me, and it makes me wonder if I *did* deserve to be stabbed. This is obviously a trick. This entity, this powerful being that's meant to only exist in stories, this being that has supposedly taken down full gods, is trying to weaponize me. He wants *me* on his team, when I've only ever been nothing more than an abnormal creature with a girl's soul who abandoned her family for the enemy. I'm not even that good of a warrior. These facts make me wonder if there is something much bigger than me brewing, and he needs all the help he can get.

"Anything?" I ask, and I know I shouldn't. But this being that stands in front of me could let me see my brother again, could let me see Milo again, could let me have whatever I wanted. Heck, he could maybe even end this useless war that we're fighting in, all inevitably leading to our deaths.

Everyone dies at some point, though. This isn't the happiest thought, but it's true. So, really, what's the point in fighting for this guy? Entities may be all powerful and all knowing, but that doesn't mean they're worth fighting for.

"Anything," Merrik confirms, a slight smile playing on his lips. He knows I'm interested, and he will use it to his advantage.

Anything. Is the cost of seeing my brother again, seeing my friends again, really worth fighting for this entity, knowing he is not who I want to fight for, knowing it will get me killed?

"Think about it," Merrik says, disrupting my thoughts. "You'll live for a little bit longer; I can feel it. Once you decide, just call out my name. Then we'll talk about the other...chores."

And with a final wink, Merrik disappears. Lillian returns, holding fresh gauze and a new set of clothes. She follows my gaze to the spot where Merrik was standing just moments before.

"Is something the matter, dear?" She notices how tense I am and rushes over to ease me back onto the bed. "Whenever you're ready, change clothes, okay? And if you help, just call."

She must be able to tell I'm not going to answer her question, so she leaves the room again, leaving me with the gauze, the clothes, and my thoughts.

And I'm betting she, as she leaves, realizes how disastrous that will be.

CHAPTER 2

AMEER

I must say, I never expected Camp Serenity to be the way it is.

The campers are scared of me. I admit I understand why, though the weak frame Finn caused is not too intimidating. I am a king, and they are campers at a camp run by a *princess*. I'm willing to bet they had no idea Elysian was even a princess anyway.

I think this while my fists slam into the punching bag outside of my 'cabin.'

Elysian offered to let me stay with her in her cabin, but I can tell she's been super busy with the campers and Xelma's death and her new girlfriend and me, and I figured the last thing she needed was another person disrupting her from getting a good sleep. After all, she built a home for herself from nothing. She is stronger than I ever will be.

So my cabin is in the woods.

It used to be the meeting room (and maybe still is), but Elysian said she'd happily move me in there. She said I was sleep-deprived enough over the past year, and I didn't argue with her. She found me a few sets of pale green T-shirts and joggers that I could wear, a few pillows, and two blankets, and that was it. Of course, there's water and food in the room already, and the training area to help me get stronger is right outside the door. But it still feels like something's strange about me living here.

Eventually, I will have to go back to the castle. I'm going to have to be king.

King.

It makes me want to bash my head against a wall, and so I hit the punching bag harder.

And when a scared camper shows up, wincing every time my fists make contact with the bag and saying meekly that dinner is served, it only makes me more unsettled.

Regardless, I make my way to the mess hall.

My sister's camp is impressive. All the cabins are in perfect order and the mess hall is made of marble, towering over everything. She's a perfect leader, just as she has always been, since she was seven years old, since the day she was born. Even though I am the next in line for the throne, she has always been a natural ruler.

When I enter the mess hall, heading for our usual table before I get food, I see Elysian sitting down, her glasses on, hunched over a notebook. She scribbles furiously, and as Ash sits down, she lifts her head for a second to say 'hello.'

Ash and Milo and their campers spend most of their time at Camp Serenity, since it's bigger, but at night, they head back to their camp to sleep. Ever since they rescued me, the camps aren't really separate camps. They're combined now, and I don't think anyone really cares if anyone disobeys the rules. We're one big family, and after all the chaos, we need the support. We all do.

"Hey," Ash says when she sees me. Her eyes flick over to my sister. "She's in a mood," she whispers, but Elysian's head snaps back up and she smiles at me.

Then she sends a pointed look to Ash. "Is that good enough for you?"

"No," Ash responds simply, leaning back in her chair. She's wearing a warm outfit today, considering the sun that beats down on us relentlessly, despite it being mid-October. She's wearing a red sweater and jeans, and she seems at ease. I'm glad. When I saw Ash for the first time, she was running from my father and Finn.

And she was fifteen, like me.

And she was in trouble, like me.

Elysian rolls her eyes. "Sorry, sorry," she says, putting the pen down. "I just don't have enough time to do *anything* anymore. It seems like everyone needs me for everything. I just want to take a long nap."

She rests her head on Ash's lap, and a small smile curves the corners of Ash's mouth. But then she knocks on her head like she's rapping at a door, and Elysian's eyes shoot open as she groans.

"You're so mean," she protests, and Ash doesn't say anything— just tries to suppress a smile.

Milo comes up to our table. He sets his plate down and starts eating without saying anything. It makes me feel sorry for him.

Ever since Selena died—Selena, one of my father's best soldiers who betrayed him and Milo was drawn to—he's been quieter than usual, kept to himself. I see it as going through grief after the traumatic accident has already happened—now that she's dead and they're not on a death quest to save me, which still makes me feel a huge amount of guilt, he has time to remember her, to grieve her.

It's happened to me before.

It's happening to me *now.* This sort of emptiness just stays with you, no matter what you do, until you learn to move on. And moving on is by far the hardest part about going through grief.

I don't say anything. I know nothing I say can help.

Instead, I look away from him. I don't know Milo well. In truth, I wasn't even aware he existed before I met him through my sister. We—my father and I—never really kept track of all the occupants of the kingdom. But now, I wish I had. Then, hopefully, I could've killed Finn before he could do anything, before he could meet my father.

Of course, though, I can't change the past.

"Milo?" Ash says gently. "I have a question."

Milo's head snaps up, his eyes softening. "Yeah, Ash?"

"Are you going to eat the rest of your chips?"

Quickly, Milo shoves all of his chips into his mouth and smiles widely. Elysian turns away, mumbling about how disgusting that is. Ash grimaces.

"Where's Sage?" I ask Elysian.

She's writing again. "Oh, uh—I don't know." She glances at me and pushes her glasses up. "She was teaching a class in the woods. I don't know where she is now, though."

I frown. Sage is always on time. Despite the fact that she's probably gone for a good reason, it's still odd to me. The whole incident with Finn has put me on edge.

Elysian sends me a glance. "Why?"

"Just wondering." I shrug, pretending it doesn't bother me. "I'm going to go get food."

I walk over to the table by the meat bar and pick up a plate. I pile some steak, lettuce, tomatoes, and corn on a plate. I hesitate, wondering if I've taken too much. Normally, Finn wouldn't feed me anything but slabs of meat that were either rotten or slathered in disgusting things, like blood and waste.

Now, the food looks perfectly clean. It seems like they're fully cooked, too.

When I get back to our table, I set down my plate and search the woods with my eyes, looking for something. I'm not sure why, but I can't tear my eyes away from those woods.

"Beautiful, aren't they?" says a voice in my ear, and I whip around, coming face to face with just the girl I've been subconsciously looking for: Sage. Her red hair is a flame in the form of a tight ponytail, her clothes the exact green color of the leaves that remain on the trees. Her pale skin has more freckles than usual, and her eyes follow my gaze to the vast forest. "The trees."

Red crawls up at my neck at our proximity. I take a step back, bumping into the table. "I—uh, yeah. They're beautiful."

My sister sends me a weird glance. Then her eyes flick over to Sage. "What took you so long?"

Sage shrugs, sitting down at the table. *Right next to my seat,* I think nervously. I'm much more hesitant to sit down now. But Ash is studying me for any weird movements, so I sit, making sure to keep my arms as close to my body as they can be. "Class ran a little long."

Elysian frowns. "It never does."

She shrugs again. "Did today."

"Is this about—"

Sage clears her throat and stands from the table. "I'm getting some dinner," she declares before walking over to the other side of the mess hall.

I drag my eyes over to Elysian. "About what?"

"It's almost her ex boyfriend's birthday," Ash explains. "He, uh, he died in August."

My eyes widen. "That's horrible. When's his birthday?"

"The twenty-first," Elysian says. "Sometimes, especially with his birthday getting so close, she goes out to the woods and just *talks* to him. It sounds weird, but it's the only thing she has left of him. She loved him."

My heart sinks, feeling Sage's heartbreak.

"Did he—the guy—like the woods?" I ask, surprising myself.

Elysian chuckles lightly, but there's sadness in her laugh. "Not really. The woods, though, are where Sage feels the most comfortable.

I nod shortly and let the topic be dropped as Sage returns with a plate. Before she can sit, I steal an empty chair across the table and sit there instead. Ash raises an eyebrow at me knowingly. "I'm begging you," Elysian whispers in my ear, "do *not* mention it. Sage will knock you unconscious."

"Sage will what?" Sage asks, leaning forward on the table.

She must have amazing ears.

"Nothing," my sister says calmly, returning to her work. She pushes her glasses up again and begins to write.

Ever since the mission ended, Elysian's been working on new laws for camp, camp-leader things—and the book she's writing, one she talks about constantly. She's a little obsessed. For example, the other day, she stormed into my room talking about her character, and so, when she said, "She's dead! She's gone!" without any context, I was seriously worried one of the campers had died.

But, of course, no one died but a bit of her soul that day.

I glance over at Sage nervously. She cocks an eyebrow. "Yes?"

My eyes widen and I look back down. "Nothing. Sorry."

"No, there's something," she insists. "What is it, Ameer?"

"It's nothing," Elysian interjects. "Leave it alone, Sage. He's just nervous."

"I can't imagine why. It's not like this is the first dinner he's had here." Sage studies me carefully—every movement, every bite that I take from my meal, every breath, probably. It makes me uncomfortable, and I shift. "What is it, Ameer? Do I make you nervous?"

I stare at my dinner. "The woods are...nice. They look nice."

"I asked you a question," Sage demands. "What is your problem, Ameer?"

"Okay," Ash says, standing giving Sage a weird look from across the table, "we're done here." She lifts me out of the chair by my shoulders and walks me, my plate in her hand, back to my cabin.

Once we get there, Ash stands in the doorway while I set my plate down.

"Is she...mad at me?" I ask her. *It sure seemed like it.*

"Maybe." Ash shrugs. "Sage is hard to read. She's a little confusing, especially now with the grief and the stress and all that. We're all under stress. I wouldn't worry about it, okay?"

"I don't want her to be mad at me."

"Why's that?" Ash acts casual, but her eyes are teasing. "You got a little crush on her?"

I feel my face getting hot. "Of course not. She's the junior leader of this camp, my sister's best friend, and she can kill me. Excuse me for not wanting to be on her bad side."

"Okay." She laughs, holding up her hands. "Sorry. Just wondering. Enjoy your dinner, Ameer."

"You're leaving?"

"The campers get restless after a while," she explains. "Plus, it's not like they can be exactly *trusted* on their own, considering the last time I left them unattended, a wicked dodgeball game resulted in seven bloody noses and ten broken bones."

I snort. "You go right ahead."

"See you soon," Ash tells me."

"See you soon," I promise.

She winks before jogging to Camp Havoc.

* * *

I'm dreaming again.

In my dream, I'm standing on a battlefield. Ghosts of the past float up from the dusty ground, chanting my name over and over. And yet, somehow, it's not mine. My mouth curls up in a smile as I survey the ghosts around me.

Though I'm the one smiling, it's not my doing. Almost like someone else is in my body.

"Yes, my children," I say to the ghosts, motioning to the wasteland around us. "Soon, we will rise. If I can just use what I need, *whom* I need, then it will be sooner than you've expected."

The ghosts laugh. One in particular comes forward. His face is pale and covered in blood. His eyes are wide.

"Are you..." The man swallows. "Merrik?"

"Yes," I say. "And you are the man I've been looking for, the one my wife has been talking about—Finn?"

"Finn Brocker," the ghost says, and a chill runs down my spine. Deep inside, my real brain, not this *Merrik's*, is screaming in fear. "My name is Finn Brocker...sir."

Even though my instincts scream at me, my smile grows wider. "Good."

"*Good?* How long have you been looking for me?"

"Finn, you are strange," Merrik says. "Determined, unwavering, lovesick. It's admirable, I must admit. But it can also be the death of you. I know you are angry, and I am asking you, *pleading* with you, to let me help you. You'll never get what you want without me."

Finn's ghost considers it. "And if I don't agree?"

I feel a flare of anger run through me. Merrik's voice echoes in my mind: *We've had too many rejections.* "You wouldn't dare." The statement comes out more like a threat than anything else. "Do you know what I am, boy? I am the brother of the father of the gods. I am more powerful than all of them combined. I have been on this planet, on every planet, influencing decisions and choices since the beginning of time. You would be deeply mistaken, *insane* to refuse my offer."

Finn tries to say something, but Merrik cuts him off.

"I understand Eliana has already spoken with you," he continues. "You have learned from my wife, yes? Learned the things I can offer you, learned the risks you will take and the opportunities you will have?"

Finn nods.

"Then I must ask you, Finn, what else would be better?"

Finn considers it again. His eyebrows furrow as he thinks. Finally, I feel a sensation run through my body and I understand: *he's going to say yes.*

"I'll do it," Finn agrees, flames beginning to rise in his eyes. "I'll be your soldier. I'll get Ashlyn in my grasp. I'll win this war."

Merrik holds out his hand, shaking Finn's, which has solidified. "Perfect."

The dream fades into another.

I find myself on the Camp Havoc grounds, glancing around. I'm not completely a person—I'm something like one of Merrik's ghosts, it seems—but I can see perfectly fine. I believe that's what I need to do, especially as my eyes adjust to the torches in the distance and the sound of voices chanting Merrik's name fills my ears.

I'm confused for a moment. *I thought I left that dream,* I think. But then I realize the chanting is *really happening* as campers turn on their lights and step out from their cabins, squinting at the figures marching toward the camp. The figures that are chanting Merrik's name and carrying torches.

Fear fills me slowly. It takes me a minute for me to realize what's happening, but once I do, I want to wake up. The figures are Merrik's ghosts, and they're putting their torches to the ground and lighting the forest on fire.

This is bad. Really, really bad. What if the campers die? What if Ash or Milo dies? What if the fire spreads to our camp?

Wake up.

My eyes snap open, and I run, without shoes, to Elysian's cabin, knocking wildly on the door. The door opens eventually and she blinks at me tiredly. "Ameer?" my sister says. "What is it?"

"It's Camp Havoc," I say frantically. "They're in trouble."

CHAPTER 3

ASH

THREE HOURS EARLIER: 9 PM

There's a candle lighter in my hand.

I'm not exactly sure why. All I know is that it brings me a sense of joy, pulling the trigger and seeing a spark, because it reminds me more of the campfires at Camp Serenity. I left earlier tonight, so I didn't have to see it, but I still wish I had. Those campfires are the best part of the camp by far.

Other than my girlfriend, of course.

Elysian is everything I've ever wanted. She's smart, funny, and is incredibly powerful and independent. She's perfect. She truly is. But there's something that's been plaguing my mind recently: a small thought that might bring the entire world down if I express it with her. At times, Elysian can be a little *too* powerful. That's all right, so long as I stay far, far away from the path down which she is sending her overbearing anger.

There's a knock at my cabin door. I stand from the bed, tossing the lighter onto my desk as I pass it, and open the door to Elysian's face. She's giddy and smiling. She's been like that pretty much ever since we rescued Ameer, and that's why I think it'll be so hard to tell her about what I've been thinking of lately.

"Hey, Lys," I say, kissing her hair.

Her smile grows. "Hey, Ash."

"I'm happy you're here," I tell her, "but *why* are you here? I thought you were busy with your work."

"I was," she says, weaving around me to get to my bed and then flopping on it, "but then I decided I was done and I needed to come see my favorite person."

I won't be your favorite person for long, whispers a traitorous voice in my mind.

"Me?" I tease. "I'm flattered. I thought for sure you meant Ameer."

"He's a close second." My girlfriend shrugs. Gods, I *love* saying that word. "But you're first."

I try to hide the huge, dopey grin that breaks out on my face. "Is that all? You look…weird."

"Very descriptive."

"You know what I mean!" I protest. "There's something wrong, isn't there?"

And, to my surprise, she sighs, sitting down at the edge of my bed. "Yes, there is. I was meaning to talk to you about it. That's why I'm here."

"Well," I say, sitting next to her and resting my elbows on my knees, "what is it? Anything bad? Anything damaging?"

She shrugs. "Not technically."

I raise an eyebrow. "Technically?"

Elysian's dark hair is pulled away from her face in a messy ponytail. She's wearing a pajama shirt that's baggy and worn from being washed so frequently and athletic shorts. Though she looks quite comfortable, she squirms like she's anything but. "It's something you may not want to talk about. Something that may, if used that way, bring down our relationship."

"Bread? Bread will bring down our relationship, simply because you like it cold and plain, you weirdo."

"You're the weirdo! You're the one who likes toasting it. Then it's not bread, it's toast." She sighs. "This is serious, Ash. It's about my brother."

I tense. *How did she know that's what I wanted to talk to her about?* I start to talk way too quickly. "What about him? I think he's perfectly fine. I think he's happy here. Sage doesn't seem to like him, though. You should talk to her. She freaked out earlier at dinner."

"That's exactly why I wanted to talk to you," she starts, and it's clear she isn't stopping. "Sage clearly has something going on. Do you? If he's too much trouble, I can...I can ask if he'll live somewhere else...back at the castle, maybe." She chokes on her last words, and it makes me realize how much she trusts me. She doesn't want to lose her brother, and I don't want her to, either, but she's willing to give him up if I simply decide I don't want him at her camp. She's trusting, but strong, and it only makes her more attractive.

My eyebrows crease. "Lys, I love you. And I think if you want him here, keep him. Who cares what Sage thinks? He's *your* brother. He's your family. I don't expect you to do anything that will hurt him. But..."

She stares into my eyes, confused by my contradicting words. Her eyes are like a clear blue sky, but I know eventually that blue sky will be covered with storm clouds. "But?"

"Is he hurting you?" I ask. "I mean, you just seem so tired and stressed. For the gods' sakes, Lys, you put him in the forest because you didn't have enough room. Your camp is already a full-time job, and with the book you're writing and being social and now your brother, I just...I don't know...you seem like you're stressed beyond belief."

I see her getting angrier the more I explain myself. *So much for trusting.* Elysian gives me a nasty look. "*Stressed?* Because I want to do nice things for my brother?"

"I know it sounds wrong." *I knew you were going to react this way.* "But, really, you should give yourself a break."

"Give myself a break?" She stares at me like I've grown another head. "You don't get it, do you? He's my *brother,* Ash, my *brother.* I can't give myself a *break*. I love him, and I think my stress is worth it, even if you don't."

Her words ring in my ears. "Okay, I'm sorry. I was just trying to maybe help you, but I see how unwilling you are to be helped."

Elysian clenches her jaw. "I'm sorry I don't want exactly what you want all the time."

"That's not what I—"

"I just think maybe," she mutters, "since I'm so stressed and all, we should stay away from each other. It could be better for the both of us."

I glance at the floor. *She can't be serious.* "Well, if that's what you want."

"It is," she says quickly, too quickly for me to believe it. Even then, it still stings. It feels like she's thrown my heart into a lion's den to be eaten and now she's stabbing it with her dagger. "It is."

And that's it. She leaves, and I'm left a puddle on the floor, watching her leave. How is it possible that something so good can turn so rotten in such little time? How is it possible that even with her flaws, *our* flaws, I still want her to be with me?

CHAPTER 4

ELYSIAN

PRESENT TIME

I stare at my brother. I'm wearing my pajamas, and the chilly air blows into my cabin. I shiver. "What…what do you mean, they're in trouble?"

Ameer's face is pale. He's sweating, I realize with a start. "Merrik—he's after them."

"Merrik?" Even as I say it, the word sends a chill through me, and I don't understand why. "Who—*what* is that?"

"Does it matter? We need to get there, *right now*. The ghosts from my dream are carrying torches and heading toward their camp, chanting his name, and he's in an alliance with Finn, and he's—"

"Of course it matters! You're talking about ghosts and armies and torches and *Finn*—Ameer, are you okay?"

"I'm fine," he says, growing annoyed, "but in a few minutes, Milo and Ash and the rest of the campers aren't going to be. Heck, the ghosts have already invaded their camp! Please, Lys, you're my sister, and Ash—she's your girlfriend. Don't you trust my word? Don't you want to help her?"

She's not my girlfriend, I want to say, but I don't. *At least, not anymore. I don't* think *she is.* "Of course I do! But...how do you know what you're saying is true?"

I really don't want to have to save her life after I just broke up with her.

Before he can respond, there's shouting, a rising rhythm of pain and surprise, coming from Camp Havoc. I feel the blood drain from my face as I register the severity of the situation we're in. And then, *Oh, gods, he was right.*

I rush out of my cabin, now squinting through the nearly bare trees at Camp Havoc. There's the glow of flames and I can just barely see transparent figures, holding the torches that the fire rests on.

"Ameer," I say quietly, eyeing the beings carefully, switching from them to the torches to the fire and back again, "are those the ghosts and the torches you were talking about?"

He gulps. I can hear it, even though I stand a foot away from him. "Uh, yeah. That's about right."

And then we're off, sprinting toward the camp, the chilliness and the fact that I'm wearing nothing more than my pajamas forgotten. I run, not just because of the danger, but because *how could I let this happen?* A sense of dread settles in my stomach, and with the way things are going, it seems it's going to find a good home there. The grass below my feet grows less soft and more burnt as I approach Camp Havoc. The cabins are perfectly imperfect, as

Ash said the day I first met her after losing my memory, all different heights and colors and shapes. And I notice with a start, my eyes sweeping over the cabins, that most of them are empty, the doors ajar, or the lights are on. *Thank the gods.*

I see Sage, already holding a weapon, looking perfectly deadly next to the flames. She uses her powers of the earth to try to topple rocks on top of the incoming ghost-soldiers, but I can tell she's getting weaker the more power she uses. Ash is fighting, too, and she looks magnificent, the way the fire turns her eyes fierce and feral and alight. She looks at home here, despite the ghost-soldiers, for the fire, in a way, is her home. Milo speaks desperately to the air, to no one in particular, yet his eyes are set on the soldiers, and he looks like the opposite of peaceful, a vein bulging in his neck.

"Oh, gods," Ameer breathes. "This is…a lot worse than I expected."

I curse under my breath. "This is great," I say sarcastically. *Why am I not fighting right now?* I ask myself.

"Yep." Ameer scans the scene, and his face only pales more. It looks like, in the heat of the fire and the heat of the moment, more sweat has appeared on his skin now, making his T-shirt and pajama pants stick to his body like they're glued there.

My hand tightens around my dagger, which I grabbed before I left my cabin. I press the button on the hilt, and my dagger turns into a sword, elongating until it's thirty inches long and intimidating. I run to catch up to Ash, and she almost cuts my head off.

"What happened?" I yell at her.

She says nothing, instead shouting directions at her campers, telling them to line up around the cabins. I realize her plan.

"Are you *insane?*" I scream. "You're going to get yourself killed!"

The fire roars louder, and Ash's expression turns grim. She mutters something, something I can't hear. "What?" I yell.

"I said, good!" she screams, turning to face me. "Good, because I would rather it be me who dies instead of my campers, instead of you! Are you happy now?"

"What's your problem?"

"What's *my* problem?" She stares at me like I'm stupid. It makes me uncomfortable. "Just three hours ago, you stormed into my cabin, talking about your brother, and broke up with me. Then, you come storming into my camp, only to question me and interject where you're not needed!"

I wince. "Look, I'm sorry. I was sensitive and scared and, you're right, stressed, and I still love you, Ash, even though you don't think so. Please, just let me—"

Her eyes blaze, and the fire in front of us begins to burn so hot that it nearly singes my eyebrows off. *She can control fire, even if it isn't hers.* "*Leave,* Elysian. *Get out of the way.*"

An idea forms in my brain. It's a stupid idea, one of my stupidest, one that might get me killed, but it also might work. "Why?"

She sends me a poisonous look, turning back to the soldiers, calculating her next move. "*Why?* Because you're going to kill yourself."

"You care about me?"

"Of course I care about you," she says, so sharply that it neglects the meaning. "Go away."

I pretend to think about it. The plan is becoming better the more I talk. "No."

Now she focuses all her attention on me. *"No?"*

"Yes. No."

"Gods, you're difficult. You know that? I'm trying not to get you killed, and you're telling me *no.*"

"Why would I be killed? Are you going to kill me, Ash?"

"It's definitely looking like an option right now," she mutters. "Go away, Elysian."

A grin spreads across my face. Slowly, I say, "I said, *no.*"

And at that, she erupts in shouts and curses. The fire in front of us grows so large that it reaches the ghost-soldiers in the forest and swallows them whole. Ash watches, the anger fading from her face and the curses dying at her lips. Finally, the soldiers are reduced to ashes.

"That—" she whispers, but she can't get the rest of the words out.

I nod, understanding what she means.

Ameer, Milo, and Sage drift over to us. "Did—" Ameer asks Ash, motioning toward the forest, "did you do that?"

Ash swallows. "I don't know," she says desperately at the same time I say, "Yes."

"She did?" Milo asks, sounding impressed.

"I did?" Ash says.

Sage closes her eyes, exasperated. "Lys, please tell me we don't have to call *her* in."

"She's not that bad."

"She's horrible!"

"I'm sorry," Milo says, his eyebrows creasing. "Who are we talking about?"

✳ ✳ ✳

"My mother."

Max Kheefe sends me a confused look, his eyes flicking from my face to Sage's. "You want me to invite my *mother* to a meeting?"

Max is the best Healer we have with Sorin gone. He's the Healer who helped bring Ash back fully after she was bitten by that wolf. And his mother, in some strange turn of events when the camp first started, is the supervisor of Camp Serenity. Anne Kheefe has been the number-one supplier of our money for years, and she doesn't know anything about Finn or anything we've gone through, which is probably why Max is staring at me like I've grown another head. But…

"We need her, now more than ever." I try to convince him. "She owns most of the buildings in the kingdom. If we get her opinion on this and her support, we'll have so many fighters."

"*Untrained* fighters," Max points out. "They barely know how to hold swords. Plus, didn't you create this camp because most of the kingdom doesn't support Magics?"

"Exactly," Sage puts in. "They don't support us because they're *scared* of us. With their king dead and the next-in-line here, they're out of options. They're terrified. All they need is a little push in the right direction."

"And that *push* is my mother?" Max raises a skeptical eyebrow. "Please, don't make her do this."

"We literally have no one else." I take over the conversation. "And, if the plan doesn't work out, we can still talk about what's been going on, leader to supervisor. Good?"

"That's not a real question, I take it," Max says.

"Wise," I respond. I can see Sage giving him a look out of the corner of my eye.

Finally, he sighs. "Fine. But I am not asking her. That's up to you two. Understand?"

I hold out my hand. "You've got a deal."

* * *

I find myself sitting in the meeting room (and Ameer's bedroom for the time being) as we wait for Anne. I study my dagger, and a few campers—one of the top Healers, the top fighter, and the top scribe—talk in hushed voices in the corner. I glance around the white room, at the green details, the swords in their sheathes near the corner of the room.

The door opens.

The few campers that have been talking rush to their seats, staring attentively at the door.

She walks in.

Anne Kheefe handles herself with grace, despite the scars that trail the length of her face. They are white and complement her startling green eyes. She wears a navy-blue blazer over a white blouse, and her skirt matches the blazer. Her dark hair is pulled away from her face, slicked back into a tight bun. Her eyes sweep carelessly over us—every single camper staring up at her with wide, admiring eyes. And then she meets mine, and a small smile curls the corners of her lips.

"Elysian Viggo," she greets, holding out her hand.

"Anne," I reply. I shake her hand.

"I was expecting something from you in the past week, possibly." Anne waves her hand as she sits, and one of the campers rushes to hand her the glass of water I asked for before she arrived. "Especially since you've been so quiet lately."

"That's actually what I called you here to talk about."

"Starting off strong," she notes. "That's why I've always liked you so much. And yet no pleasantries, my child?"

"Would you prefer I tell you about the recent events or spoil you with 'hello' and 'goodbye' and 'thank you for coming'?"

She gives me an admiring look, taking a sip from her glass. "All right, fine. What were you wanting to talk about?"

"The attack."

Two simple words, and yet they make the glass in her hand crack. Water spills onto the table, but Anne doesn't care. She stares straight at me, her eyes murderous and dark. "Attack?"

"Late last night, at around midnight, my...friend was attacked by soldiers in the form of ghosts," I tell her. "They were transparent, and yet they held torches. Her camp would've been invaded if she didn't use the power she had to get rid of them." I lean forward, setting my elbows on the table. "Now, I'm not asking you to figure it out, but I do think we need to handle it, for the safety of the camp, of the campers, of all Magics in the kingdom. We need your help."

"And what are you planning to do?" she asks, her eyes clearing once again. "Form an army?"

I grin. "Precisely."

* * *

"But that's insane. You told her that?"

Max stares at me wide-eyed as I wait for the line at the meat bar to clear up.

"Yep." I study the food that's already on my plate with intensity—I never noticed corn could be so interesting.

"And? What did she say?"

"She said she'd think about it."

He frowns. "That's it? Normally my mother is much more *expressive.* Did she tell you how stupid and careless of an idea that is?"

"Actually, she was quite open to the idea," I say. I'm still looking at my corn. "She said she'd go to work and try to fix it."

"And?"

"And then she left. Sorry. Were you expecting something else?"

I raise my head just soon enough to see Max's eyes dimming. "No. That seems like my mother."

"She did leave a message for you, though, if you were wondering."

"She did?" Now he looks simply bewildered.

"She did," I confirm. I pull the note from the pocket of my fleece jacket. Max reads over it quickly, and then crumples it up, throwing it on the ground.

"Thanks," he mumbles, and he leaves the line.

I pick up the piece of paper, my eyes skimming the graceful script.

Max -

I'm sorry I couldn't talk, lovely. I hope to see you again soon, especially considering your sister has been missing you lately. In case you do happen to return, there's one thing I'd like you to know.

If your sister mentions your grandfather at all, I'd like you to know – he sadly passed away a few weeks ago.

I'm so sorry that I didn't tell you earlier, lovely. But if it makes you feel any better, you are the fortieth to know!

- Mom

Sometimes Anne can be a little clueless, especially when it comes to her own kid. That's why Max lives here, at Camp Serenity. But he often visits his parents' house to see his sister and Orange, his orange tabby cat. Other than that, though, we are his family, and the wild creatures that roam the forest are his pets.

That's just how it is when you're outcast from your own kingdom for something you can't control. That's the way it was for me, except I never got to return home. And now, thinking back on my family life and what a horrible person my father was, I'm glad I didn't.

I make my way to my table, Sage and Ameer eating across from each other, perfectly silent and avoiding one another's eyes. I roll my own and sit in one of the chairs.

"Lys, thank the gods," Sage says, eager to say something. "I wanted to ask you how the meeting with Anne went."

"Oh," I say. "It was good. She's willing to consider it, but I have to make her a pros and cons list by Monday."

She rolls her eyes. "Be serious. This is the future of our camps we're talking about."

"And this is the important organization needed in said camps *I'm* talking about," I retort. "In all seriousness, she'll consider it. She says she'll get back to us as soon as she's made a decision, and then we need to find people."

"Have you…" Ameer trails off, noting the attention is on him now. "Sorry, I know it's not my business, but have you talked to Ash about this stuff?"

I hastily look down as Sage says, "I'd like to know the answer to that myself, actually."

"No," I say finally. "But I was going to eventually."

Ameer gives me a disapproving look. "Well, you should've done it before you scheduled it. I know you've been fighting, but you're still dating, right?"

"Of course we are," I say, a hint of anger in my voice.

"Okay," he says, holding up his hands. "Sorry. Just wondering. But you haven't told her, even though this is a problem that surrounds the attack on *her* camp?"

"I know how it sounds," I start, "but really, I don't think she'll care."

"*I* think she will," Sage interjects, "and she's not *my* girlfriend."

"Fine. You wanna know the real reason?" Despite my voice being flat, Ameer and Sage nod. All their attention is on me. "I really just don't want to talk to her right now. We're not in the best place in our relationship."

"And that means you don't tell her important things?" Sage raises an eyebrow.

"I tell her the *most* important things!" I argue. "Plus, I was going to talk to her tonight at the campfire, while everyone's enjoying s'mores."

"To soften the blow?" Ameer asks.

"Exactly." My stomach is starting to hurt.

"Well, that's going to be hard, considering she isn't coming to the campfire," Sage says.

I stare at her. "What?"

"She hasn't been here all day," she continues. "She hasn't talked to anyone at Camp Serenity, and neither have her campers. She's *really* mad at you for...whatever it is you did."

"That's insane. Does she realize how insane that is?" I glance at Ameer, maybe to have support, maybe just to look away from Sage. I'm not sure.

"She's angry," Ameer says with a shrug. "Hasn't said anything to anyone. And something tells me you're mad, too."

"What?"

"Why won't you tell us what happened during your meeting with Anne?" Sage asks. "It's weird. You love the details. Something happened."

"You're accusing me of *hiding something from you?*"

"Yes, I am," she continues. "Because you *are.*"

My jaw clenches and I sigh, giving in. "A ball."

"What?"

"A ball. Anne says she will do this for us if we have a ball at one of the ballrooms she's rented. She says she will cover the transportation and the catering. All we need to do is be there."

It's silent for a second. Then, both Sage and Ameer say, *"What?"*

"That's crazy!" Ameer protests.

"She can't be serious," Sage agrees.

"And she just thinks we'll do it?"

I wince.

"Elysian Viggo," Sage says, "is there something else you're not telling us?"

"I may have…already…possibly…*agreed.*"

"Okay," says a new voice, Max's, from the corner of the room. He's relaxed, and it's clear he's been monitoring our conversation for a while now. *Creepy.* "Now, you should *definitely* tell Ash. About...everything."

CHAPTER 5

SELENA

It's late the next time Merrik visits me.

Outside the open window, the birds that were chirping before the sun set are completely silent, replaced by the sounds of angry cicadas. Lillian has left me a bottle of *soigner*, which sits on my nightstand alone. I've moved my ratty, bloody clothes onto the floor after changing. I don't want to see them. They bring back bad memories.

His light hair is messy, and his white grin is confident and wide, cocky, and it sends fear coursing through my veins, which mixes with the pain. "Hello, Selena."

"What do you want?" I respond flatly. I'm tired. This is the fifth time he's visited me in the past three days, and I'm not very excited.

"How kind of you to assume I want something," he says, and his grin grows wider, impossibly wide. "I'm just here to check up on you, my moonshine. All I ask is that you cooperate."

"During?"

"Your death, of course," he says, slowly, deliberately, like it's obvious. He's teasing me, making me believe something just to scare me. It's what he wants to happen. He wants me to believe he's going to kill me, and then he wants to revel in it.

It's working.

Over the past few days, I've been weak. I hate to admit it. My eyes widen as I register what he's saying. "Are you going to kill me?" I ask, trying to stay as calm as I can.

"*I'm* not." He stares right into my eyes. It's unsettling. "But as far as I'm concerned, there are several people that would just *love* to get their hands on you, dead or alive. Plus, I'm sure plenty will be surprised—angry, even—to discover that you're alive." He grins, so quickly that I almost miss it, but I don't.

"Finn." My realization is quick. "He's alive?"

"And fighting for me," Merrik confirms with a nod. "He has made the smart decision, the one that will keep him alive. The real question is if you are willing to make it, too."

"I would rather die than fight for you," I snarl, and Merrik's jaw clenches slightly.

"Again?" he says, and he's angry, I realize, despite his teasing tone. He wants me on his team, wants me to agree. But why? "If you wish to kill yourself in this battle, to never get revenge, to never get justice for your brother, then…well, it's not my battle to fight. Not my war."

He turns, and I call out. "Wait. What was that about my brother? He died because of a stray arrow, not because of anything Finn did."

I hear Merrik chuckle—a low, intimidating sound that makes the hospital floor shake. I watch as the glass bottle of *soigner* wobbles before falling to the floor and shatters. *Great.* "Didn't you know? He ordered that arrow. Ordered your brother to be killed."

My heart drops into my stomach. "Why?"

He's silent.

"I'm not asking again," I force out. "Why?"

"He figured it would lead you right to him." Merrik's voice is soft at first, but as he continues to talk, it grows louder, harsher, angrier. "He figured that if there was anything that would make you angry enough to come after the castle when you were already having doubts about coming, it would be that. Figured your brother being shot by a Royal guard was enough to lead you there."

My jaw clenches. "You're kidding."

"I don't *kid,* Selena."

"So…everything you're saying about my brother's death, about being led into a trap—all of it is true? You're not just making up a stupid little story to get me on your side?"

"I don't lie, either, Selena." His stance is calm, but his eyes are crazy, a slow fire burning behind them. "Everything I say is true. Everything I tell you, everything I offer, is sincere. I want you to get revenge, not just to be my soldier. I want you to help yourself, Selena, in the way you know best. Fighting, killing, being the person you know you are inside. Is that really too much to ask for?"

"Yes," I say quietly. "That *is* too much. I'm not a fighter anymore, and I don't want to be."

"I never expected you to turn down the opportunity to help your brother, Selena, after you've been gone for so long." His eyes flash dangerously, a warning. "But, alas, I suppose you have always been…unpredictable."

He turns away, leaving me with my thoughts, and yet he hesitates. He stands there for a second, staring at the window before he vanishes.

Lillian enters the room immediately after. "Good evening, my dear," she says cheerfully. "You're sitting up—that's good. You're making progress. Soon we can let you go. Is there anywhere you *can* go after you're healed, honey?" She applies *soigner* to my stomach wound, her calloused fingers brushing over the healing skin.

"No," I say, shaking my head violently. I want to throw up. How *dare* Merrik talk about my brother like that? How dare he mention Finn's name? How dare he even talk to me? "I don't."

Lillian tenses, just slightly. "Well, then, we'll have to find a place for you to stay inside the hospital, okay, dear?"

"Okay." I'm not listening to her, though. Wincing with bursts of pain flickering every now and then as she tends to my wound, I glance out the window at the scenery. The hospital is close to a field (which is where they get their *soigner,* as it grows on vines) and there aren't too many trees surrounding the small amount of rough dirt roads that lead to the entrance. The hospital reeks of manufactured flowers, thanks to the cans of scented spray in nearly every room. But the smell of death—unmistakable, rotten, horrid—hangs in the air like the plague.

It makes no sense how I got here, or why I'm here. Lillian keeps telling me that the spirits of Room 106 brought me in, but I can't understand why, if that's even the case. I was half-dead and dying still on the floor of their place. Perhaps they didn't want my blood spilling anywhere else, or maybe they were nice ghosts. Either way, it doesn't make sense.

Lillian notices how tense I am. "Are you all right, darling?"

"Yes," I say quickly—*too* quickly, based on her suspicious look—and Lillian stands.

"Your wound should heal soon," she tells me. "But just to be sure, the hospital brought in one of our top Healers. The staff believes you're an odd case, and so does he. So he'll look at you in the morning."

"What's his name?" I ask.

"He'll tell you," Lillian says, and then she ducks out the door and walks briskly from the room.

The *soigner* on my stomach burns, but I'm glad for it. It means it's healing. And the quicker I heal, the quicker I can get out of here. And then it dawns on me: *they're not going to let me go.* At least, not while they believe I don't have anywhere to stay. I need to track down Lillian.

I step out of bed for the first time in days and the muscles in my stomach tighten instantly. I'm still not used to moving around. It works my injury, and I almost double over in pain, but that would only make it worse. Besides, I need to make sure I get out of here. I walk slowly to the door and out it. I stare at my feet so I don't trip when suddenly I run into someone.

The person in front of me drops their papers and a mug full of coffee that shatters. I grimace.

"Oh, gods, I'm sorry," I say.

The person curses, once, and I hear their voice. *His* voice. I start to profile him when I realize—gods, I need to be finding Lillian.

I'm about to rush off when he says, "You're Selena, right?"

I do nothing to indicate he's right, and yet he nods anyway.

"I'll be seeing you in the morning," he continues, his back still to me.

You're the doctor? I want to ask, but I don't, instead running down the hallway. He calls, "You really shouldn't be running right now," but I'm gone, going as fast as I can with my stomach screaming in pain.

And then I run right into another person, except this time it's Lillian, and the cart of medical supplies that she's pushing falls over.

Oh, no, I think, and my hands launch forward on their own, trying to grab all the *soigner* before it hits the floor and breaks, but it's no use. I fall to the floor with the cart, embarrassment mixing with the agony, and Lillian gasps.

"Oh, my gods," I say, glancing at the situation. The cart has fallen a little away from me—two feet, maybe. I wince. "I'm so sorry, Lillian."

Lillian frowns down at me. "What in Adar's name were you doing out of bed, Selena? You need to let the medicine sit! Now it's not going to work." Even though her tone isn't angry, it's disappointed, which is worse somehow.

"I'm seriously sorry," I apologize again. "I wanted to tell you that I have a place to go. Really. And I was looking for you and I didn't know where you were or if I would ever find you, and I met the doctor that's going to check up on me tomorrow—"

"What?" Lillian asks. Her face pales as the blood drains from it. She looks surprised, and—frightened. "You *found* him? He's in the *hospital?* Right now?"

"Yeah." I remain staring at her. "Is he not supposed to be here?"

"No, no. He's fine. I just…wasn't expecting him, that's all. Why don't you head back to your room, and I'll get someone to reapply your *soigner* soon enough, okay?" She smiles tightly at me, a signal that I should go, and I hop to my feet and walk back to my room, trying to at least numb the pain in my stomach with all this walking.

* * *

Later, when the sun is beginning to rise, the new doctor comes into my room. I know it's him because he announces himself before he strides—rather proudly—into the room, and I begin to study him.

The guy is tall, taller than most of the men in the Royal guard. His hair is light and his eyes are dark, and he has skin tanned by the sun. I assume he's come from Ruri, the kingdom of sunlight. He's wearing a stark white lab coat over a light blue button-up, and he makes it look…decent.

"I'm Dr. Ben Abott. I'll be looking at you today, Selena—studying your health, your heart rate, things like that."

I nod.

"But first…" He scoops some *soigner* out of a glass jar and lifts my shirt, and somehow it's weird when he does it instead of Lillian. His fingers slide over my scars easily, like that's what they were made to do. "Lillian told me you had a little accident with *soigner* last night."

"Yeah," I admit half-heartedly. I watch his hands as they trail the length of my scar, and I want to look away but I can't.

He chuckles. "Well, let's try to avoid glass bottles for a bit, eh?" I murmur words of agreement and we're silent until finally he removes his fingers from my stomach and runs them under the sink across from my bed. It's beside that sink where Merrik normally stands, and that thought alone is enough to make me snap out of whatever trance I've been in.

"I'll do a few tests, see how good your health is." He nods to me, and I nod back, just because I have to. He's a doctor, for the gods' sakes, and he's here to help me get out of here—something I've longed to do since I woke up here.

He straps a contraption to my wrist, sticking a needle into the vein. "This thing helps keep you hydrated," he explains. "It transfers liquid into your veins and allows you to live longer."

"And why do I need it?" I ask, regaining my voice. My tone, I notice with an internal wince, is sharp.

"Because, Selena, when the hospital staff brought you in, you were *dead*."

I stare at him like he's grown another head. "That's impossible. Nobody can be brought back to life."

"You're a miracle, then," Dr. Abott says, "because *you* were."

"How? Was it the spirits? The doctors? The *soigner*?"

"No *soigner* has the powers to that extent," he explains, sitting on a stool positioned next to my bed. While he speaks, he monitors my heartbeat with a stethoscope. "At least, not one that is powerful enough to heal Magics like yourself."

My eyes widen and I sit up. He carefully pushes me back onto the bed by my shoulders.

"Relax," he tells me. "I'm one, too. So is Lillian. We're Healers, and I'm a sun manipulator. There's a lot of them in Ruri, where I grew up. Anyway, when you were brought in, they noticed you were practically dead in their hospital. The staff told me immediately, and I rushed here as fast as I could, but horses don't exactly move like machines do. We don't know who brought you in, but they kept saying that you weren't meant to die yet, that they were from Room 106, and then they vanished. Lillian was assigned to you. Slowly, not without our help, you regained your senses and woke up from an injury-induced coma after two months. And here we are."

A pang of panic hits me. "I'm sorry, what? *Two months?*"

"Just about. You were brought in on August sixth, and now it's October eleventh, so I would say around two months. But you've spent over a week here while awake already."

"A week?" I never knew it was *that* long. Milo—my friends—the campers—they must think I'm dead. What if something bad happened? What if Milo's dead, died the same way Sorin did? What if he's in danger? What if—what if—

What if I can't save him, just like I couldn't save Sorin?

But that's impossible. It has to be—*has* to be impossible. Otherwise, I've failed. Failed everyone, failed everything. The Royal guard would laugh if I called myself a soldier.

"Selena," he says, snapping me out of my trance. "Are you all right?"

I nod and swallow down my fear, but he doesn't believe me. His eyes narrow slightly, but when he speaks, his voice is only kind, not accusing.

"No," says Dr. Abott, rather sadly. "No, you're not. Your heart rate accelerated tremendously when I asked you that question. Selena, please, don't lie to me." He looks away from the monitor in front of him and instead focuses on me, brown eyes studying mine intensely. His eyes, the same color as Milo's, only remind me of him, and my heart skips a beat in my chest.

"I'm fine," I force out. "Now, can we continue these tests? I want to get out of here."

I face the wall again, and after I do, I feel Dr. Abott's eyes on me—sad, pitying me. I don't need his pity, nor do I want it. How does he think it feels, anyway? Just splendid? I *died*. I was dead. My brother's gone, Finn's still alive somehow, and I was helpless and weak enough to be taken advantage of, to be killed.

"I'm going to ask you simple questions," Dr. Abott says. "You have to answer them honestly. It'll show me if there's anything wrong with your mind."

I say nothing, do nothing. I just want him to leave.

"How old are you, Selena?"

"Twenty-three," I say.

"What is your full name?"

"Selena Jane Torsney."

"Where are you?"

"A hospital."

"Why are you here?"

"Next question."

Dr. Abott opens his mouth to say something, but I send him a harsh look and he closes it again. He looks as if he's checking things off a list mentally and then continues to ask me simple questions.

"What is my name?"

"Dr. Ben Abott."

Dr. Abott stares at the monitor for a bit before asking me the next question: "Do you have any siblings? If so, what are their names?"

I tense. My throat constricts. "No," I say. "No, I do not have any siblings." *Not anymore.*

When my brother and I were little, we didn't think about the future. We were just kids, after all. But one night, I realized I'd forgotten how to swim. While I was in the water. I would've drowned had my parents not discovered where I was. That night, Sorin and I talked about funerals and what would happen if either of us died. He said he wanted a nice funeral, and he wanted all his friends to go. He always wanted everyone to like him. He never wanted anyone to give up on him.

And I'm not ready to give up on my brother either. Not ready yet.

So, then, after Dr. Abott moves onto the next question, I clarify my answer.

"I have siblings," I say, to his surprise. "I have a brother. But he's dead. And I really want to have a proper funeral for him. So could you put aside whatever else you're doing in the near future and help me?"

He's silent for a bit. Then, finally, he says, "Sure."

CHAPTER 6

ELYSIAN

Ash stares at me like I've gone crazy, which, considering the situation, I probably have.

"You want me to invite my campers, my *warriors*, to a ball thrown by another camp's supervisor?" she asks, raising a confused eyebrow. Sure, I deserve this distance that she's putting between us. After all, I asked for it. I asked if we could stay away from each other, and now I'm making that incredibly difficult. She has every right to be mad at me. *But please, Ash, not now. Not when I need you the most.*

"Yes," I tell her. I talk about Anne Kheefe and her visit to our camp, and I talk about the agreement she's set. She will help us only if we help her: by dressing in our best outfits and heading to a ball Anne is throwing.

She bites her lip, considering. I wonder how she's not frostbitten yet. The temperature, though only being early into October, not yet the time for winter, is drastically low, nearly freezing, and yet Ash is wearing a flannel shirt and jeans, not as warm as my sweater. She looks content, though. That's something, I guess, that I've always admired about her: her lack of feeling when it comes to harsh temperatures.

"It's insane," she tells me, stating the obvious. "You know that, right?"

I nod.

"And you already agreed."

I nod again.

"And you said *I* would be there."

I nod yet again.

"Are you crazy?" She stares at me hard, the considering look leaving her face. Her brown eyes, the ones I always adored, the ones flecked with gold that contrast from the dark brown of her iris, are even darker and more intimidating. "Seriously, have you gone insane? We—you're—*I* have nothing to do with this. This is your camp, your supervisor, not mine."

I shiver as a harsh wind blows past us. It's probably my fault that the wind is blowing so intensely, but it's not my fault that we're sitting in the cold meeting room with the windows propped open. I requested a private meeting with Ash without Milo or their supervisor or any of the other campers, because I knew she was going to react this way. "It wasn't *my* camp that was attacked," I say. "It was yours."

"Exactly," she shoots at me, "so stay out of it. I didn't ask you to do any of this."

"Because you're so stubborn that you'd rather die before you ask for help!" I lower my voice. "We're not getting anywhere arguing. If you don't want to go, I'm sure I could tell Anne and maybe she'd understand, and I guess I'll see you…around."

I readjust my belt that has my dagger strapped to it and turn to walk out the door, when I hear Ash sigh from behind me.

"Fine. But you are not controlling what I wear, and there's nothing you can do about that."

I smile faintly, manipulating my tone so I sound grudging. I know it'll satisfy her if she thinks she has the advantage over me. "Fine."

I leave the mess hall, feeling Ash's eyes on me as I do.

* * *

"Gods," Sage says, a curse following it. I'm sitting on her bed as she digs through a massive pile of clothes in front of her closet. Her cabin is decorated with many different posters and works of famous geographers and writers, most of the smart people in the world. She has tapestries and colored lights hanging around her room, most themed colors like white and green. Her hair is pulled up into a beautiful bun—it's Ball Day, as several campers have been whispering around campus, and a beauty-manipulation Magic named Lylah is great at doing hair. "Why, *why* would you let me bring so many clothes when I first got here?"

I chuckle. "You were a smart kid. I figured you knew what you were doing."

"Well, obviously, I didn't." She tosses an ivory dress at me and I catch it just before it hits me in the face.

"You're not wearing this, are you?" I hold it up before me and squint. "You'll probably blend in."

"Splendid." Sage whips around and steals the dress from me, throwing it on the ground with force. "This was a possibility, but it's not anymore. It's like I own nothing."

"That's because most of the stuff in here is stained with blood, ash, or is from when you were fourteen."

She flops on the bed. "I don't know what I'm going to wear to this thing, Lys. Sorin would help me out if he was able to. I don't even know who I'm going to go with. I mean, I could go with you, but you're probably going with Ash, and I guess Ameer doesn't have anyone but I don't know him that well and…I don't know what to do."

"There's always Milo," I tell her softly. Sorin and his absence is a sensitive subject for Sage.

"Do you really think it would be wise to go with him when he's still not over Selena?"

"You don't *need* to bring anyone, do you?"

"Of course I do! I need someone to dance with. What's the point of a ball if you can't even dance?"

"I can't dance," I say. "Ash can't dance. And I'm not sure I'm going with her."

"What's going on between you and her?" Sage, suddenly intrigued in the topic, leans forward on her elbows and glances at me. "You're strangely distant, yet you're doing all of this for her. And for some reason, you're not going with her. I thought you...you know, loved each other."

I'm about to say something in response, when a head appears in the doorway. Lylah Berkley is wearing a tight beige coat, puffy and fur-trimmed. Her dark hair is pulled away from her face, which is red from the cold, and she scowls, yelling, "Don't you dare mess up your hair, Sage!"

Sage rolls her eyes. "Go to archery, Lylah. Remember, you have my class later today."

Lylah crosses her arms over her chest. "Classes are canceled because of the ball."

Sage raises an eyebrow at me. I give her an apologetic look.

"Then...go do someone else's hair," Sage says. "I'll give you a hair tie."

"No, thanks," Lylah replies. "I've gotta find my dress, and then I'm going to study for the test tomorrow. *Do not mess up your hair.*"

"I wouldn't dare," she murmurs under her breath. Lylah leaves, eyeing Sage skeptically. "She scares me," Sage says when Lylah's out of earshot.

"Me, too," I say. All of the beauty-manipulative Magics are terrifying, and not only because of their sharp but amazing looks.

"Back to what we were talking about," she says quickly. "Don't you love her?"

"Of course I do. We just got into a fight, that's all. I went to her camp after the meeting with Anne and talked to her, and she said she would go, but I don't really think she wants me to go with her. It's not like the world is ending."

She sends me a weird look, a sad one, as if the world really *is* ending. "Lys. Don't you get it? In order for our camps to fight together in harmony, to not go back to the hell that we were before you and Ash fell in love, to even live against this new threat and these ghost-warriors, then you have to maintain a good relationship with her." She grabs my hand. "Your relationship is so important, which is what makes it strong. If it breaks, then it breaks, and the relationship between our camps breaks, too."

"That's totally not a lot of pressure."

"I'm just saying. It means a lot, not just to you and Ash, but to both of our camps." She winces. "I'm not helping, am I?"

"Not exactly." I chuckle. "Are you going to ask Lylah to help you find a dress?"

She opens her mouth, most likely to say she's not going, but I send her a warning look, and she sighs. "I'm going to ask someone else."

"Who?"

She doesn't tell me, but I understand who she's talking about immediately.

"Sage..."

"I want his opinion," Sage says.

"He's—"

"I know what he is." She diverts her eyes. "I know what he is, I know he's dead. I know. But these visions I see—these visions he sees me in—they're real enough. I still love him, and I want his opinion."

I sigh. Sage has been having dreams lately, ever since the beginning of August, in which Sorin Torsney, her ex, the former best Healer of Camp Serenity, talks to her, visits her, catches up with her. It's good for them to have closure, but she's getting attached. I want her to not get caught up with him—not for a second time, not if she's going to be damaged. Finally, I say, "He's going to say a green dress."

A look of surprise passes over her face.

I continue talking. "He's going to say a green dress with your hair up all nice and pretty, no makeup so your freckles stand out. He's going to say, if he doesn't, that you go as you are, since you're already perfect. He's going to say, most of all, that you're the love of his life, and that he wishes he was there in person to help you through all this. He gives his love to me and Ash and Milo and Selena, and he kisses you, and he says you're beautiful, and you wake up. That's what's going to happen, Sage. I knew Sorin for *so* long, and I know him. I know him. And I know that's what he'll say." She's still staring at me like I've grown another head, or I'm spouting nonsense, and, maybe I am. "But I know you, too, and I think I've known you for longer. And I know this is important to you. So I'll do whatever I can do to help you. Even pretending Sorin has any fashion sense."

She laughs, throwing one of her ironically sage-green pillows. "You're insufferable."

I smile, throwing a pillow back at her. But my focus isn't on the pillow fight. It's, unsurprisingly, on Ash, as it has been for the third time today. What would she say if I asked her what to dress in? And would she go with me if I, say, wondered aloud?

I don't know, but I want to find out.

* * *

"I need to speak with Ash."

Milo stares at me. His hair has grown longer, almost reaching past his ears. His eyes are less brown, somehow, but the sun is bright today, despite the chill that floats through the air, infecting passersby. He doesn't seem to look cold, though, but it's probably the suit that he's wearing that's aiding him.

"Are you...sure?" His jaw flexes. He's uncomfortable.

"Very," I tell him firmly. "I need to see her before..." I motion to the two of us. I'm wearing a sky blue, floor-length gown, my hair pulled up into an intricate twist, and I feel like an *actual* princess. "This."

He nods, leading me over to her cabin, where the door is shut tightly, the window blinds pulled all the way down. "Good luck," he says, then walks off to talk to some other campers, studying the outfits of others.

Not only did Anne invite me and Ash and the Junior Leaders of our camps, she also invited the rest of our camps.

"Ash! Are you in there?"

"Of course I am!" she yells. Her voice is slightly muffled, and she sounds annoyed. "Go away! I'm getting dressed!"

"I want to see you!" I yell back.

"Why?"

"Because you're still my girlfriend!"

She's silent. Then, she opens the door a crack. Her face is red with anger and I see her dark hair, braided close to her head. Her face has little makeup on and she looks absolutely beautiful, even though I can't see her outfit. "What do you want?" she asks.

"You look pretty," I say, feeling as if the breath has left my lungs.

Her look drips with venom.

"I'm here," I say, a slow smile spreading on my face, "to bring you to the ball, of course."

"You're my date?" She raises an eyebrow, a look of amusement passing over her face. "When you can barely walk in those heels?"

"You bet," I say cheerfully. "I'm going to be your escort. I'm going to take you to the dance, I'm going to dance with you, and you and I are going to mend this little issue that we're dealing with right now."

"Why are you doing this?" she asks. "Why are you trying to make up? I thought you were perfectly fine with this whole thing—the space that I'm giving you. I thought that's what you *wanted*."

"Of course it wasn't," I protest. "It's not! You—Ash, gods—I love you."

She bites her lip. "Fine." She smirks at me. "You may escort me to the ball."

She holds out her hand and I take it gladly, pulling her out of her cabin just to kiss her in front of her cabins in our fancy up-dos, to kiss her like there was never even anything wrong with us ever.

CHAPTER 7

SAGE

The carriages that line up outside of the massive ballroom are huge and gilded in gold. I wonder where Anne got the money to fund all of this.

The ballroom looms in front of me: intimidating, marble, lively and filled with brightly colored lights. Campers inside share secrets and drinks and dizzy dances, and I watch from my carriage as they converse amongst one another, wishing I was on that dance floor, doing the same thing with Sorin. He told me, just as Elysian had predicted, that I would look beautiful in whatever I wore, but I should wear an emerald green dress to match my eyes. So, using the oath she made to help me, I had Lys get me a floor-length emerald green ball gown, the exact shade of my eyes. And, of course, it's what I wear now, my green heels resounding against the floor of the carriage with a satisfying but depressingly lonely *click*.

"What's a pretty girl like you doing all the way out here, alone?" A tall boy appears in front of me, wearing an emerald suit, like we were destined to meet. He has messy blonde hair and alarmingly blue eyes, and as he studies me they grow wider. I'm assuming he's just now realizing the tears that run down my face, just as I am. "Are you okay?"

"Fine," I manage, and yet he still sits next to me in the carriage, wiping away my tears with one of his calloused hands.

"Why don't you go inside?" he says. "Why *aren't* you inside? I assume it's your friends that are in there fighting."

"Fighting?" My eyes widen. "They're fighting? Who's fighting? Two girls? One in black, one in blue?"

"Those are the ones," the guy affirms. "However, no one else seems affected. This happen a lot?"

Regaining my senses, I glare at the boy. "None of your business."

"I wouldn't be so feisty, pretty girl," he says with a laugh. "You're supposed to have fun. After all, it *is* a party." His eyes gleam as he says it, and then he's pulling me away from the carriage steps, leading me toward the ballroom.

"What are you doing?" I ask him suspiciously.

"You want a drink?" The boy smirks. "You wanna dance, pretty girl?"

"My name is Sage," I tell him, resisting the urge to roll my eyes.

"I prefer 'pretty girl' more. That's what you are. A pretty girl." He grins alluringly, still pulling me toward the music and the heat of bodies talking and dancing. It feels strange to want to be led into this mess by this guy and not my Sorin, but I suppose he'll have to do. I mean, he kind of looks like him, in a way.

"You know how, right?" he says. "How to move that gorgeous body of yours?"

I feel my cheeks heating. "Your name?"

When he says nothing, I repeat myself, more firmly this time. "Your name."

"Merrik," the boy, Merrik, says finally. "Sage, I must admit, you *are* persistent. I don't think anyone I've danced with tonight has gotten me to say my name."

"And you don't think that's a problem?"

"I think I do what I have to do to stay alive," Merrik tells me, his eyes suddenly serious. We're inside the ballroom now, the high, arched ceiling raining beams of light from crystal chandeliers upon us.

"I admire you for that," I say. He's started to circle me, and my dress swishes as I turn to face him. "Most wouldn't think before they act."

"I'm mostly careless," he tells me. "But you…you're different, you know that? Careful, always analyzing. It's something that's obvious about you. Something your enemies may use against you."

The topic of conversation has changed drastically, and I make sure to point it out. "Enemies? And you know so much about my enemies?"

"Of course I do."

He takes me in his arms, and we fall into perfect synchronization, dancing like we were made to. Merrik twirls me and I fall into his arms in a flawless dip, right as the music turns from fast-paced to a slow dance.

"After all, I am one."

I feel all the color draining from my cheeks but leaving now would be idiotic. There's too many people surrounding us, and, despite every other sense screaming at me to get out of there, my useless, lonely heart whispers, *Stay.*

"Now, I expected more of a reaction from you," Merrik hisses in my ear, his breath warm on my neck. "It's not every day that you get to meet your new nemesis."

"And you're so sure that you're going to be my enemy, *why?*" I ask him, stalling for time. The music grows louder as we converse while dancing, moving swiftly across the floor. Others make room for us and Merrik puts on a show, twirling me until I'm dizzy and I hear a few shouts of praise.

"I have done some things to your little…group—camp— whatever you call it." He flashes his blindingly white teeth and waits for me as I fall into step with him once again, making our way past the wine. I make a mental note to grab a cup of that if I can before we leave. "Not things you'd approve of," he adds, like I need the clarification. A minute ago he was calling me careful and considerate, and now he's talking to me like I can't even form full sentences.

I shouldn't care. He's just trying to get under my skin.

And yet it's working.

"I got that," I snarl through my teeth, and my heart pounds in my chest, not just from adrenaline and anger. There's attraction pulling me toward this man that claims he's my enemy, says he's not good for me.

I hate it.

Finally, the show ends. The music stops abruptly and Merrik's grip on me slips. I pick up my dress and try to move as quickly yet as carefully as I can in these tall heels to Elysian, talking with Milo in the corner of the ballroom, holding a glass of champagne.

I grab the glass from her and drink the remaining drops all in one gulp. "We need to leave."

"I don't see why," she tells me, raising an eyebrow. Elysian's eyes travel over to Merrik, where he watches me, satisfied, a smile curving the corners of his lips upward, like this is exactly what he expected me to do. "You looked like you were enjoying yourself."

"Nice dancing, by the way," Milo adds, flashing a grin at me. "I didn't know someone could spin so fast so many times without falling."

I glare at him, which confuses him, and turn to Elysian again, my look changing into one of desperation. "Seriously, there's something wrong with that man. He's—"

"Smoking hot," Elysian says, cutting me off. When Milo and I give her a look, she raises her hands. "I'm very loyal to Ash. I was just saying it because you weren't going to."

"Okay, fine, sure," I say. "He's cute. But that's not the point. The point is he's saying he's our enemy. *My* enemy. He acts like he knows everything about me, and he keeps hitting on me, and I…just feel uncomfortable."

Her eyebrows crease in concern. "He said stuff like that?"

Yes. "Yeah."

Her jaw works. Elysian turns to Milo. "You ready?"

"I'm good to go. I'm just not sure *she* is." He nods toward Ash, who is staring at Elysian while talking to a camper. She's obviously bored with their conversation and seems to be pleading with Elysian.

"She wants me to dance with her," Elysian says flatly, reading Ash's expression plainly. "I'm going to tell her that we have to go."

She walks over to Ash, an amused look on her face. Ash is definitely drunk. Her cheeks are pink and she seems to have trouble standing straight.

Merrik eyes me and begins to walk over to where I am, and my hand travels down to my hip, where my dagger is settled in its sheath. "Easy," he says soothingly when he gets to me, like I'm a wild animal. "I don't bite."

I shudder internally.

Milo gives me a look. He's asking me if this is the guy. I nod shortly and his eyebrows raise, just a fraction, before he puts on his friendly smile and holds out his hand. "Milo Belittle. Are you a friend of Sage's?"

"Not yet," Merrik says, leaving out the fact that he said not minutes ago that I was his enemy and he mine. "I hope to be, though."

You won't. I chuckle, like I'm flattered. By the way Merrik's eyes narrow when I do, he can tell it's fake. "Not in any universe," I hiss under my breath, my hand feeling for the hilt of my dagger.

"So quick to dismiss me." Merrik speaks quietly, blatantly ignoring Milo's hand. "Why is that?"

"You're insane."

"Maybe so. But don't you think I deserve a fair chance?"

"Never."

We're getting nowhere, and he must sense it, because he asks, raising his voice, "Another dance, Sage?"

"No, thank you," I say politely as people turn their heads to watch us. "I believe the alcohol is getting to my head."

"Then you shouldn't have any more." Merrik grabs the glass from my hands—a goblet made of the toughest glass in the kingdom—and shatters it without even glancing at it. "Come on, just one more dance? This is my favorite song."

I glance over at Milo. "Can I talk to Milo for a second, Merrik?"

His voice is tight when he says, "Of course." Merrik scampers off, still watching me somehow. I feel his eyes on my back when I turn to talk to Milo.

"This might get us information," I say.

"Or it might get you killed," he reminds me. "I see the hungry look in that man's eyes. There's something about him…" He trails off and shivers, though there isn't even a light breeze tonight.

I nod. "We should go."

Ash and Elysian are coming back anyway, Elysian hauling Ash toward us while she protests in drunken anger.

I move toward the door and Merrik is there in a flash, standing in front of me, a dark look in his eyes. He studies me, then Milo, and his eyes turn a colder blue somehow, like he's turned to ice.

"Move," I growl, my hand finally closing on the hilt of my dagger.

Before I can order him to move again, he grabs my hips and whisks me away to the dance floor and we're dancing wildly, him twirling and spinning and dipping. My feet have begun to hurt and my dress almost rips as it catches on one of the tables and yet he doesn't care. He's still dancing, and I'm still dancing with him.

His grip is like iron clamped onto me, and I quickly grow uncomfortable. My hand tightens around my dagger's hilt and I get ready to yank it from its sheath, when he spins me once, so if I try to reveal it, I will cut off my hand.

Dancers, like before, begin to clear the ballroom floor, and I hate it. Why can't they tell that I need help?

"Can't you see, Sage," Merrik finally says as we dance, "that I am remarkably like him? Can't you tell I'm exactly what you want, what you need, but what you can't have?"

I don't answer his questions, and it only makes him angrier.

"Can't you? Don't you see him?"

"Of course I do." My words are quiet but heavy with grief, and it's suddenly like a huge weight has been put on my shoulders. "Of course I see him. I see him in everything you do. This dancing, this banter. I see him. Why?"

"This is not just a simple coincidence," he tells me. "I am powerful. I am designed, as I was at the dawn of time, at the beginning of your entire world, to be exactly what everyone feared the most. And your fear, lovely Sage, is seeing Sorin again."

"How do you know that? How do you know anything about me?" He's slowed because I've started to yell, so I yank the dagger from my sheath and put the blade to his neck, though it feels like a blow to my gut. "How do you know his name? How, in that twisted mind of yours, can you believe that it's *okay* to speak his name? How *dare* you utter his name?"

And for a gratifying, beautiful second, Merrik looks utterly and completely shocked.

But then anger takes over in its place: red hot anger, anger that grows the more his perfectly blue eyes travel from my dagger at his throat to my eyes, the ones Sorin adored. I see the anger.

I *feel* the laughter.

It's low at first, startling me so much that I almost remove the dagger from his neck, but then I remind myself that's exactly what he wants. I press it harder into his perfectly tanned neck, his skin the same color as *his*. Sorin's.

His stunned mouth curls into a smile; a horrid, wretched smile that makes me want to throw up. He grows older in front of me as he laughs, older to the age of around mid-twenties, where his hair turns brown and his eyes chocolate and his skin deathly pale, the perfect opposite of Sorin. He's immortal and yet he seems so *old* somehow, as opposed to my perfect ex-boyfriend. His grip feels foreign and unwelcome, uncomfortable and weird. "Let go," I hiss, and he obliges, but carefully, so I'm still in his reach under the circumstances that I try to escape.

"What do you want?" I demand. "What do you want from me? What do you want from us?"

"Nothing," he says, still laughing under his breath. "But you will want something from me. And it will tear you apart."

He vanishes, and I sheath my dagger, yelling for the campers in the ballroom to get out before he returns.

I watch Milo and Elysian and Ash start running and I run behind them faster than I ever have, even in heels, so I catch up to them quickly. There wasn't a breeze before, but there is now—blowing through the trees and rustling the leaves and causing several campers to shiver and try to cover their bodies with their extra layers.

Adrenaline pumps through my veins, hot and yet exciting, thrilling, something I wish to experience more. Milo next to me glances back as if to see if I'm still there, and I nod shortly. I have no idea where we're going or how long it's going to take to get there or if Merrik will scare me while I sleep, but I don't care. All I need is to get away from the ballroom, to get away from the memories that haunt me even now, as I think back on that night sitting around the campfire. It makes me run faster.

Finally, a large building looms over us from out of the darkness. It's lit brightly and through the windows I can see it's busy with people. Above all that, it reads GRAYMONT HOSPITAL.

"We're at a hospital?" I ask Milo, coming to a slow.

He nods. "Apparently."

"Good," I say, glancing over at Ash. "Hopefully they have something to help her get over this alcohol."

He nods again.

We walk into the hospital.

Almost instantly, I find a doctor. She's dressed in blue scrubs, her graying hair pulled back. "Hello," I greet. "We're here to—"

"See the new patient?" the woman asks me. "Oh, yes, I suppose you are. Everyone's here to see Selena. She'll be waking up soon enough."

For the second time tonight, my face pales. "I'm sorry, wha—"

"Her room is room 27, and Dr. Abott is seeing her," she continues. "Have a good night."

When I make my way back over to the group, I can only manage a few words: "Guys, I think Selena is alive."

* * *

"Coffee?" a doctor asks me as he passes, sending me a questioning look. "Doesn't coffee shrivel your insides?"

Inside room 27 where Selena lay with tubes attached to her veins, it's stuffy. It's quiet and uncomfortable and not somewhere anyone in their right mind would want to be. I had to get out of there. That's why I hold a steaming cup of black coffee in my hands, staring at this doctor. And I am *really* not in the mood to let people judge me.

"Well, I just found out that my dead ex-boyfriend's supposedly dead sister is not actually dead, and coffee may shrivel my insides, but it is the only thing keeping my head attached to my body. So, yes, I guess it does."

Instead of staring at me like I'm insane as I suspected or walking away like I hoped, he laughs. "Yeah, that's an appropriate response."

"I wasn't going for *appropriate*."

"And I wasn't going for sarcastic," he tells me, a dorky smile still on his face. I let my eyes sweep him: his dark eyes; his blonde hair; his easy-going smile; his white lab coat that reads ABOTT. He notices me looking. "Dr Ben Abott," he says, holding out his hand.

I regard it absently, taking a sip of my coffee. "Sage."

"Do you have a last name, Sage?" When he says it, though, instead of it sounding like teasing, it sounds like an actual question.

"I don't see how that's any of your business." I glare at him.

"All right." He smiles, flashing white teeth. "I'm actually Selena's doctor."

"Now, how, Dr. Abott, did you know that's who I was talking about?"

"From the way you described the situation, I got a pretty good idea," Dr. Abott tells me. "Call me Ben, please," he adds. "Dr. Abott is only for patients, and you look in pretty good health."

"Thank you," I say, then dryly add, "Considering I just ran from an ambushed ballroom in high heels, that's flattering."

He gives me the once-over, probably just now realizing that I'm wearing a full-on ballgown. "You're welcome."

He looks like him, *too. Is this another trick planned by Merrik?* "Can I go now?"

He flashes me another smile. "Mind if I walk with you? I'm headed over there for a cancer patient."

"Do you get many mortals in this hospital?"

"Not exactly," he says, pushing his blonde hair away from his face. It painfully reminds me of Sorin, and I push the uneasy feelings that surface away with a force. "We get mostly Magics, as our staff is Magics—I'm a sun-manipulator from Ruri—but we do get some mortals mistaking the hospital for their usual, run-of-the-mill hospital, which makes sense, considering we have a rating system."

"Seriously?" I laugh.

"I'm kidding." He's still smiling. "Only the mortal hospitals have ratings. Plus, ratings are only for distant kingdoms—not the higher, more sophisticated people of the non-ratings."

I laugh again. He has Sorin's humor, and almost all of his looks, except the eyes. Though, in a way, it's a good thing that he's not exactly like him, for I don't know how I'd be able to stand it.

"Are they at least good ratings?" I ask, actually curious.

"No. Actually I'm pretty sure they'll need to remove the one-star options on those papers."

I crack a smile, then ask, "So, what did you do with Selena? As one of her doctors, I mean?"

"Well, I ran tests on her. I know enough to know her brother's dead, whom I'm guessing is the ex you were talking about. And I know she's…she *was*, at one point, very, very dead."

I stare at him, almost dropping my coffee. "How is that possible? She was dead, and now she's alive again?"

"Room 106, right next to the Castle of Buit—that's where you were, right? When she died?"

"Yes."

"The rumor going around is that the spirits brought her back to life."

Is he insane? "You're kidding. Those spirits—they're evil. They'll take you all the way across the globe without you asking."

"And," he says patiently, "they may think of that as a sign of helpfulness."

"Maybe," I argue, "but they're literal spirits. They've transported dozens and dozens of people to distant kingdoms and countries. Plus, they were living at some point. Don't they understand that people don't *want* to be taken away from the ones they love?"

"There's actually no scientific proof that the spirits that haunt Room 106 even lived at all." Ben isn't looking at me. *He must sense that I get scary when I make valid points*, I think sarcastically. "They might have spawned there when the kingdom of Buit was discovered. And didn't you notice, which I'm guessing you didn't, that most people scared out of their minds are unusually quiet? It's not like, when being faced with actual real spirits, they're going to suddenly grow a voice and beg for mercy."

"You've thought about this a lot," I note, a hint of skepticism sneaking into my voice.

"Well, when you're a doctor dealing with traumatized patients and a bored kid with a huge library, you learn a lot."

"You lived somewhere that had a huge library?" I whistle. "Milo would love that. Milo is—"

"Selena's boyfriend, I know." He's still not looking at me. It's making me uncomfortable.

"I don't think so," I tell him. "After she...died, I guess, Milo kind of shut up when it came to her. He only talked about specific topics, and when we brought her up, he'd go silent or change the subject. He was really upset."

"She murmurs about him in her sleep," he says, almost absently, like the tapestries that announce the hospital's title hanging from the ceiling above us are fascinating, something he can't tear his eyes away from. "I noticed that while I was doing a nightly check on her and had to wake her up."

"I bet she didn't handle that well."

He laughs. "It went swimmingly." Turning his head ever so slightly, he shows a purple bruise on his cheekbone. "She's also a sleep fighter. Did you know that?"

I chuckle. "Nice. You could say you got that in a fight with a rabid animal, make yourself seem cool. Considering that you work in the middle of nowhere, I doubt people will think anything else."

"I better head to my cancer patient," Ben says finally, sighing.

"And I should head back to Selena's room," I agree. "They might have ripped her head off already."

"Or maybe it's the other way around," he reminds me, and I laugh before he keeps walking down the hall, a smile curving the corners of his lips.

I walk the rest of the way to Selena's room, and I almost miss it when I hear her name. Milo is standing in the corner of the room, saying nothing. Ash and Elysian, Ash drunk, Elysian trying to reason with her, are arguing, the excitement and happiness of earlier tonight forgotten.

I throw my coffee cup away and sit on the metal chair next to Selena's bed, grabbing her ghost-white hand and squeezing it.

"You're freezing," I remark, and her head snaps up, relief filling her face.

"Oh, gods, Sage." She leans forward and wraps me in a hug. "I'm so sorry. Are you okay? I've missed you so much. All of you."

I smile. "I missed you, too, Selena. We all did. I'm okay. How are you? After all, you're the one who *died*, not me."

She chuckles lightly. "I guess that's fair."

"So? Grief latch onto you too tightly?"

"Considering I didn't have too much *time* to grieve, not really. I'm a little sick, but at least I'm well-rested."

I give her a look. "Let's be serious here."

"Sage, my brother learned every joke he knew from me," she chides. "You really think I'm going to be *serious* about this situation? It's the perfect opportunity."

"I hardly think this is the 'perfect opportunity,' but I'll take your word for it."

"You should. You're always so serious, Sagey. You always have been." She cradles my jaw, pulling out of the hug, and I watch as her eyes brim with tears. "You have no idea how much I missed you."

"I think I do," I retort. "You literally *died.*"

"Can you both stop with the sappy stuff?" Ash asks us, a look of anger and smeared mascara on her face. Selena's hands pull away from my face. "It's gross. Makes me want to throw up even more."

"You need to lay down," Elysian tells her softly. "Please, Ash, you're still drunk—"

"No, I do not!" Ash's voice is shrill, and I wince. Elysian grabs her hand and leaves the room, closing the door behind her.

"Milo," I say, pretending I just noticed him for the first time. "Did you say hi to Selena?"

"Not yet," he murmurs.

Selena's face dims. "It's fine," she says quietly.

I try to make it seem like I believe her, but it's hard, considering the previous relationship she and Milo had before the situation at Room 106 and the battle and her death. "You're freezing," I repeat. "Do you need a blanket, a jacket?"

She avoids my question. "Why are you all dressed so fancy? Wanted to look nice for me?"

I hear Milo choke from behind me. "A ball," I say shortly.

"And I wasn't invited?"

"I would've invited you if I thought you were alive, promise." I flash a smile. "But, honestly, I don't think you would've wanted to go."

"Bad?"

"Bad."

"That sucks. I'm always looking for opportunities to show off my dancing skills." She glances at the door. "What's with those two?"

"Elysian and Ash are fighting. Apparently they were together and then they broke up and, well, no one really knows what's happening between the two of them."

Selena opens her mouth to ask me another question when the door opens so quickly that it slams into the wall.

Elysian is in the doorway, her face deathly pale. Ash is standing next to her, looking as confused as the rest of us. "*Ameer.* Where's my brother?"

CHAPTER 8

AMEER

By the time my carriage pulls up to the ballroom, it's empty,

flickering candles the only things illuminating the place. It's been

completely deserted, tables turned over, ripped fabric hanging from

dozens of places.

"You're sure this is where you're supposed to be?" the driver of

my carriage asks me, his eyes narrowing as he studies the sight in

front of us.

I nod. "I'm sure."

I step out of the carriage, trying not to wrinkle my suit, and

enter the ballroom. It's a beautiful place—or at least, it looks like it

was before it was left behind. There's wine glasses shattered in one

corner of the room, and glass on the floor everywhere I turn. I try

my best to avoid it. The ceiling is high and arched, beautifully

painted with patterns of Cupid and his arrow. The structure is

painted gold and decorated with splotches of red wine and

champagne and other kinds of alcohol, and I see a bottle that I pick

up and gulp from, trying to steady my nerves. My sister has to have

been here, right? She told me this is where she was going to be. I hope nothing bad happened to her. But she knows how to handle herself, especially how to survive after being ambushed.

Where *is* she?

I set the bottle down, trying to focus, when something whooshes past me, barely a whisper of a noise, but for some reason, it's now all I can think about. I stumble toward where it's headed—the entrance of the ballroom—as someone materializes in front of me.

He's tall and mysterious, with hair and eyes the color of the night outside. His skin is bronze and smooth and a contrast from the white shirt he wears under his blue blazer. Even though he's nice to look at, he's still a surprise, and I jump upon his arrival.

"Where are you going?" the boy asks me, a slow smile spreading across his face. "Leaving the party so soon?"

"I hate to do it, considering it's the rager of the century." I motion around us at the empty ballroom.

He raises an eyebrow in surprise. "Sarcasm, eh? Well, you're partially right about that. You can't see the spirits partying right now, but that's only because your ignorance doesn't allow you to."

"Spirits exist?" I ask him suspiciously, and I hate it when I am suddenly reminded of the dream I had not too long ago, of the battle with the ghosts and the torches.

"Of course they do, silly." The boy flashes me a grin. "They're all around us. You have one. We will all be spirits eventually."

"What do you mean, I *have* one?"

"Everyone has one. Everyone's spirit is reflective on themself as a person, and that's why there's different kinds of spirits."

"Do you have a spirit, whoever-you-are?"

"Let's just say," the boy says with a sinister look, "all of the spirits you see here are mine."

Suddenly, the ballroom is filled with all kinds of people in fancy gowns and high heels, the perfect picture of dancing sophistication. They talk in hushed tones and drink alcohol, and their eyes keep traveling back to me as they whisper.

"Are they talking about me?" I ask no one in particular.

The boy hooks his arm in mine. "Let's meet everyone, shall we?" he says, deflecting my question.

The boy and I begin to walk across the room to a couple wearing blood-red clothing, their dark hair pulled away from their similarly dark eyes.

"The Longreys," he tells me, then turns to them. "How are you?"

"Fine, thank you." The woman, Mrs. Longrey, sends a glare to the man. She's distracted, probably by the fight they've just ended. "And you?"

"You didn't let me answer," Mr. Longrey hisses. *Or maybe the fight they're still having.*

"And you had something that just *desperately* needed to say? *'Good,'* maybe? Because that seems to be the extent of your vocabulary!"

"Longreys, Longreys, please," the boy says, a charming smile on his face. "We have a guest. Meet Ameer Domhnall."

I ignore the weirdness of the fact that I never told this guy my first name, much less my *last* name, and politely hold up a hand in a half-hearted wave toward the fighting Longreys. As soon as they see me they both close their mouths and their eyes widen.

"He's the one?" Mrs. Longrey asks the boy quietly. "Ameer? The king?"

"Now, now, Mrs. Longrey, let's hang on a second," the boy scolds. "Ameer is a guest. Let's leave him and the topic of politics alone."

"But you said—" Mrs. Longrey protests.

She closes her mouth when she notices Mr. Longrey and the boy glaring at her.

"Of course, sir," Mr. Longrey says to the boy, and they continue fighting as the boy brings me to another group of lively, drunk people. These people are dressed in midnight blue and they have lighter hair, hair so blonde that it looks almost silver in the moonlight.

One girl in a blue ball gown brings a glass to her lips and laughs at a joke. She's gorgeous, and her eyes widen when she sees me, not unlike the Longreys. "Sir!" she says, catching the boy's eye. "I didn't know you were coming tonight."

"I had to be there to escort our special guest," the boy tells her with a fond smile. "This is Ameer Domhnall. Make yourselves known, now."

"I'm Mia." The girl, Mia, motions with her wine glass to herself. "I didn't know *you* were coming tonight, either! Being in the same room with you is a gift, apparently, since we all know what you're capable of."

"Capable of?" I send a weird look to the boy. Leaning close, I ask him, "How do these people know what I'm 'capable of'? I'm not even sure *I* know what I'm capable of."

"He tells us very much about you, Ameer," Mia explains, glancing between the two of us. "Has he not told you?"

"Not yet," the boy tells Mia, and he seems calm, but there's a point to his expression.

"You talk about me?" I ask quietly, shocked.

"Goodbye, Mia," the boy says dismissively, and we move to a different table.

The man stands by himself, watching the few couples dancing with a longing, wistful look. He has a champagne glass partially up to his lips and when he notices us standing in front of him he almost drops it. The look on his face turns into a fake, obviously forced smile.

"Hello, sir," the man greets, raising his hand and the champagne glass with it. "You look great."

"You flirt, Matthew," the boy says, his body tensing. *"Stop it."*

Suddenly, Matthew's face turns white. He goes slack, and when he returns to his body again he's smiling like nothing happened. "Have we met before?"

It takes a minute before I realize he's talking to me.

"Uh, no," I say cautiously. "I don't believe so."

"Oh, that's a shame! You seem like such a great person."

"So do you." I tip my head toward him, smiling, though nothing here prohibits a smile. He takes a sip from his champagne glass and instantly grimaces, spitting it back into the cup. "Something wrong?" I ask.

"He's not a drinker," the boy tells me quickly, before Matthew can respond. "Light stomach. You know how they are."

I chuckle. "Yeah, I'm one myself."

"I don't believe that, considering the bottle that's already halfway empty over there," Matthew cuts in.

I feel the color drain from my face. *Have they been watching me?* "What?"

"He doesn't know what he's talking about," the boy says hastily.

"No, I think he does," I respond sharply. "What do you mean, Matthew?"

"Call me Matt. Matthew is only for the boss."

"Boss of what?"

"I can't tell you that."

"Tell me *what?*"

"We see you."

Matthew vanishes. He's gone so suddenly that I wonder if he was even there at all. But then I see that everyone else who was in the ballroom—Mia, the Longreys, *everyone*—is gone. The boy still stands next to me, though, and his face is ghostly pale.

"It's started so soon," he says quietly.

"Started? What's *started?"* I glare at him.

"You hate me already."

"Yeah, I do. There's so much you're not telling me, obviously. Matthew—what was that all about? And you—*you*—something's going on with you."

"Of course, something's going on with me," he bites back. "I don't have experience in this area of human manipulation. I knew Merrik hiring me was a mistake—I shouldn't have asked him—but Matt recommended it—and the hating has started already."

"Human manipulation? Merrik *hired* you? Matt recommended what?" I stare at the boy, turning to face him. "Who—*what* are you?"

"I'm like you," he tells me. "I'm human. I'm loyal to my friends. Loyal enough to get roped into this job—the job I didn't even want! Who *wants* a job like this? Leading people on, getting them to like me, fall for me, even, and then sending them on their way with this stupid thing so Merrik can trap them!" He motions to his dog-tag necklace, which I now realize he's wearing.

"So, this stuff about the spirits—they don't exist?" I ask cautiously.

"Of course they exist!" he yells. He's fired up now, and I make no move to calm him. "And I was supposed to show you that, drive you insane, and make you the perfect victim for Merrik. I've failed, and now he'll kill me. He'll kill me, and I'll be dead."

"That's usually how that works."

He glares at me.

"Look, while that doesn't sound like the most fun thing in the world, I just want to get this straight. Everything I've seen exists. You were supposed to lead me through here, drive me insane, give me that tracking dog tag necklace, maybe make me fall for you, and send me home all happy and dandy so that I could be a victim to Merrik?" I demand, confusion showing itself in my voice.

"You've heard of him, then? Oh, this will make things so much easier. When you're being offered your new job as the head of the 'Camp' department, put in a good word for me. Tell Merrik *I* was the one that gave you the dog-tag necklace. He'll surely reward me."

"*'Camp'* department?"

"Merrik—he made a whole department because of you and your friends and that sister of yours," the boy explains. "He's crazy about the lot of you. Insane."

I stare at the boy in front of me. "What's your name?"

He looks excited suddenly. "Did you just ask me what my name is? Are you *agreeing*? Oh, please tell me you are." When I say nothing, he says, very quietly, "My name is Adam."

"Adam, good." *We're making progress.* "Do you, Adam, by any chance, know how *crazy this is*? And you think I'm just going to agree? Do you know how crazy *you* are?" I sgih, trying to control my tone. "Okay, Adam. You like Merrik, right? You're a follower?"

He sends me a reproachful look.

"Of course you are. But, anyway, you're loyal to Merrik. If he said to let me go, would you?"

Adam nods.

"And if he said to kill me, would you?"

"He would never say that. He wants you and your sister and the rest of your little clan alive."

"Hypothetically. But why would he want me alive?"

"He thinks you're useful, needed for a project he wants to pull off," Adam says. "If you're not alive, he can't use you."

"Project?"

"To create an army."

"An army?"

"There's a war stirring," he continues. "Everyone knows that. Merrik knows it, especially. He wants to be ready. He knows that your sister's powerful, and he knows that her girlfriend is powerful, too. He knows it, and he wants to use it."

"Use it? What do you mean?"

"He wants to drain them of their power or use them as warriors," he explains. "Merrik says Magics are valuable, and it's clear that when he says he uses valuable resources, he really does. But..."

"But?"

"There's a way you can stop him."

"And," I start urgently, "that way is?"

"Merrik's main power is fear," Adam says, and I'm afraid for a second that this is his way of leading me on. "He feeds off of it. It's what fuels him. If someone doesn't fear anything, he's powerless."

"So you're telling me that in order to stop Merrik from draining my sister and her girlfriend of all their powers and using it in his war, I have to learn to fear nothing?"

"That's exactly what I'm saying."

I stay silent.

"It's not supposed to be easy," he tells me impatiently. "It's supposed to be a challenge. That's exactly why he rules over it—so that he can never be defeated."

His necklace grows dangerously, and he cries out in pain, reaching up to cradle his neck. "You need to take this, quickly," Adam says, holding out the necklace.

"No!" I say, aghast.

"Fine," Adam says, suddenly very bitter. "But he practically already knows where you are, and once he finds you, it's only a matter of time before you die, along with all the rest of your *friends!*" Then he vanishes, leaving the ballroom in shreds and a giant weight on my shoulders.

A light flickers in the distance—a blindingly white, blindingly bright light—and, like a moth drawn to a flame, I follow it. The smell of burning as one of the ballroom's tapestries catches on fire reminds me of all that I have learned—and all that is at stake.

CHAPTER 9

MILO

Selena being helpless is tearing me apart, and there's nothing I can do about it.

She's just been laying there in that bed for days—weeks—*months*—and I thought she was dead the entire time. I gave up on her when I shouldn't have, and the thought alone is enough to make me want to literally tear my heart out and splay it on the bed in front of her, to repeatedly tell her that it's hers.

But I can't do that.

So, when I see the cup of coffee in Sage's hand, I leave the room to get myself a cup. She's been pushing me to talk to Selena, and I would—I would whisper to her until my voice grew hoarse—but I can't. I just *can't.*

If I tried that, I would break before I had the chance to.

I walk the halls for a bit, mulling the events of the past few days over and over in my mind, scrutinizing every detail until they feel like distant dreams more than memories. A nurse finds me, glares once, and allows me to keep walking. Eventually, I come across the coffee machine and pour myself a cup, downing it. The burn of the hot coffee hits me like a freight train, and it's like waking up from my horrible, horrible dreams.

Where are we going to sleep? How long are we staying here? Do we need medical help? Is anyone hurt? Did I do a headcount? How is this ever, even in another reality, going to work?

"Excuse me," I say to a passing staff member, pushing a cart filled with mushy stuff that I think is food. "Do you know where I can find any clothing?"

She nods and motions to follow her. I oblige and listen to the clanging of the cart as it rolls over the floor tiles. We finally stop in front of a closet and she ducks inside, handing me hospital gowns. I take them from her gratefully, but not before asking if there's any other clothes the hospital has.

She nods again and I follow her without needing to be told. She stops before the cart does, and it rams right into the next closet door. Inside of this closet is scrubs that she gives me four pairs of, like she knows exactly who I am and what I'm talking about.

"Thank you," I tell the woman, and she nods for the third time.

And then she's gone, back on her way with her hopefully edible food in tow.

I wonder absently if that woman has ever been in the situation I'm in. I wonder that simply because I need to wonder something, even if it's preposterous. I need to get my mind off this situation.

I make my way back to Selena's room, the coffee in my cup looking pathetically up at me—well, at least, the last few drops that are left look up at me pathetically. I speed up, not quite wanting to be in a hospital room that has Selena's name written on the door, but also not quite wanting to be in the middle of a hospital with no coffee and scrubs in my hands.

I crack the door open. It's just Selena. Sage is gone. She's probably at the coffee pot. I place the scrubs and the empty coffee cup down on the foot of her bed and sit down in the chair farthest from her, making sure not to look her directly in the eye.

The truth is, I'm afraid. I'm scared. I don't want to get too attached, in case something like this ever happens again. I don't want to lend my heart to someone when I'm so permanently scarred. And maybe that makes me sound shallow or like a control freak, needing everything to be perfect. But I do. I need it to be perfect for her.

"Are you afraid of me?" Selena asks suddenly, breaking the silence. "Are you scared, Milo?"

It's like she read my thoughts. "Of course not," I lie.

"Then why won't you look at me? Why won't you touch me? Why won't you even sit by me?" She motions to the distance between us, and I still keep my head hung low, afraid. I'm a coward, and I hate it. I hate it.

"Say something," she pleads. "Please."

She coughs violently, and my eyes finally snap up. I rush toward her when I see the blood on her bed.

"D-did—was that you?" I ask her.

Selena avoids the question. "I don't have a lot of time. My power is draining, I can feel it. I'm dying, slowly. I want to make sure I have enough time with you. And if you keep pushing me away, denying my company, avoiding my eyes and avoiding *me*, then I'm not going to have that. *We* aren't going to have that."

I stay silent, staring at her face. There're freckles on the bridge of her nose and on her cheeks, I notice. They weren't there back in July or August. She looks tired, not just physically. Her eyes are exhausted, weary. I realize what she's saying is true.

And I hug her.

She's too stunned to do anything for a moment, but then I feel her arms wrapping around me. She hugs me tighter than I'm hugging her, which seems nearly impossible. And suddenly I'm crying, tears hitting her shoulder.

I sniffle. "Selena, I missed you," I tell her. "I missed you so much, and it tore me apart. Gods, I missed you."

At those words, she hugs me even tighter. I know my fancy clothes are probably wrinkled but I don't care.

I pull away from her slowly, and her eyes are sad, but she's smiling. "I missed you too."

And I realize how much she missed me when her lips crash against mine.

My hands instantly come up to cup her face. She sighs, and for a second I'm scared that I'm doing something wrong, but when she doesn't pull away I'm pretty sure I'm doing everything right.

The kiss ends, and the world comes back, but slowly—I register the hospital bed and the room itself distantly, like it's an illusion. "How's that for missing you?" she asks me, a stupid grin on her face.

"P-pretty good," I stammer.

Someone bursts through the door and I snap out of whatever trance I've been in, rushing back to my chair.

"I got you that fruit cup you asked for," Sage tells Selena, handing her one of the items from the cart I saw earlier. "Pretty weird request, considering that it's one in the morning and they're still giving out fruit cups."

It's one in the morning? "Seriously?" I say, surprised that it's already so late.

"Oh, Milo, didn't see you there," Sage says, not answering my question. "You're so quiet. Have you talked to Selena yet?"

My eyes dart to hers, to that stupid grin still on her face.

"We...talked," I say.

"What's the grin about?" Sage asks Selena, and Selena simply says, "I just...*really* love fruit cups."

I clear my throat, changing the subject. "Where's Ash and Elysian?"

Sage says, "They're outside. Ash is smoking, Lys is telling her about the negative side effects, the usual. But every few minutes they'll stop and stare at each other. It's weird."

"Well, they're not the most normal people," Selena points out.

"None of us are." Sage shrugs, sitting in the chair right next to Selena's bed. She grabs her hand and begins talking to her, but even after they're deep in conversation, I can still feel Selena's eyes on me. I leave the room, deciding to put on my scrubs and call it a night.

* * *

I could talk about how bad sleeping in a hospital is, but then I fear that I would regain memories, and those are some that I'd like to block out.

My back hurts once I wake up. The scrubs I have on are tight, fitting too close to my body for comfort, and I groan as I spot the only other clothes that I have.

I decide to change into my dress shirt and slacks, without the tie or the jacket. They're not comfortable, either, but they'll have to do.

Ash groans as she wakes up. She's sleeping next to Elysian on an air mattress on the floor. She spots me and asks, "Why is your shirt tucked into your pants *this* early in the morning?"

I don't respond, instead leaving the room to get another cup of coffee. I sneak a glance at Selena before I leave—she's incredibly pale, and her lying in that bed like she's dead makes me want to look away again. But she's still Selena, and I smile at her.

Maybe it's my exhaustion making me delusional, but I swear she smiles back.

I find Sage at the coffee station, leaning against the table while she sips. She's changed into scrubs now, but she's wearing her heels.

"Why are you wearing your dress clothes?" she asks me immediately.

"You and Ash have very similar minds," I tell her, pouring myself a cup.

"I seriously doubt that." She throws away her cup. Sage must notice my tired eyes, because she says, "Long night?"

"Long night," I agree. "How long have you been here?"

"The entire night."

"So it was an even longer night for you."

Dr. Abott, Selena's doctor, passes by us, and I can't ignore the way Sage's eyes catch on him and follow him. I give her a weird look.

"Do you like Doctor Abott?" I ask her, resisting the urge to smile.

"Of course not," she says sharply, glaring at me. "That's stupid. Why would you think that? Of course, I don't *like Dr. Abott.*"

"Sorry, sorry." I hold up one hand in retreat, then take another sip of my coffee. "I just wondered. You don't exactly stare at everyone like they're an exhibit at a museum, you know."

"Your references really need some work," she retorts, but she's not denying it.

"Maybe, but I don't think I'm wrong."

"The wrong people never do." She shakes her head, but there's something with her. She seems more scattered, somehow.

Am I wrong? I ask myself.

No, I don't believe so.

CHAPTER 10

AMEER

I walk for a bit before stumbling across a large clearing, seemingly deserted.

There's a few bits of trash on the ground, but nothing too extreme—no other signs of life, at least. The sun is beginning to rise, and yet I still find one of the trees to rest against and close my eyes.

Finally, the sound of rustling wakes me up.

The afternoon sun is hot on my cheeks. My dress clothes feel hot and stuffy, and I relentlessly toy with the collar of my button-up. I remember what woke me and glance around wildly.

Then I see an arrow positioned at my head.

"Who are you?" the person holding the bow demands. A boy, by the looks of it. He has short blonde hair and eyes a grayish-purple color. My mouth opens and closes as I decide what to say.

The boy takes a step forward, so the arrowhead is nearly touching my forehead. "I *said*, who are you?"

"No one important," I manage.

He glares at me. "I don't believe that."

"Who are *you?*"

"*You* are the one trespassing in *my* forest," the boy says, his expression hard, eyes calculating, yet there's a hint of curiosity in them. "I believe I have the right to question you."

"*Your* forest? Is your name on it? What *is* your name, anyway?"

The boy lowers his bow partially. "You're strange. But don't think I'm letting you go this easily. You will tell me what I want to know, or I'll kill you."

"Go ahead and do it," I tell him. "Please, I beg you. These last couple of years—my whole life, actually—have been filled with all kinds of misery, and now I'm being stalked by a guy with a ghost army. Kill me, please. It's my only request."

He rolls his eyes, dropping his bow completely. "As tempting as that is, I can't. Not while you're that pathetic. Seriously, if you want someone to kill you, at least *pretend* to put up a fight. It'll make you seem more...killable."

"How flattering."

He squints suddenly, scrutinizing me. "I know you from somewhere. Somewhere...distant."

I suck in a breath. So far, I haven't been recognized yet for being a prince (other than by those spirits), but I feel like I'm toeing that line right now, as this boy studies me.

My cheeks flame.

Eventually, he decides. "I think I've seen your tribe wandering around in these woods. You come from the Combatants Tribe, don't you?"

"Yes, of course," I say, nodding hastily. "I come from the...Combat Tribe."

"Combatants," he corrects me.

"Doesn't that mean 'fighters' in French?"

"Yes, it does." His eyes narrow. "But I'm sure you're well aware of that. After all, you *are* a member."

"Uh—"

"And since you're a member, you know that the Combatants' rival is the Pugnatores, and that they are very serious about the land they inhabit, and they absolutely *hate* strays and Combatants?"

"Um—"

"And you would know, were you an actual member, that I am the son of the chief of the Pugnatores tribe, and I am known to be vicious and unforgiving, correct?" The son of the chief of the Pugnatores tribe leans close so he's whispering in my ear. "And, by the way, I *really* hate liars."

He slams his bow into my head, and I pass out.

* * *

When I wake up, my hands and feet are tied behind my back. Several men and women stand over me, and when my eyes open they back away like I've wounded them. One of the men calls for an Andrew, and then there's a younger boy standing over me, staring into my eyes.

I recognize this boy from before. I groan as my head throbs. "Why did you knock me out?"

The boy, Andrew, grins. "I hate liars, Prince Ameer."

I tense at my title. I guess after he figured out that I lied about being a Combatant, he also figured out really quickly who I was. I mean, I have the face for being a prince, considering I am one. "Don't call me that," I say.

"Pretty bold words coming from the boy who's in the infirmary right now with his arms and feet tied behind him," Andrew retorts. "I can get you killed in two seconds, so I would refrain from telling me what to do if I were you."

I swallow, glancing down. I'm in a white bed, sure enough, but I'm propped against the pillow and not really relaxed. And it seems like this is a pretty scarce infirmary, considering it's just a patch of land in the Pugnatores' headquarters.

"Where'd you get the bed?" I ask him.

He begins to loosen the rope around my feet. "From my friends," he says. "The Pugnatores tribe has areas in many different kingdoms, and many different areas around *this* kingdom. Just because my father is the chief *here*, that doesn't mean there's several other chiefs everywhere else, all of which would have the sense to rip you apart as soon as they saw you."

"I'm guessing I'm not that well liked within the community?"

"Especially since you lied to the son of a chief," Andrew confirms.

"Word spreads fast around here," I note.

He moves to my hands. "Yes, it does. Mostly because the people in this tribe are the nosiest people I have ever met. I can't say the same for you. How many of the stuffy Royals that you talk to gossip?"

"Most."

"That's what I figured." He steps back, dropping his hands at his sides. He's wearing a simple leather outfit, but the fabric looks strong enough that not even the sharpest blade could cut through it. I notice that his hand stays positioned strangely, right above his hip. I assume that's where he's stashed a dagger or weapon of some kind. "We're going to hold you hostage for a few days, see what you know. Nothing too extreme. Then you can go."

I consider telling him about last night's events, and even though something tells me that it's not a good idea, I say, "I don't have anywhere else to go."

"Princey was thrown away?" Andrew teases. "Well, guess what? So was everyone else here. Figure it out. You leave on Wednesday."

I send him a confused look.

"You leave at dawn three days from today. Today is Sunday."

I nod. "Okay."

Andrew rolls his eyes. "Unless..."

"Unless?"

"Unless you were so helpless that I just couldn't find the heart to kill you, that you were writhing on the floor in agony at the thought of being sent away. Then, I would be exiled for forcing out a prisoner."

"You can force out a prisoner?"

"In this society, you can, yes. But you're missing the point, Princey."

"Oh, yes, of course." I writhe on my bed. "I don't want to leave!" I cry, hoping my voice carries far enough for others to hear me. "I have nowhere to go! I'll be killed! Please, Andrew!"

"Andy," Andrew corrects quietly. "Just Andy."

"Oh, okay. Andy!"

He smiles, though grudgingly. It seems like the act is foreign to him, and I bet it is., with the amount of blood that has stained his hands red.

Then Andy's gone, and I stare at the wilderness ahead of me before passing out again.

* * *

Someone is pouring a bowl of steaming liquid into my mouth when I wake again. Andy stands above me, a scowl on his face. "Do you know how difficult you are? I tried to feed you this soup, made by me, and you kept spitting it out, despite the fact that you weren't fully conscious! It was really offensive to my cooking."

"I think I'll refrain from drinking anything that's been given to me by a stranger, thanks," I say, pushing myself up onto my elbows. "Why are you helping me anyway? I thought you hated me."

"Not necessarily," Andy tells me, sitting on the foot of my bed. "Granted, you did come into my woods unannounced, and I thought you were threatening me, but I'm willing to give all of my...guests...chances to improve themselves. And right now, you're not making that good of an impression."

I look down. "You know, I appreciate keeping me around like this, but I'll have to leave eventually. My sister—"

"The princess?"

"Yes, the princess. She'll be looking for me. I need to get back to her soon." I glance up to see Andy's reaction. He's staring back at me, his expression unreadable. "Except...I don't know where she is."

"I've never met the princess before," he says thoughtfully. It's all he says.

"Well, she was taken away from the castle when she was seven, and then...Why am I telling you this?" I question, mostly to myself, but Andy answers.

"Probably because you're a little messed up in the head."

I stare at him, trying to keep my expression impassive. "Andy…" I say. "I need to leave. Soon."

"I know," he says. His eyes are hard again. "Where are you going to go, Princey?"

"I was kind of just guessing I'd wing it."

"Oh, yeah, that sounds like a great plan." Then he sighs. "Look, I know you don't want to stay here. I don't want you to stay here either. But I promised my father you'd be interrogated. If I let you go now without questioning you, my father…well, he's not the best person. He's executed the people in the past who have lied to him."

"But it's not necessarily *lying*. It's just…making an assumption."

"It's making a promise, Princey." Andy stares hard at me. "Promises can't be broken when it comes to my father. It's a binding oath."

"Binding oath?"

"I'm sure you don't know this, considering the insufficient amount of information you know about the tribes in your very own kingdom, but the Pugnatores tribe is *very* serious about the promises its people make. Promises are so much more than the loose offers you grew up with. In a way, they're contracts, a simpler way of saying, 'I will do as I say.'"

"You can't just say, 'I will do as I say'? It has to be a binding oath?"

He glares at me. "The questioning starts today. If you don't answer the way we want, then you'll be tortured. Do you understand?"

I glance around the forest, spotting two Pugnatores tribe guards, watching me with threatening looks. One of them cracks their knuckles when he spots me looking at him.

"Uh, sure. Yeah, I understand," I say, but I'm not really listening to him. My eyes are on the guards that are clearly wishing to kill me, but the son of their chief is stopping them.

I turn back to Andy. His jaw is clenched, and he's standing now, reaching out for me so he can haul me to my feet. The forgotten bowl of soup sloshes onto the white sheets as I am pulled to the ground, and then Andy drops my hand like it's acidic, motioning with a nod to the guard to tell them to start walking. They do, and Andy whispers something to the one who cracked his knuckles at me, and he stops so he's behind me, waiting to see if I try to make a run for it.

I don't. I'm not really nervous about this questioning. I mean, I've always been a truthful person. I try my best not to lie, so this won't be bad for me. Besides, how will anyone know if I lie? Isn't the point of a questioning to find out more information, not ask questions about things you already know about?

The guard's hot breath is on my neck. When Andy and the guard in front of me stop suddenly in front of a large, metal building seeming like it's made for torture, I lose all my confidence in my safety during this questioning very, very quickly.

The guard grabs my arms, twisting them behind me, and shoves me into the room after the other guard opens the door. I'm thrown to the floor, and my hands are chained. I just now realize that the ropes around my limbs have fallen off, probably because Andy loosened them before.

"Andy?" I say, and the door is closed, bathing me in darkness. My voice grows more anxious. "Andy!"

"Shut up," one of the guards hisses, and there's a stinging pain in my back. I realize I've been cut with a knife. "You stay quiet and this will be quick. You talk, and it'll only make it a lot longer and a lot more painful for you."

Suddenly there's a blinding light in my eyes. I squint, resisting the urge to whimper, and then Andy's standing in front of me, holding a knife, the glint of the blade matching the evil glint in his eyes.

"What do you know about Finn Brocker?"

I feel the color drain from my face. *Okay, maybe it'll be harder to lie than I thought it would be.* "He...kidnapped me, not too long ago. I was held hostage for over a year."

He doesn't look satisfied with my answer, based on the grim expression on his face. "The princess. What magic does she have? What kind?"

"Uh…I don't know."

There's more pain in my back. I cry out. *How do they know I'm lying?* That causes another shock of pain to rise up my spine. "Okay, okay, I know! She's a weather Magic. She can control the weather."

"And?"

"I—I don't know!"

More pain.

"I was *talking* about the extent of her power," he says sharply. "Does she cause storms? How powerful is she?" When I don't answer immediately, he demands, *"Well?"*

"I've never seen the extent of it. I'm pretty sure she's like most of them—can cause storms and immense damage if she wants to— but, like I said, I only knew her until she was seven. We just recently reunited, but our house was a sheltered one, and we were never allowed to display magic publicly."

"I didn't ask for a life story, did I?" He leans forward, whispering in my ear. Then he suddenly rears back. "So you believe she's like every other one of them, huh? You don't know anything about her?"

"Nothing," I say, thinking that's the right answer. Of course, with this violent side of Andy, *nothing* seems to be the right answer.

"Then you're of no use to me," he says with a wave of his hand. "Guards, kill him."

"Wait!" I cry. "You said—you promised your father not to kill me! You promised to let me go!"

"I did nothing of the sort," Andy says in a cold tone. "And as for my father, I simply promised that you would be questioned, not set free. And, didn't *you* agree to the torture that would happen here? Why, this is simply the penalty that you are facing for intruding into my forest. Guards."

He leaves the metal room, leaving me alone with two blood-thirsty guards, both of whom have their swords raised.

I reach for my sword—and then I realize that I'm wearing dress clothes, and that Andy and the Pugnatores tribe probably stripped me of all the weapons that I might have had when I entered their home.

Panic grows in my chest, rising to my throat like a title wave, causing it to constrict. I try to put on a brave face, but then my eyes land on the doorknob. It's locked with four locks. I couldn't even break them if I used all my might.

The guards advance on me, their swords raised. I stand there, paralyzed in fear, ready to accept my fate of dying young, afraid, and cornered. Not exactly the way I want to go, but it seems like the only option right now.

And then something unexpected happens. The guards freeze. Literally. Ice crawls up their limbs and the blades of their swords, stopping them completely.

I stare at my newly-made ice statues, the panic in my chest not leaving but growing.

I was really getting used to the thought of dying mostly peacefully.

CHAPTER 11

AMEER

I stand there frozen, shock painted on my face.

I glance around at my surroundings. The door is locked, so there's no way I can use that to my advantage. There are barely any windows except one that *also* has a lock on it. There isn't a way out.

Unless...

I try out my powers, willing the guards to unfreeze. They launch at me, and I close my eyes tightly, opening them when the sound of the guards' grunting comes to a halt. They stand there, frozen, and I claw the icy swords from their hands, surprised that the coldness of the ice doesn't register with me.

My entire life, my sister was the one with the power. She was always the strange Magic whose existence was a mystery. The citizens didn't question it, though, because of the sheer fear that developed inside them when my father's name was uttered. But I never suspected—never dreamed, never hoped—that I would also have a strange power that people would question.

Even though the main inflictor of my pain is dead, the thought of him finding out about *whatever* this is makes me shiver. Okay, maybe the cold that's suddenly in the metal room *is* getting to me.

I will the guards to unfreeze, then use my frozen sword to plunge into his abdomen and kill him. Then I freeze his friend.

I lean down, reaching into the dead guy's pocket. I fish around for a key ring, and then I come across it, pulling it out and using it to unlock the door.

I try my best to stay unnoticed, but as a captive with knife wounds holding a sword covered in thawing ice, that's a little difficult.

A member of the Pugnatores tribe stops me just as I'm getting to the edge of the woods. She's wearing leather, like most, I've observed, of the Pugnatores, and she stares at me like I'm something disgusting on the bottom of her shoe. She must know I'm an outsider.

Sure enough, she says, "Who are you? You are not from here."

"I'm, uh—"

Suddenly her eyes widen. "I know who you are. You are the prince—the one Captain Andrew brought in." Then she does something unexpected. She leans down so far that she's on her knees on the ground.

This lady literally just knelt before me.

"You—you can get up now," I tell her, trying to put on my brave face. I resist the urge to tell her that there's no need to bow before me, that if she found out what I'd just done, she would probably kill me. "I'm just on my way back to my castle."

"The fight," the woman says. "I heard about the fight, about your father dying. Good man. Those Magics think they can do whatever they want—" She stops herself, starting again. "I'm sorry for your loss, truly. We all respected King Cirillo, even if he did not show much interest in us."

That sends a pang of guilt through my heart. I wish I had had the opportunity to learn more about my kingdom. If I had, then I would've known about the Pugnatores and the Combatants, and I would've been able to lie my way through Andy finding me in the woods. Knowledge about my subjects would've made everything so much easier.

But I'm just as clueless as ever. Well, maybe a little less.

"Oh, uh, thank you," I say to the woman when I notice that she's staring at me expectantly, waiting for my acknowledgement of her well wishes. "I appreciate it, really. But, uh, I'm kind of in a hurry here, so if you wouldn't mind..."

She's still kneeling on the ground, and when I try to take a step forward, she catches my foot. "Oh, please, King-To-Be, won't you dine with us tonight? It's the least we could do after your loss. This dinner may help you! And it would make us just so very happy."

I consider my choices. Going to dinner with this Pugnatores lady probably isn't the best idea, especially considering the circumstances. But she looks so pathetic, and she's holding onto my foot with an iron grip. If I refuse, she may very well rip it off.

So I sigh. My sword's ice coating is starting to melt. I clench my jaw and say tightly with forced enthusiasm, "I would love to."

There's nothing forced about her enthusiasm when she gets to her feet and begins to drag me to the dining hall n the middle of the Pugnatores tribe campus, right across from the metal room that has its doors wide open, giving me a perfect view of all the things that may get me killed very, very painfully.

* * *

Dinner actually isn't that bad.

Andy isn't here, and neither is his father, thank the gods. They would recognize me, definitely. I sit with the woman and her friends, and they all try to kneel but get stopped by the table in front of them, which I'm thankful for. I don't know how many people kneeling before me it would take before I went insane.

The food is great. I'm actually pretty sure that it tops Camp Serenity's food, which is saying something, because their food is *delicious*. I have the time of my life, sharing stories of my childhood, having girls finally show an interest in me. And when dessert is brought out, I'm so happy and delirious that I decide to make a speech.

"I would like to thank the beautiful woman who brought me here." I speak loudly enough and make sure I stand high enough (on top of the table) that my voice carries through the entire mess hall. I feel high right now—high on happiness and good food. "I loved this dinner and meeting all of you. Actually, I wasn't even *going* to meet all of you. When this woman found me, I was fleeing because I'd just killed some guards! But it's nothing to worry about. I mean, one of them isn't *fully* dead. Just frozen. And that's another thing! I discovered I have magical ice powers and I'm actually a Magic, and now I'm pretty sure my dad's ghost is going to come back and haunt me because of that. But you know, that's normal in my world."

The crowd starts to murmur. Taking this as a sign to continue, I start to talk even louder.

"My father was a horrible person. Seriously, who do you guys worship him so much? He's dead now, though, so I guess it doesn't really matter. Point is, I'm grateful for your hospitality."

Behind me, someone clears their throat.

I whip around. There stands Andy, arms crossed, glaring at me.

"And now I've gotta go," I announce, stepping off the table and running from the dining hall, my hand clasped tightly around my sword.

Andy shouts orders to guards from behind me, and I glance back. Guards looking just as menacing as the first two race after me, their swords raised, and I close my eyes tightly.

When I open them, expecting the guards to be frozen, and notice that they're not, my heart stops. I run until I get to the clearing that I first met Andy in, and I look behind me again, when I suddenly notice a tall building reaching over the top of the trees, and hoping it's safe enough there without any blood-thirsty tribes, I start running again.

* * *

"No weapons are allowed in here, sir," a sullen woman wearing blue scrubs tells me as I step inside the building called GRAYMONT HOSPITAL.

"Oh," I say. "Well, ma'am, I just escaped a whole bunch of murderous Pugnatores—"

"Murderous *what?*"

"—and they're after me, so…I kind of need this with me, in case they find out where I am."

The woman rolls her eyes. "Fine. Leave it at the door." She leaves me at the entrance then.

I walk up to the reception desk after setting the sword down by the door. "Excuse me? Can I have a room to stay in? I don't know where I am or what I'm doing here, and I'm pretty sure that I'm going to be in very bad health soon enough."

"'Soon enough' isn't soon enough," the receptionist spits at me, a twisted expression on her pinched face. "If you're really sick, then I'd be happy to have an employee escort you to a room. But if you're *pretty sure* that you're going to be sick, then you need to get out and find another hospital that accepts walk-ins with weapons."

Suddenly, a man in scrubs stops. He must've heard the situation. He comes to stand next to me. "Now, Agatha, I'm sure you know that isn't the case. This young man is here to Selena Torsney, just like all the rest of them. Aren't you?"

The doctor sends me a pointed look, like he's saying, *Agree or else.* I nod quickly. "Yeah. I'm here to see Selena Torsney. Wait, *Selena Torsney?*"

"I'll lead him to the room where she's staying now," the doctor continues. "No work needed on your part."

Agatha considers it. Her eyes nearly roll into the back of her head as she thinks. But then she says, "Fine. Go ahead."

The doctor sends a charming smile her way before wrapping an arm around me, pushing me down the hallway labeled ROOMS.

"You're lucky I'm friends with your sister," he hisses in my ear, though how he knows who I am and who my sister is makes me a little suspicious of the situation.

"My sister?" I say.

We stop in front of a wooden door, the name of my dad's best guard written on it in blocky, bold lettering. Since the paint hasn't faded, I assume that she hasn't been here for long.

"But—but how? She's dead."

"She *was,*" the doctor clarifies.

He cracks open the door and shoves me through.

My eyes land immediately on my sister, sitting on a mound of blankets, drinking a steaming cup of coffee. Then I see Ash, lying next to her and snoring loudly. I see Sage, staring at the sleeping Selena with a sad expression on her face, but I don't know why. And finally—finally I see Selena.

She's in a bed, the white sheets and pillow not too much of a contrast from her skin tone. Her black hair stands out against the whiteness of the room like a shadow. She looks on the verge of death, but her chest rises and falls, so I know she's only sleeping.

"Quite a sight, isn't it?" the doctor says in my ear.

Elysian's eyes are wide when mine finally return to her. She sets her cup on the floor and rushes toward me, wrapping me in a bone-crushing hug. "I thought you were dead—or still at camp—or—or—"

"Lys, I'm fine, seriously," I whisper, but I hug her back anyway, because I need it.

"Ben," Sage says, standing from the chair she's sitting in. She stays where she is, though, not managing to greet me. "Have you heard anything?"

"Well, until we're sure she has somewhere to go, then we can release her," the doctor, Ben, replies.

"But she has somewhere to go," Sage argues. "She has Camp Serenity."

"And Camp Havoc," Milo adds, who is in the corner of the room, so quiet that I didn't even know he was here.

"That's great. I believe you." Ben sighs. "But as for the board of the hospital, the board that controls all of the hospital's decisions—they believe that these camps don't exist."

"What?" Elysian says, crossing her arms. She drew away from me a while ago, watching Ben intently.

"Well, there isn't much evidence of these camps," he explains. "You all just showed up out of the blue, somehow knowing Selena. You've all been wanted by the Royal guard at least once, which seems pretty suspicious. From what I've heard, these camps are protected by magic, meaning they can't be found. I wish I could help, but this situation is *very* sticky."

Everyone just stares at him for a bit. Finally, Selena's voice says groggily, "That's idiotic."

"Good morning," Sage greets flatly.

"I'm sorry for the bad news," Ben says, and he looks like he really means it.

Sage says nothing in response. She returns to what she was doing before—staring at Selena. Except now, they talk in hushed tones.

Ben sighs.

"Thanks for bringing me," I say to him, "and saving me from Agatha. That lady is *scary*. It's like all she does is glare."

"Well, I imagine you just intimidated her," he responds. "Agatha is a little bit of a bully sometimes." Then he leans forward, speaking slowly. "Don't tell her I said that."

I laugh, causing a smile from him, and he leaves the room, shutting the door softly behind him.

"So?" Elysian says as soon as the door is closed.

"So, what?"

She sits on the blanket mountain that she shares with Ash, who is unaffected by everything that's just happened. She still snores just as loudly as before. "Tell me everything."

CHAPTER 12

ELYSIAN

For a frightening second, I really believe that my brother has lost his mind.

As we sit in Selena's hospital room on the pile of blankets I slept in last night, he tells me about the Pugnatores tribe, which I had no idea existed, and a boy, the son of the chief, who he thought was his friend until the boy tried to get him killed. He talks about discovering the powers he has by using them, first, on the guards trying to kill him, and second, on trying to get out of the woods. He explains his dinner with the Pugnatores and his stupid declaration, and I know everything about it is true because I know he would never lie to me, not without good reason.

"So...you're a Magic? And you didn't know it?" I say eventually, after I process all that he's said.

"To put it simply, yes," Ameer says. "And before all that, I went to the ballroom that the ball was supposed to be held at, I met this guy—"

He breaks off suddenly, like he's remembering something.

"What is it?" I ask, studying him. "Did something happen?"

He opens his mouth like he wants to say something, then must decide otherwise. "It's nothing."

"You went to the ballroom, and you met a guy…"

"Never mind," he says, avoiding my eyes.

"What were you going to say, Ameer? Is it something I wouldn't like?" When he doesn't say anything, instead studying the hardwood of the floor, I say, *"Ameer?"*

"The guy told me Merrik wanted you," he tells me, growing very somber. "You and Ash."

"Merrik? What is a *Merrik?*"

"He's not a *what,* he's a *who.*" Ameer sends me a look. "Merrik. He's the leader of the ghosts. He's the one I saw in my dream the night Camp Havoc was attacked, except I *was* him, and…oh, gods."

"What?" We're getting somewhere, and I don't want this to end so soon.

"In the dream, Merrik was talking to someone," Ameer says. "He was talking to *Finn.*"

"Finn *Brocker?*"

"It was like he was alive, but he wasn't, clearly," he continues, "considering Merrik was making a ghost army and all."

"You're saying that Merrik is this magical person who's creating a ghost army and using Finn Brocker, who's supposed to be dead, to do it?"

"Not a person." Selena says it this time. "Merrik, he isn't a person," she clarifies when she notices me and Ameer staring at her like she's grown another head.

"You've heard of him?" Ameer asks, bewildered.

"I've heard of him." She gains a sour expression, like even talking about the guy is enough to get her upset. "He's visited me a few times."

Ameer's face pales.

"What do you mean, he's *visited* you?" I question. "And if he's not human, then what is he?"

"He's come and talked to me about joining his army, I guess," she says. "He's an entity. He's not a god, but more powerful."

"Merrik," Sage says, hearing the conversation. She's chewing her lip. "He danced with me at the ball. He told me he was what I feared the most."

"So, everyone pretty much knows who this Merrik guy is?" I say.

"Trust me, Elysian, you don't *want* to know him. He's horrible," Selena tells me.

"What are we supposed to do to stop him?" Milo says from the corner of the room. He's been watching the conversation closely, waiting for an opening.

"In the ballroom, the guy told me something about Merrik. He said he's fueled by fear," Ameer says. "If someone fears nothing, then he doesn't have any magic to help him. He's weak."

"We have to learn how to not be afraid of anything in order to defeat him?" I ask, making sure I've got it right.

Ameer nods. "Unfortunately."

"Well, that's just great," I grumble.

Milo's face pales. "What do you mean, we can't be afraid of anything? Are you sure this is the only way we can defeat him?"

"I'm sure." Ameer gives him a sympathetic look.

"Well, you know what that means," Sage says glumly. "We're going to have to beat our fears—and fast."

* * *

"How can you drink that stuff?"

Ash stares at me, an eyebrow raised, as I take a sip of coffee from the cup I'm holding. She hates coffee. She says it's bitter. I practically live on it.

Besides, I deserve it, anyway. After what Ameer told us about Merrik and our fears, this coffee is quite literally the only thing keeping me sane.

"How can you sleep past eleven in the morning?" I retort.

"Touché."

There's an awkward pause, and I hate it. I *hate* it.

She glances away from me, and I resist the urge to make her face me again. I consider doing something reckless, something to make her look at me, but we're in a hospital and I really don't want her angry at me—not now, not while our relationship is so fragile. I think back to what Sage said the day of the ball: *"Your relationship is so important, which is what makes it strong. If it breaks, then it breaks, and the relationship between our camps breaks, too."*

That seems like so long ago, but it's only been a few days.

"I've been thinking," she says suddenly, snapping me out of my thoughts.

"Yeah?" I take another cup of coffee, loving the way the heat of it burns my throat. I'm thankful for a distraction. "About what?"

"Us."

My heart drops, and I know what she's going to say next. "What about us?"

She looks back up at me. "You know, Lys. It's not going to work. We fight all the time."

"So…so you're breaking up with me." It's not so much a question as it is a statement. "You're breaking up with me."

"We were practically broken up anyway," she tells me. She's only making it worse. "We knew it wasn't going to last long. We rushed into it. You were grieving and working and we were both stressed, and maybe we just didn't see the reason in our choice."

She's talking about it being a choice. *Like I* chose *to be in love with her, to be hated even more for something I just can't control. Does she know how many campers I lost when they found out we were dating? Does she know that even though losing those campers broke me, the fact that she was with me was enough for me to not obsess over it? Does she know that I didn't care about what others thought because we were happy and we were* together? *She thinks that's a choice?* "Sure."

Ash sighs, pinching the bridge of her nose, like she has a headache. "It's for the best. You know that, don't you?"

"Sure."

"Please, Lys, say something else."

"Sure, I know that. But I also know a lot about you, and I love you, and I don't want what we have to end just because of one stupid fight. We started out enemies, and I don't want it to end that way. Heck, I don't want it to end at all. But here we are. And if you think it's the best thing that we can do right now, then sure. Sure."

I take a last gulp of my coffee and she turns away, a sad look in her eyes, the most beautiful thing about her. She leaves me by the coffee machine.

I sniffle. Tears form in my eyes and I try to blink them away to no avail. They drop into my coffee cup, and I gasp, trying to keep my crying silent.

Am I not good enough? Does she seriously think that we'll never get past this? Why now? Why *ever*?

I throw the cup in the trash and walk down the hall to the entrance of the hospital, leaving the building. With my tears start the first few drops of rain, but then as my weeping turns to sobs, the sky overhead turns to a rough, dark gray.

Sage finds me outside. She doesn't ask questions, just hugs me, and I cry into her shoulder. Drops of rain hit us hard and soak our clothes but she doesn't stop hugging me—doesn't stop hugging me, because I would do the exact same for her.

Because I *did* the same for her.

And now, as I sit in the rain, my clothes soaked through, I'm grateful for it.

CHAPTER 13

ASH

I feel miserable.

I hate what I did, I hate having been so sensitive, and I hate the silent tears that roll down my face as I walk back to Selena's room. I can feel my heart breaking, like it's being torn apart, and it's almost like I can hear my mother whispering in my ear, telling me I'm weak, that this is nothing.

I hate it.

Sage comes storming into the room, completely soaked and scowling. She grabs my arm and yanks me out of the doorway, leading me to another hospital room—except this one is empty.

For a second, I'm scared she's actually going to kill me. But then she releases my arm, closes the door behind her, and yells, "Are you out of your mind?"

I'm stunned for a bit. "I'm sorry?" I say eventually.

"You better be." She glares at me. "My best friend is *heartbroken* and you're just going around acting like everything's fine! I thought you loved her! You—you're so screwed. Do you know that? The camps will become rivals again. We won't have an alliance anymore. We'll be attacked. Campers will die. People—innocent people—will *die*. Do you *want* that?"

"Of course I don't want that! But how does that have anything to do with me breaking up with Elysian?"

"If your relationship falls apart, your camps fall apart." She somehow glares harder at me. "Your safety falls apart. Wow, you were stupid when you decided this."

"It wasn't a *choice*," I bite back. "Elysian told me that she wanted to take a break, and I wasn't ready, I guess, to keep living like we were strangers. I *had* to break up with her."

"Gods, you're an idiot. She just caused a whole thunderstorm—probably a tornado too—because you were broken up. She's dying inside right now, and I'm guessing you're not much better." She gives me a knowing look.

"Is it that obvious?"

"Ash." Sage sits on the hospital bed. She sighs. "You and Elysian—you're made for each other. But sometimes people that are made for each other can't see that immediately."

I did see that immediately. I loved her immediately. But she wants a break, so a break I will give.

"She wanted this," I tell Sage sourly. "She wanted to take a break."

"As someone who can literally never be with my boyfriend ever again, I think you're taking this the wrong way. Couples take breaks.

It happens. But that doesn't mean they don't love each other or—or that they're not made for each other. In fact, I think it's the opposite. All healthy couples have a few bumps in the road. Wouldn't you say so?"

"You dragged me away for a counseling session?" I ask her, raising my eyebrows.

"No," Sage says, sighing. "I'm telling you that this is a mistake. I get that you're angry, and I get that you're hurt, but you're going to regret this."

I stare at her, a grim expression on my face. "I know that."

"And you don't care?"

"I care. I'm just not talking about it anymore. Thank you for the wonderful insight on *my* relationship—"

"—or lack of one," Sage interrupts, and I glare at her.

"—but I think we should just drop this," I continue, giving her a hard look. "It's not making anyone happy, talking about it, so just...let it go, okay? Forget about it. And if Elysian wants to talk to me about it, then she can handle it herself."

She lets me walk to the door, and then she says, "You are a coward, Ashlyn Kave. I hope you know that."

She pushes past me, her shoulder hitting mine as she walks back to Selena's room. I stare after her, a bitter taste filling my mouth.

I know. Trust me, I know.

"Well, if you ask me, it sounds like you're being a little overdramatic," Milo says, filling up a cup with coffee. I watch as the dark color floods the cup, taking over everything. I feel like that now. Darkness is taking over everything—all my reasonable thoughts, emotions, my ability to feel things.

"Overdramatic? That's really what you think?" My eyebrows crease. My scrubs are too tight, and I think the waistband is cutting off my circulation. I struggle for breath as I stare at him, so neutral, so calm, so *him*, in the middle of...whatever this is. *I don't have the mental stability for this.*

"You love each other, and so you should be together," he continues, and I can tell he's still not fully paying attention. Selena really took a toll on him, still *is* taking a toll on him.

When I say nothing, his plain expression falters. "You *do* love her, don't you?"

"Yes, I do," I say, almost absently. I watch the paintings on the walls intensely. "I love her. But...she hurt my feelings, and she has to apologize."

"Ever heard of being the bigger person?" he suggests, and his tone isn't unkind. "Maybe *you* could apologize to *her*."

"Why would I do that?" The words that fall out of my mouth are sharp, sharper than I want them to be, and I sigh. "I'm sorry, seriously. I'm tired, and this stupid argument isn't helping things."

"Except," he says cautiously, "this wasn't just an argument. This was a break-up. Something that caused fifty deaths in the next kingdom over from a sudden natural disaster."

I wince. "I don't want to hurt her, Milo," I say quietly. "I just...I've never been this expressive with my emotions. I've never tried to communicate clearly with someone, and it seemed like things were going pretty well...but then...I ruined everything." I put my face in my hands.

He stares at me sympathetically. "It's not your fault, Ash," he tells me, and he's lying to my face.

Still, despite this, I raise my head and reply glumly, "I know."

"Ash," he says in a warning tone.

"What?" I say, and he opens his mouth to respond. But then he spots Sage coming toward us and motions for me to go back to Selena's room with a tip of his head. I do, gladly, thankful for the distraction. Milo may be disappointed in me in every way possible at times, but he's still my best friend, the person I chose to build my life with. And I know that he'll be there for me.

Selena's door is cracked open when I get there. I push on it and enter, closing the door behind me in case she's asleep.

She's not. She's wide awake, staring ahead at...

Oh, gods. *What the…?*

My *mother* stands in front of Selena, smiling at her. Blood drips down the side of her face and there are flames crawling up her leg, but she doesn't seem to notice. She's wearing the same dress she wore the day that I killed her, and I realize with a start that she's *her*, the day that I killed her.

I swallow back my fear and step toward the bed. My hand instinctively goes to my hip, where my sword should be, but then I remember I'm in scrubs and the hospital staff didn't let us have weapons inside the hospital. I notice a sword sitting next to the door and grab it, though I'm confused on how it got there or whose it is.

"Who are you?" I ask my mother, my hand squeezing the hilt of the sword so tightly that my knuckles turn white.

"Ashlyn Kave," my mother says without looking at me. When she finally does, her eyes are black pits, and her mouth is curved up into a terrifying smile. "How nice to finally meet you."

"Finally?"

"Oh, yes." My mother laughs, and the sound taunts me, reminding me of the memories I had when I was a child of her laughing with my father. "I forgot. Who do you see me as, dear Ashlyn?"

It finally registers completely that the person standing in front of me is *not* my mother, and they *are* meeting me for the first time. I should be scared—I should run away, even—but I don't. I glance at

Selena, her face as white as a sheet, and decide it wouldn't be fair if I fled just because of *my* fear. If I see my mother, I wonder who she is seeing. Her brother, maybe, or the captain of the Royal guard?

"Who *are* you?" I repeat, trying my best not to look at the slow drip of blood from a crack in my mother's skull.

No, she's not my mother. Whoever this is isn't my mother. It's an illusion, nothing more. But, still, when I look at her, I realize how *real* it seems. She has the scar I gave her from the time we were practicing and I accidentally turned my sword the wrong way. Her face is already wrinkled and she has the same warm-toned skin that I have, proof that I got my complexion from her and not my pale father. I swallow the lump in my throat and stare at this person head-on, not willing to let my barriers fall and show how truly vulnerable I have become at the sight of her.

Selena says something, but I can't hear her.

Then she repeats it.

"Merrik," she breathes.

The man—no, *entity*—that we were talking about earlier, the one that feeds on fears, is who stands before me as my mother. I have to say, for an entity whose looks are always changing, he makes his illusions pretty believable.

"Yes," he says with a smirk, glancing at Selena. "I am Merrik, entity of fear and destruction."

Entities are the fathers and mothers of the gods. Some stories claim that the stars are actually the parents of our gods, but most talk about the main entities: Jaava and Sawn.

Jaava is the mother of the gods of nature and peace, and Sawn is the father of war and battle, of hardships. The two fell in love—which at the time (before the universe was created) was a little scandalous—and together made the gods that we worship now. There's Adar, the god of war and fire, and Isla, his wife, the goddess of ice and darkness. There's Adelyn, the goddess of nature and outdoorsy things like picnics, and Eve, the goddess of the holidays. All of them have the ability to bless humans the minute they are born, rendering them with magical powers and making them Magics. The point is, the gods as we know them were created by *something*, and those things are rumored to be entities. Of course, no one believed the stories. No one is more powerful than the gods. That's what we were always taught. But someone—something, rather—that is more powerful than the gods stands before me, looking exactly like my mother did as she died.

Great.

I suck in a breath just as the door bangs open.

I whip around, so that I am now facing Elysian.

"Lys, you have to—" I start, but a gust of wind sweeps by me, nearly knocking me off my feet, and I stop.

"What...is *that?*" She points at Merrik.

"Oh, goodie," Merrik says. "The two people I was just hoping to see."

He waves his hand, and Selena shrieks, but then she disappears. In fact, the whole *room* disappears. My eyes have been closed, and when I open them again, there's only white surrounding me.

I glance behind me and see Elysian standing there.

Oh, great. Way to rub salt in the wound, Merrik.

"Where are we?" Elysian demands.

Merrik smiles evilly. "Welcome, my dears, to my meeting."

Suddenly, the room morphs into something that looks remarkably like a basement. There's a table in the middle of the room that several translucent men and women talk over. They converse in hushed tones, like they're scared they're going to wake someone up.

A few start to notice Merrik and straighten, silencing themselves. Eventually everyone catches on, and Merrik takes a seat at the head of the table.

Is it weird watching my mother command the respect of hollow people? Yes. Is it exactly what I would expect of her, though? Also yes.

Elysian steps forward until she's standing next to me. Just looking at her is like pressing on a raw injury.

I can't make myself turn to look at her. I stare straight ahead at the table, watching Merrik wait until the entire night is listening.

Elysian is so close that I can feel the heat of her body, and I see her dangling hand in my peripheral vision, but I'm not brave enough—or stupid enough—to reach out and lace her fingers in mine, like I did just two months ago.

I thought breaking up was what she wanted, what would be better for her. Elysian has always been independent. She doesn't need anyone. And she was still writing her book at the end of the summer and we just rushed into it. I keep telling myself this like an explanation for why we broke up will fix everything, but it won't. I know it won't.

I push that thought from my mind and focus on Merrik.

I scan the attendants of the meeting. Several are people I've never seen before, and most avoid eye contact with everyone else, staring at the table. But my eye catches on one face in particular.

Finn.

I look away. Elysian seems to notice him, too, because her jaw flexes.

"I am calling the meeting to order," Merrik says from the front of the room. "What is the topic at hand?"

"The two girls," one of the members says quietly. "The two you wish to have in your possession."

Merrik grins maniacally. "Yes?" His eyes travel over to where Elysian and I stand.

"They are not at their camps," the member continues. "The camps are...completely deserted. No one's there. We searched the entire area."

"No one living there *at all?*" For a moment, Merrik looks honestly confused. But then he regains his senses. "Go on."

"Everything is still where it was before, but it's empty. There's no one." The member shrugs. "I'm not sure why."

My heart aches for the campers that were at the ball. If they haven't returned to the camps yet, then where are they? They're not in the hospital, as far as I know, so they must just be...homeless.

My stomach lurches.

"Well, figure it out!" Merrik slams his hands down on the table. Several of the people at the table startle. "I need this information. I need to continue building my army."

"But you have us," says another member further down the table. Once she says it, though, she winces, like she knows she's made a mistake.

"You aren't *good enough!*" It seems like the entire table shakes now, just from the vibrations of his voice. "I need an army of *Magics*, an army that can actually do more, an army that can hold more than useless *torches!*"

"That's not nice," says one of the members with a reproachful look in Merrik's direction.

"Did I *ask* if I was being *nice*, Matthew?" Merrik seethes. "No, I didn't. Now, if you can't handle this job, then I'll send you away. All of you!"

The table members wince in unison and the meeting is adjourned.

Slowly, the hospital room comes back to us.

And Merrik is gone.

I look around, expecting to see him behind me or something like that—but nothing. He's gone.

Elysian looks around at the empty room and groans. "Is this some kind of cruel joke?" she demands to the sky, to the gods, which is very dangerous.

"Lys, maybe you shouldn't—"

"Don't tell me what to do!" she says to me, barely trying to hide the pain that is written plainly on her face. "I know what I'm doing," she tells me, quieter this time, but her hard stare still bores into me, like she's analyzing every flaw that I have and judging it silently.

I wouldn't be surprised if that were the case.

"Do you?" I say, surprising myself and her. But now, once I've started, I can't stop. "Do you know what you're doing? You're running around, causing tornadoes, cursing the gods, all sorts of things, just because you're too fragile to handle a simple break-up? It's not a big deal, Elysian, so stop making it one."

"Making it a big deal?" she breathes. I would've been less intimidated if she had yelled. "Oh, yes, because *I'm* the problem here."

"Maybe you are." I match her tone, and her lip curls. A sour expression replaces the one of bewilderment.

"If this is how you're going to be, then you will leave me alone." She glares, her voice turns to ice. "Otherwise, who knows what could happen to you."

Is that a threat?

I stare at her as she turns and leaves the room.

CHAPTER 14

SELENA

"What an eventful morning," I say to Milo, and he smiles faintly.

"Right you are." He hands me a bottle of water, setting his cup of coffee on my nightstand. He's been surviving, lately, on coffee and hospital food, and I feel bad for him. He can leave—he can *try*, at least—but he doesn't know where he is, and Camp Serenity and Camp Havoc are supposedly deserted.

He looks distracted, I note. "Are you feeling okay, Mi?"

"Mi?" He raises an eyebrow.

"New nickname, just trying it out," I retort quickly. Making my tone softer, I ask, "So that's a no on the nickname, then?"

"That's a no," he says, chuckling. Gods, I love Milo's chuckle. And his smile. And nearly everything about him.

We've only kissed once, and I want to do it again. But I'm not that bold.

"Well, are you okay, *Milo*?" I ask gently, placing my hand on his arm. His body heat seeps through my fingertips and warms my hand, and I am thankful for him, for the contrast that we are.

He changes the subject. "I'll have to leave soon."

"I know that."

"I'll have to leave *you.*"

"Just the duties you have when you're big and important." I grin at him, and he doesn't return it.

His eyes are serious, yet soft. "I don't want to," he tells me, and his hand rests on my shoulder.

I sit up straight, lean forward so I'm so close to him that I can feel his body heat through my hospital gown and his dress clothes.

And he kisses me.

He kisses me, and there's an unmistakable warmth crawling up my body, choking me. It's starting to *suffocate* me. I pull away and all he does is put his hand on the back of my neck, kissing me again. I try to tell him, but it's like there's fire in my lungs—fire everywhere.

I wake up.

The sky outside is pink, yet rain falls down, a shattering, splintering sound that I can hear even through the musty glass of my window. I gasp for breath and am pleased to find that my lungs work perfectly fine, that they're not filled with fire. Milo's gone, I realize, looking around at the room. Sage is gone, too, and Elysian and Ash and Ameer.

They're all gone.

Maybe my nightmare meant something. Milo talked about not wanting to leave me, and now he's gone. He's left me.

I climb out of bed slowly, wincing as the muscles in my stomach flex uncomfortably. I walk toward the door, but stop, turning suddenly. I remember that they left their dress clothes in one of the cabinets when they left. Maybe—hopefully—I'm the same size as one of them.

I search through the pile of dresses, finding Elysian's pale blue one that shimmers in the early-morning sunlight. It looks about my size.

I tug it on, loving the way the silk feels against my skin. I've been trapped in that hospital gown for who knows how long, and I really wasn't wanting to get changed into tight scrubs.

Then again, maybe I *should* wear scrubs. The gods know how bad the weather is, how cold it's getting...

Suddenly, there's a knock on my door, and it opens.

Milo stands in the doorway, raising his eyebrows when he sees what I'm wearing.

He's beautiful. His hair has grown since I saw him last, and a few of his curls hang in front of his dark eyes. His skin is smooth and clear, just the slightest hint of stubble growing on his chin. He's changed into a simple gray sweater and black joggers, but somehow, he still makes that look good.

"Wow," he says, walking over to me. That's all he says.

There's a mirror in my hospital room above the sink in my bathroom, and I stand in front of it, studying myself. My imperfections stand out like a sore thumb. The dress is too small and makes my skin look too pale. The black boots that I wear, standard uniform for Royal soldiers, look horrible with the dress. But Milo doesn't seem to notice. He circles me and wraps his arms around my waist from behind, setting his head on my shoulder.

"Wow," he repeats. "You look amazing." He says it in my ear, and a shiver runs down my back.

"So do you," I say softly with a smile—a real smile, not one that I learned how to force from years spent with the Royal guard.

I think about my dream, and suddenly he feels too close, and my lungs feel like they're on fire again.

"Selena?" Milo crouches down as I slide to the ground, clutching my throat during a fit of coughs. "Selena, are you okay? Do I need to call a doctor?"

Then it stops abruptly, and I'm left reeling. Milo's arms are still around my waist, I realize, and I blush furiously, turning my head away from his confused and worried stare.

"No, no," I say. "I'm fine."

"Are you?" His eyebrows crease, like he doesn't believe me, but he relents, releasing his hands from my waist. I'm actually a little disappointed that he does. "What was that?"

"It started…just now."

"You've never had it before?" If possible, Milo looks more nervous now. "So, it was just a cough?"

I look down at my stomach, where I was stabbed, the reason why I'm in here in the first place.

Milo seems to think the same thing as me. "Not just a cough," he says. "You think it has something to do with Finn stabbing you?"

"I think it has to," I tell him. "Hopefully, though, Lillian can get some *soigner* to help."

He nods. Then he says, "Lillian?"

"The nurse that takes care of me."

"Oh." He looks down, fiddling with his thumbs. "Well. The dress looks good on you."

"It's Elysian's."

"Still looks good on you." He raises his eyes, just for a second, to sneak a glance at the dress again. When they start to drift back to his hands, I grab his chin and lift it up so he's looking me in the eyes.

"There's something you want to say," I guess, and I watch as Milo's throat bobs. "Say it."

"I'm not allowed to," he tells me, and a stupid bird chirps outside, completely ignoring the mood.

"Not allowed to? What, like you follow rules?" I give him a look, but then I say, "Oh, wait. Yes, you do."

He chuckles, but it's forced.

"Milo." My voice is serious. "You're leaving."

His eyes widen. "Did someone tell you?"

I resist the urge to tell him about the dream. Instead, I just shake my head. "Just a feeling."

He sighs. "Sometimes I forget how smart you are." He pokes me, and I smile.

"You're leaving," I say. "With Ash and Elysian and Sage and Ameer."

"Yes," he says with another sigh. "We're leaving, but not because of you."

"Well, then, why?"

"Dr. Abott."

I stare at him like he's gone insane. "Dr. *Ben* Abott?"

"Yes." He starts to explain. "He said, after Elysian and Ash fought, that it wasn't safe for either of them to stay there. They met Merrik, and they told Dr. Abott about it. He told them to leave. He's coming with us."

"And I'm not?"

"That's why I came back," he tells me, and my heart nearly melts. "We'll pack a bag with *soigner* and all kinds of things that you need for your stomach and your muscles and pain, everything you need, so don't worry about it. We'll have a doctor with us and—"

"I'll go," I say immediately.

"But I have a whole bunch of other reasons why you should," he says, like he's almost disappointed.

"I'll go," I repeat, leaning my forehead against his chest.

He brings his arms around me and hugs me close to him. He murmurs against my hair. "They're waiting outside. Dr. Abott found some normal clothes for everyone, but I'm all for this punk-princess look."

I laugh softly. "I'll take the normal clothes, please."

He smiles. "Okay, then. Let's go."

When I get outside, Dr. Abott's lips part slightly, like he wasn't expecting me to go with them. *I'm not staying here by myself, not after I've seen my friends. No way, never.*

Milo's right about the 'normal clothes' part. Ash is wearing jeans and a long-sleeved shirt, like Sage, but hers is red and Sage's is green. *Fitting.* Elysian is wearing leggings and a light blue sweatshirt, and she eyes the dress I'm wearing, *her* dress, and I look away, self-conscious. Ameer is wearing joggers and a T-shirt, like Dr. Abott. *They're going to freeze.*

"Selena." Sage offers me a change of clothes, and I nod, ducking back inside the hospital to get dressed.

She handed me leggings, like Elysian's, and a black sweater, soft to the touch. When I put it on, it fits perfectly, and I wonder where Dr. Abott would've gotten these clothes. I sling the bag holding ointments and things like that over my shoulder and, with a final glance at the front desk, leave the hospital, starting to walk next to Milo.

"So, Dr. Abott, where are we headed?" Elysian says, breaking the silence.

"I have a few friends in the next kingdom over," Dr. Abott says. "We're headed to Ruri. Oh, and, please, call me Ben. Dr. Abott sounds so formal, and I already quit."

"You're not working there anymore?" Sage asks, her eyebrows meeting. "Aren't we going to stay in a motel or something in Ruri? None of us have any Ruri money."

A smile quirks the corners of Dr. Abott's—no, Ben's—lips. "You'll see."

CHAPTER 15

SAGE

Walking in the woods like this is a painful reminder of everything I went through just around two months ago.

We know where we're going, and I burned my map whenever we got back to Camp Serenity, but it's pretty similar. Especially as we enter the woods that lead past the castle of Buit to the castle of Ruri, just over the border.

I glance over my shoulder at Ben. He's not wearing the white coat, but I still see him as a doctor, as *Selena's* doctor. There's just something about him that makes him seem smarter than the rest of us.

"How far away is Ruri?" I ask him. I don't want to think about doctors and sickness right now.

"Not many miles from here," he says, staring straight ahead. He's incredibly handsome, with a sharp jaw and muscles that I couldn't see when he was wearing his white coat. About two or three. It'll take a few hours because of the terrain, and then we'll stop to train. I have a friend we can stay with."

"And your parents," I say. "Do they live in Ruri?"

"Ruri is my hometown," he explains. "I grew up there. Since Ruri is the kingdom of sunlight, I was gifted powers from Aelia, the goddess of the sun. I'm a sun-manipulator."

My heart aches for Sorin. "Cool."

"Selena…" Ben pauses, gathering his words. "Selena told me she had a brother, Sorin, who was a sun-manipulator too. She said you liked him."

I glance over at him and see that his cheeks are flushed. This obviously isn't a very comfortable topic for him, either. "I did," I say shortly. "But he died in August."

"His birthday…it's soon, isn't it?"

"In a week."

"The twenty-first."

"Yep." I shrug, like I don't care.

"Selena wanted to have a proper funeral for him." Ben clears his throat, glancing at me quickly enough to make me think I've imagined it. "She said you didn't have the time. I was wondering if you want to attend."

"It's being held on his birthday," I say, "isn't it?"

My voice is dull but Ben still winces. "Sorry. Is that too soon?"

"No, no, it's okay," I respond. "I'll be there."

He looks relieved. "Okay, good. It's going to be a small ceremony, and if you have any belongings of his that you want to give that we can bury…"

I think back to the pen that sits on my nightside table, the pen that I named Sorin's pen. I wouldn't give it away for the world. "Not with me, no. Sorry."

"Oh, it's okay," he says. "I'm sorry. I just...I thought you would. But it's okay."

At Camp Serenity, Sorin's cabin is uninhabitable. It has most of his belongings and his clothes, which smell like him—the unmistakable smell of cheap cologne and outdoors—but it stays honorary. He was the best Healer we had. Plus, if the campers tore it apart, I...I don't know what I'd do.

Sometimes I go in there. I go in there just to look at what it was like before he died. I was never allowed in his cabin after he came back, after I became Junior Leader and he didn't, and once in September I noticed there was a portrait of me and him inside, hanging on the wall. We were children, just barely fourteen, painted when we got to Camp Serenity. We stood next to each other, smiling awkwardly. His hair was ruffled, and he fidgeted a lot, so the area around his hands was blurry, deeming the portrait 'imperfect.' But he'd kept it. I took it off the wall and hung it in my cabin, right next to his pen. I scribbled the date it must've been made on it—December, because of the snow in the background—and let it stay there next to my bed, because it means so much to me. *He* means so much to me. A proper funeral is what he deserves, and I'm thankful for Selena because she's trying to give it to him.

"Sage?" Ben asks, snapping out of my thoughts.

"Yeah," I say.

"Did you hear what I said? About making things he liked out of paper?"

"Oh, sure." I shrug. "That sounds fine."

"Are you okay?"

The question catches me off guard. It's not really something you want to hear from a doctor, considering they're usually the ones who tell *you* if you're okay. "Oh, yeah," I say. "I'm fine."

The backs of my eyes start to burn, and I will the tears back. I glance around at the trees and the sky, watching the pale blue color of it and the white clouds as they move away from Ruri, away from the sunlight kingdom.

To distract myself, I ask, "Has there ever been rain in Ruri? Any snow, anything other than sunlight?"

"Not to my knowledge," Ben answers, and he seems grateful for the subject change, too. "While I lived in Ruri, it was always sunny. No matter what. The kingdom is blessed by Aelia, so it's protected from the other weather conditions. You might think that's cool at first, but it's basically like living in a huge drought. Most of the time, the servants of Emerald, the kingdom to the south of Ruri, will bring over gallons of water in huge shipments, and we use that to water the people and the crops. I moved away because I didn't want to wait for them to bring over water before washing my hands."

I grimace. "Sounds horrible."

He shrugs. "Ruri isn't entirely like that, but that's mostly the premise. Sure, it's nice in the winter to always be warm no matter what, and we have some breezes that blow past thanks to the good weather, but largely it's a huge pain. I moved here also because I wanted to see snow for the first time."

I glance at him. "Sorry to take you away from that."

"Oh, it's okay," he says with another shrug. "I lived in Ruri all my life, and I never saw snow. Not once. Now…" He glances up at the sky, smiling slightly. "Now it looks like it may snow before we cross the border."

I follow his gaze up to the dark storm clouds ahead of us. I wonder for a second if Elysian's doing this, but then I remember how much she hates the snow.

I look back to the rest of them. Elysian is walking next to Ameer, who looks dangerously pale. He might be the one causing the weather to do this. Or he might just be cold. It's his fault that he wore a T-shirt. Ash and Milo and Selena stand next to each other in a little group, all staying silent.

I suddenly get a pang of homesickness as I remember the campfire. Every night we would have a campfire, no matter the weather, and Elysian would fend off the snow using her power. The campers would all huddle together around the fire and trade stories and toast marshmallows, and it's my favorite part of camp because of how nice it is to be surrounded by the people I love.

"Yeah," I say. "It does."

Then, the first flurries of snow start. They fall slowly, landing on my sleeves softly, like a pat. Ben smiles as he glances up at the sky, and the snow touches his eyelashes, getting caught. It's freezing but he doesn't seem to notice. He doesn't even shiver, which is impressive.

There's a gasp of surprise from behind us and soon everyone stops to feel the snow, to let the flakes tap us and decorate us in a blanket of white.

"*This* is what you moved here for?" I ask Ben, my tone light. Elysian hates the snow, but I find it beautiful—the way it settles over the disappointments of the day and fixes everything by being lovely.

He chuckles and says, "Yeah. This is what I moved here for."

"It's October and it's snowing," Elysian grumbles from behind us. "This is just great."

As if she's angered a god, which she most likely has, the snow starts to fall more quickly. We speed up the pace so we can get over the border before it *really* starts to snow.

The snow is, thankfully, still light as the tall wall that separates Ruri and Buit comes into view, looming over us. I glance up at it, my mouth dropping open. Luckily, Selena is the only one with a bag, or else we would have problems.

"We have to scale *that?*" Ameer says. He and Elysian come to stand next to me and Ben, but Milo and Selena and Ash stay behind us, studying the wall.

"Yeah, it does look a little intimidating, doesn't it?" Ben says as he approaches the wall.

"A *little?*" Elysian echoes, already bothered by the snow.

Ben ignores their complaints and finds a stone that juts out awkwardly. There's no security by the wall, I note, and I wonder why. They're just leaving it open for people to climb over? Yes, it works in our favor, but isn't that a little stupid?

There's suddenly shouting from the woods that we just walked out of, and I curse under my breath, whipping around to face the Royal guards that stand with their swords pointed toward us. *There they are.*

I draw my dagger from a sheath strapped to my waist. I keep it aimed to the ground and decide that since these guards haven't attacked yet, it's better to see if we can talk it out.

"We just need to get over to Ruri," I say cautiously. "Will you allow us to do so?"

The guards ignore me as their eyes fix on each one of us in turn. There are three guards, all wearing armor, but I notice one in the back that shivers. He must be freezing.

There's suddenly a gasp, and Elysian pushes Ameer forward.

"What are you doing?" he asks desperately, and Elysian says nothing in response.

"We have the King of Buit with us," Elysian announces. "If you kill us, he will order you to…chop your own heads off."

"We are armed," Ash says, playing along. "And he is too. If you do not oblige, *he* may chop your head off."

Something like recognition passes over each of the guards' faces in turn. The one in the front kneels. "We are so sorry, King Ameer," he says. He offers his sword to Ameer, who is now right in front of the guard, a sour expression on his face.

"No, no," Ameer protests. "I don't want to chop off anyone's head."

"Tell us, then," the second guard says. He isn't kneeling, and he has a specific pride that he holds himself with. "Do you grant these people passage over the wall?"

Ameer nervously lifts his eyes to the second guard. "Um, yeah. I do."

"And I second that," Elysian says. "I am the Princess of Buit."

The first guard, the one kneeling, is still offering his sword. "Oh, we apologize profusely, Your Majesties!"

"We did not wish to offend," the third guard says, bowing his head.

The second guard scrambles over to the wall and pushes a small button that's invisible to the untrained eye. A door appears in the middle of the wall and swings open, allowing us passage into Ruri.

"Thank you," Elysian says to the second guard, and she and Ameer go first. Ben and I follow, and then Ash, Milo, and Selena go through the door last.

Once we're on the other side, I exhale gratefully, relieved we haven't been chopped to bits or bruised from climbing that wall.

Meanwhile, Ameer looks like he's about to throw up.

"Gods, I hated that," he says, and he shakes the snow off of him.

I notice there's something wet running down my face and realize it's melted snow.

Ben opens his mouth, like there's a question or two on the tip of his tongue, but then he says, "Welcome to Ruri, the kingdom of sunlight."

Ruri is definitely not as impressive as Ben made it out to be.

The sunlight beats down on us, and I almost wish I *wasn't* wearing a long-sleeved shirt. Ben basks in it though; the relentless sun matches the tan he has. His eyes light up every time we go past another market—it's like Ruri is *made* of markets and booths and angry merchants—and he smiles faintly, as if he's remembering something.

The castle of Ruri trumps all the rest of the markets and the booths and homes, though. It's huge, with each of the tapestries that hang from the windows being a picture of a sun. It's entirely different from the castle of Buit, which has shadows in every corner and dark colors everywhere. It's painted white with yellow accents, and it stands out, though I'm not sure how you would miss it if it *wasn't* painted like a huge eyesore.

"This is your kingdom, eh?" I say to Ben.

"Yeah, this is my kingdom," he says, glancing around at the buildings. They're like the cabins at Camp Serenity—and around the same size too. They're each decorated differently, uniquely. Maybe it's just how different Buit is from Ruri, despite both being a part of the Asterian Dynasty (a collection of five kingdoms each blessed by gods), but I don't like this kingdom. It's foreign and strange, and I'm glad, at least, that my friends are with me, but it feels like there's a big weight on my chest that I can't get rid of.

"But this isn't Ruri," he tells me. "Not yet. This is just outside of Ruri. You see the castle, way over there? *That's* where Ruri starts."

I feel the blood rush out of my cheeks. "You're kidding."

"I said it would take a day at least. Did I forget to mention that? Whoops." When he glances over at me, his expression is amused. "What, you thought it was going to be *that* easy?"

Despite myself, I nod.

He leans forward, so he's whispering in my ear. "Let me tell you something: I will *never* make things easier for you. You ought to remember that."

His words make me shiver—not just because of his proximity, but the sudden change in his tone.

He continues forward, cheerful as ever, toward the castle. "My buddy's around here somewhere. He works in one of these brothels, but I'm not sure which."

"Brothel?" I give him a weird look. Around me, I notice that the buildings are bigger, made for fitting more people inside. Because of a glance through a window, I see paper money being thrown through the air and quickly divert my eyes.

"Yes, brothel." Ben grins. "Ruri may be the kingdom of sunshine, and you all may think it's so happy and perfect, but it's really a kingdom of lies and deceit. Even the *name* is deceitful. It's Ruri, which is a name meant to ward off creatures, but somehow they always manage to get inside...." He trails off, the grin leaving his face for a minute, but then it quickly returns. "I believe it's this one."

He stops in front of a bustling brothel and opens the door, the smell of sweat and stench of old alcohol filling my nose. I grimace.

The others pile in behind me. Elysian points to a tale that's empty but filled with bread crumbs, and she and Ameer rush to sit there. Selena gives me an odd look but follows, and Milo and Ash follow after her.

I trail after Ben aimlessly, looking around for someone that I would peg as Ben's friend. I try not to look at the room at all, though, so that makes it a little hard.

"Ben?" I say. "This friend of yours is insane."

"He knows," Ben says, and then whips around, hauling a guy with him.

The guy has buzzed brown hair and amused brown eyes. He's grinning ridiculously, like he finds the situation hilarious.

"You supposed to be here, gorgeous?" the guy says, and I take a deep breath, resisting the urge to punch him in the face.

"Absolutely," I say, resisting the urge to grimace, and he raises his eyebrows. *He doesn't believe me.*

"That's a new one," the guy mutters.

"Ben, can I talk to you?" I say.

Before he can respond, I grab his arm and pull him into a dark corner of the brothel.

"Are you serious?" I demand, and he looks taken aback. "That man is drunk. He's hitting on me, he works at a brothel, he's *drunk*, and you're still taking us to his house?"

"Sage, I know he's not the most trustworthy man by your standards—" he starts, and I cut him off with a snort, which he glares at, "—but he's my friend. An old buddy. I've known the guy since I was in diapers. He's my best friend. He offered to help, and *I* trust the guy, so he's pretty much our only option. In case you have a better idea, of course."

I flex my jaw. "I don't know this kingdom—"

"No, you don't know this kingdom," he says harshly, and I can barely hear him over the sound of clinking glass and men cheering. "*I* do, and this guy does. He's being nice enough to let us stay at his house. I know this kingdom. There's pickpockets and thieves and liars that will manipulate you, that will steal the clothes off your back if they have to. This kingdom, unlike yours with bumblebees and butterflies and rainbows, is tough, and if you don't think you'll survive, then you can head back to Buit and talk those guards into not killing you. I'm sure that will end well."

He turns away, like the argument is finished, but I say, "What are we here for?"

He stops, turns around, looks me in the eyes. He seems calm enough but there's something so blatantly obvious about his stirring anger, about the way his jaw is clenched or the way his hands are forming fists in quick fury.

"What is the purpose here? Why did we come here?" I continue. "Selena has a stab wound. She was at a hospital, where she was safe. I understand that you're a doctor, and, trust me, I did not want to be in that hospital any more than you did, but why not take us home? Why not just leave us stranded somewhere? Why, *why* did we come here, where everything is dangerous and strange?"

"I can't tell you that," Ben says carefully.

"Why?" I ask. "Why are you so adamant to refuse anything? Why don't you trust us? *We're* the ones who should be suspicious of you, not the other way around! You dragged us to this kingdom that most of us have never been to, and now you're just expecting everyone to go along with it, to do whatever you say—"

"I'm not expecting anything of you," he says, his tone still careful. His brown eyes stare up at me, big, vulnerable, reflecting the dull light of the brothel despite it being midday and sunny. "I'm not expecting anything of any of you. I was surprised when you agreed to it. And I brought you here to keep you safe."

"From *Merrik*? We know the solution. We just have to learn to fear nothing, and then—"

"You will never be truly fearless." Ben's expression is hard, all vulnerability lost. "No one is. You may *think* you are, until an old fear comes back to haunt you, to tear at you, and Merrik is there. Merrik appears. He haunts you, just as the fear does. And that is what makes him powerful. Even the bravest men have fears they do not know of, fears they do not speak of, fears that will eventually haunt them the same way *he* does. I brought you here to train you, to break you, but, of course, I can't tell you that, because then he'd kill me."

"Who?"

Ben doesn't say another word. He spins on his heel and walks back over to the guy without glancing at me once.

* * *

The brothel guy's house is not as nice as Ben made it out to be.

It's bigger by Ruri standards, and it's filled with junk and made from stone. It's clear that he'd had roommates before, because there's no way one singular man can make such a mess.

Beer bottles and wrappers from who knows what crowd the floor. The walls have nails stuck to them in random places and inappropriate posters hung on almost every wall. I try to keep my gaze focused on other things, but that's just it—there is nothing else.

There's a very small kitchen and a loveseat facing a small window, and that's it. There's a hallway which I assume leads to bedrooms, but from the theme that seems to be here, I'm guessing there's only a bed in there.

Brothel Guy, whose name is apparently Ethan, stops the tour after the foyer. He literally stops. Just stops walking and glances around, placing his hands on his hips, like he's proud of the place. Though I'm not exactly sure what he has to be proud of.

"Ethan, right?" Selena says. "Isn't there more to this tour, like where we'll be staying?"

"There's bedrooms down the hall," Ethan says, and I notice, now that he's slightly sober, that he has an accent when he talks. "Pick it and stick with it, 'kay? Ben tells me you're gon' be staying for at least a night."

I clench my jaw and look down at the floor.

Ben shrugs. "You heard the man. Find a bedroom."

We all head down the hallway, and I find a bedroom that's pretty decent. There's still beer bottles everywhere, but I can clean and make this room good enough for me to sleep in. Plus, I'm guessing it's the master bedroom, because it has a bathroom attached.

The door opens, and I whip around. I notice it's Ben.

"Get out," I order.

"While I would love to, this is the only bedroom that's available," he says.

"That can't be right."

"There's three bedrooms. You've got this one, Ash and Selena and Milo are in another one, and Ameer and Elysian are in another. I don't really have many options."

"Well, then…" I consider it, glancing around the tiny bed. "I'll stay with Elysian, and you can stay with Ameer."

"I really don't think moving a girl from a bed while she's sleeping after walking around for hours is the smartest move."

"You're just intimidated by the fact that she's a princess, aren't you?" I cross my arms over my chest.

"Yes," he admits, without any guilt. "Yes, I am."

I take a deep breath. "You see, there's a problem."

"And that is?"

"There's only one bed."

"I'll sleep on the floor."

"You can't *sleep on the floor*," I say defiantly. "What, do you *want* to crack your head open on a beer bottle?"

He sighs. "You're not going to give it up, are you?"

"Excuse me for caring about your health."

He sighs again but says nothing and moves to the dusty old closet on the left side of the room. I watch him carefully and then glance back at the bed.

I clear off the trash. "So it's settled then?"

"Settled? When did we settle the matter?" His voice is low and muffled as he speaks through the wall of the closet.

"You can't sleep on the floor," I clarify. "You're much too important."

He emerges, a wry smile on his face. "Gee, thanks."

"I'm telling the truth. And, besides, without you, Selena may not survive."

"Surely you know how to apply *soigner*."

"To *dummies*, yes. A real, living person, no."

He says nothing and instead holds his hand out to me. In it is a piece of fabric.

"What's that?" I eye it suspiciously.

"My shirt."

I glance up at him. He doesn't *look* shirtless. "What does that mean?"

He sighs, exasperated. "I told you earlier that Ethan's been my friend for as long as I can remember. Well, when I was just getting ready to move to Buit, I brought clothes that were too big for me at the time and hid them in this closet. I figured I'd be here again."

"And…you want me to do *what* with it?"

"Wear it," Ben tells me casually, and my cheeks flame.

"You're kidding," I say.

"I'm not," he retorts. "Can you stop being difficult and just take the stupid shirt?"

I snatch it from his hand, making my way to the bathroom before he can. I slam the door behind me.

Thankfully, the bathroom is a lot cleaner than the room itself. It looks cleaner than anything I've seen here at all, even the window.

I stare at myself in the mirror. My cheeks are slightly red, fading back to my usual pale color. My jaw is clenched, though I didn't notice. The shirt I'm wearing matches the color of my eyes, and his shirt is a navy blue. It's baggy and when I bring it up to my nose to smell it, it smells like vanilla.

I change into Ben's shirt, and it fits me loosely, but it's not baggy enough that it's unwearable. It's comfortable.

I glance up at the mirror and smile at myself. In this dark blue, I look *good.*

I open the bathroom door. Ben stares at me for a second, his eyes sweeping the clothes I'm wearing—partially *his* clothes now. His lips part like he's about to say something, but then he says, "You girls take forever."

He shoves past me to get into the bathroom and I make my way over to the bed.

I slide in. The sheets are cold, unused but obviously clean. *Maybe Ethan cares more about Ben than he's willing to let on.*

I let my head rest against the pillow for a second, closing my eyes. The bed is actually really comfortable. I'm almost asleep when the bathroom door bangs open, and Ben steps out, wearing basketball shorts and a T-shirt.

"Why'd you get the shorts and I didn't?" I ask him, leaning back on my elbows.

"I remember someone being very against wearing even my shirt," he says. "You really think you'd want to wear my shorts?"

I give him a look. "Well, not *now.*"

He rolls his eyes playfully, climbing into bed next to me. We make sure to stay as far away from each other as possible, on opposite sides of the bed. His shirt now clings to my body as I stare up at the ceiling, the sun beginning to fall.

We lay there in the mostly-dark room for a while. I suddenly notice how loud the crickets outside are.

"Early riser?" I say finally.

"Can't go very long without talking, can you, Sage?"

"Unfortunately, my competitive tendencies don't allow me to do so."

He snorts. "Tendencies."

"Well, are you?"

"Am I what?"

"An early riser."

"No, no," he says with a chuckle. "I'll sleep until twelve if I need to."

"I don't understand people like that. You get a full fourteen hours of sleep, and yet you're still exhausted."

Ben sighs. "When I was younger, my parents made me wake up at the crack of dawn every day and sprint around the house at least once."

"That doesn't sound so bad." *Especially considering the size of these houses.*

"It's worse than you think," he says. "Anyway, I did it every morning until I was thirteen. By then, it was a routine. But I've been working hard for years to break that habit, and I finally have. I'm proud of myself for waking up late, because it means no matter how bad a habit I have, I can break. It's a symbolic thing."

"I never...thought of it that way."

"Most don't. But you just have to be willing to look at all sides of the story, no matter what side someone's on."

I let that sit for a moment. Then, I say, "Thank you for the shirt."

"Thank you for...caring enough to make sure I don't crack my head open on a beer bottle."

"I'm considerate like that."

"I can tell."

My statement is meant to be a joke, but there's not anything in his voice—no hint of sarcasm or a teasing tone—that tells me he's joking right back.

"You said, earlier, that someone couldn't have zero fears," I start. "Then, later, you said you were here to train us. What are you training us for, if there's no point in trying to be fearless?"

"You can't be fearless," he says, his tone careful, thoughtful, "but you can learn to *control* fear. If you can make sure that you can control your fears enough to not let them get to you when Merrik's around, he may start to become weak enough that you can defeat him."

"That's...smart."

"Surprised?"

"Slightly. I didn't think you would be the planning-type."

"Because you are?"

I say nothing, and he seems to take that as a yes.

"Maybe we can work together sometime in the future, if you can get over your hatred for me," Ben says.

"Not…exactly *hatred.* Just annoyance."

"That's reassuring."

"You brought it up."

He turns on his side, so he's looking at me. "Yes, I did." He's grinning like a crazy person, and his brown eyes are still bright. "Good night," Ben tells me.

It takes all my willpower not to look at him directly. If I look at him, I'm not sure I'd be able to look away. "Good night."

With Ben next to me, for the first time since Sorin's death, I sleep a dreamless sleep.

* * *

When I wake up, Ben's face is inches from mine, and I suck in my breath. He smells exactly like the shirt I'm wearing does—vanilla.

He smells great.

I rid myself of those thoughts by shaking my head and climb out of bed. Outside, the sun is just barely beginning to rise. Ben may not be an early riser, but I am, and I just can't break my habit. I make my way to the bathroom and wash my face, using a new toothbrush, still in the packaging, to brush my teeth. I decide to go to the kitchen to see if Ethan has any coffee, so I leave the bedroom, closing the door softly behind me.

When I get to the kitchen, Elysian looks uncomfortable. Ethan is mostly sober, but he's still hitting on her, and once I appear, he slinks back to his room on the other side of the house.

"Thanks," she tells me gratefully. "I was about to smack the alcohol out of that guy." Then she eyes the shirt I'm wearing.

"What?" I say, grabbing myself a cup and pouring a pot of coffee that I assume Elysian has just made.

"That's not yours," she notes. "Who did you end up rooming with?"

"Oh, uh…" I make up a lie quickly. "Milo."

"What about me?" Milo asks sleepily from the hallway, coming into view. "I shared a room with Selena and Ash."

Elysian chuckles, maintaining eye contact with me despite the fact that I'm trying to look at the ground right now. "You roomed with *Dr. Abott?* That's *his* shirt?"

My cheeks start to flame.

She smacks my arm. "It totally is! Sage!"

"Don't say anything, okay?" I tell her. "Not to anyone. I don't want them to get the wrong idea."

"Meaning you don't want to believe that you're moving on from Sorin," she clarifies, and I hate how well she's able to read me. "It's okay, Sage. You can move on. You can want other things, other people, than him—"

"I don't *want* to move on," I say sharply, and the coffee I've started to pour spills onto the counter.

Elysian says nothing and hands me a paper towel.

"And it's not like that," I continue. "Not with me and Ben. He offered me his shirt, and I figured I'd use it, because it was available and I needed to."

"And the sleeping part?"

I glance up at her. "What?"

"The sleeping part. Since you're so adamantly against using his shirt, what did you do when you went to sleep? Were there two beds? Did he sleep on the floor?"

"We…slept in the same bed."

She raises her eyebrows, but doesn't say anything. For some reason, this makes me feel like I have to defend myself.

"Seriously, nothing happened. We stayed on opposite sides of the bed, and when I woke up—"

"Was it awkward?" Elysian asks. "When you woke up."

"No," I say, "because he wasn't awake yet. He's not an early riser."

"There's so much that you learn about each other when you sleep in the same bed," she muses, and Milo answers with a nod and says, "Evidently."

"If you guys keep talking so loud, you'll wake everyone up," I say, pretending to take a sip of coffee, but I'm really just trying to hide my blush.

It doesn't get past Elysian. "It's fine, Sage, to be at least a little bit embarrassed."

"I didn't—" I sigh. There's no use in arguing. "Nothing happened," I say finally. "And, please, *please*, don't bring it up. I'll never live it down."

Elysian rolls her eyes playfully. "You know we're just teasing you, right? We don't care who you shared a room with, as long as you got a good night's sleep."

I think back to the dreamless night I had with Ben by my side in his vanilla-scented shirt, and I smile slightly. "Yeah. I guess I did."

Suddenly, Ben enters the room. I glance at him, my smile vanishing. Elysian gives me a look.

"I thought you weren't waking up until twelve," I say.

"I wasn't going to," he says, "but I guess I forgot how early the sun rises in Ruri. I couldn't sleep with it in my face, and I realized you were already awake, so I decided I'd come to the kitchen and see what you were doing."

"Making coffee." I hold up my coffee cup.

"That's it?"

"That's it."

"Well, you'll need it," Ben mutters, sliding onto one of the stools next to Milo's. "We're going to be training a lot today. Facing your fears, fighting them. Things like that."

Elysian loses her amused expression. "What?"

"How, do you suppose, are we going to face our fears if we don't have much access to anything here?" I ask Ben, ignoring Elysian.

"We're not even inside the kingdom yet," Milo says, his attitude probably affected by the fact that he had to share a room with two girls who could rip his face off the entire night.

"You're right," Ben says, "but…Ethan is really important, especially to the people of Ruri, and he can call in some favors."

Elysian snorts. "You're telling me that the guy that was just in here calling me 'sweetie' is actually *important* to people?"

I wait for Ben to blow up, like he did on me when I talked about Ethan, but he doesn't. He just chuckles slightly. "Yeah, he is."

In my ear, Elysian murmurs, "I seriously doubt that."

"So your experiences with him aren't as good as mine, huh?" Ben says, pouring himself coffee. I hate how he's acting so casual about all this. I mean, he should be, but, even if nothing happened between us, *something* did. I feel it pressing down on my chest like the weight of an elephant—something so heavy that it would make sense to move it, but I just can't.

But then again, why *should* he be bothered? We barely even know each other, and there's certainly more pressing matters than what happened last night.

And he must have a high tolerance for anything like this. After all, his best friend *does* live next to a brothel….

I shake my head. *Don't think about that.*

"Sage?"

I realize Ben is saying my name.

"Are you okay? You look a little off."

"Fine," I say hastily. "Probably just drank too quickly." I hold the coffee cup as proof and then hit myself internally. *Of course he knows what you're talking about.*

Ben doesn't say anything about my stupidity. He just nods, like he understands, and returns to making small talk with Elysian and Milo.

Elysian turns to me, and in her eyes is confusion. I turn away from her, facing Ben.

"When are we starting training?" I ask, cutting him off.

He smiles. "We start as soon as the coffee's done."

Elysian sees my expression and takes the coffee pot, pouring the rest of the contents into her cup. "Done," she says. "Let's start now."

* * *

I've trained before. I've run a mile or two without stopping. I've fought several enemies head on. I'm great with my dagger. I know how to *fight*. All of this seems relatively easy to me now, after years of doing it, so I never thought learning to face your fears would be as hard as it is.

I changed into one of Ben's other shirts before training, and it's soaked with sweat. My knuckles are bruised and bloody, and my fingers ache. Apparently when Ben said Ethan could call in favors, he meant that could *really* call in favors. He hired a whole bunch of stuntmen from Ruri that have been acting as enemies. Ben wanted to test which fears we had before we started the actual training, and so far, he's learned things about my friends that I didn't even know. I never would've guessed that Milo's big fear is spiders, or that Elysian's is snakes, or Ash's is…black fabric? I wonder what that's about.

"Is that my shirt?" Ben mutters as I fight with one of the stuntmen in front of me. As the stuntman lunges forward, trying to stab me, I grab his arm and twist until he backs away, crying out in pain.

"Yes," I say breathlessly. "I couldn't find anything better."

He snorts. "Well, that's what they're for. You not 'finding anything better.'"

"I thought you'd be flattered that I even bothered to look into that musty closet and pull out one of your shirts."

"Oh, I'm very flattered," he says, his tone teasing. The next stuntman advances, and I raise my dagger, hoping my eyes show enough malice to make him want to end this fight quickly. "Just a question."

"It's a stupid one." I slash at the stuntman, but he's wearing armor, thankfully. My anger is growing because of Ben's taunting remarks, and my grip on my dragger is turning my knuckles white.

To make sure I don't seriously hurt him, I drop my dagger and step away from the stuntman. Ben glances at me questioningly, but I simply glare at him.

"When is this going to be over?" I snarl at him.

He walks closer to me. "Depends," he says, a smile gracing his light features. I'm suddenly struck by his features in his brown eyes, gold around the pupil, his hair blonde in contrast, curling up at the ends. *You're staring.* "Are you ready to quit?"

"I'm not quitting," I say harshly, turning away from him. His annoying smirk is still there, and I feel his amused eyes boring holes into the side of my skull. "Just a question."

He raises his eyebrows in response to my repetition of his words, and then he chuckles lightly. "I know this is probably really taxing for you, considering you're *fearless* or whatever you'd like to believe, but...there's something you're not telling me. Something you need to tell me in order to make progress. And as long as you refuse to tell me whatever it is you're trying to hide from me, then we will never move on."

When I say nothing, just press my lips together in silent resignation, Ben nods.

"That's what I thought."

I bite back my retort and motion with my chin for the next stuntman to come forward, picking up my dagger.

* * *

Several hours of training later, the sky has turned to a dark purple-pink, and the sun, though it's almost midnight, is still setting. I grab a coat from the coat rack next to the door and slip out of the house.

There's no chill outside. I eventually shrug off the coat and wrap it around my waist, loving the feel of the light breeze against my bare arms. I'm wearing another one of Ben's shirts, though I'm still angry at him due to this morning.

I look around and see the coast is clear—non one in sight. I duck behind a building and tie my hair up, hiding it in a ratty cap that I found in the closet where Ben's clothes are. My plan is simple: sneak into a brothel, assuming the role of an excited young man, and gather information on the kingdom of Ruri and the Royal family from the citizens. If that doesn't work...

I eye the leather pouch that I have, filled to the brim with *solis* coins, the money that Ruri uses. I'm sure, no matter where the person I ask is from, they'll benefit from some extra money. After all, Ruri *is* known for having the best artifacts in the entire dynasty.

I scan the area after hiding my hair and drawing my coat around me tightly. The most populated brothel seems to be the one to my right. I pick it grimly, not wanting to do this. But if we're staying in Ruri for a while, I need to know a little about it.

I bite the inside of my cheek and push open the brothel door. Lights and music blare. Women dance with all kinds of different props, and men watch them, the light shining off their faces, as they throw money at the ground to be picked up later.

Thankfully, there's a bar, so I can lure someone over and pretend to have a nice, friendly chat as reporter Eli Jacobs, doing a story on what really is the topic of conversation on the outskirts of Ruri.

I slide onto one of the stools, bringing out a notepad to make it believable. The bartender comes over as I'm writing a few short words on it, asking me if I want a drink. I clear my throat to make my voice lower and order shots of tequila. *Only the gods know how much I'll need them.*

I lean back against the counter to make myself look more cocky, more like a guy. Eventually, I lock eyes with a girl that's talking with a group of men. She apologizes to them and makes her way over to me.

She sits on the stool next to me. "I've never seen a reporter boy in here ever," she says thoughtfully, eyeing my notepad. "Normally they follow the queen around like lost puppies."

"Oh, I get it," I say. "Though I've always been more of a cat person."

She chuckles. "And I've definitely never seen a *funny* reporter boy in here before. Why *are* you here?"

The bartender comes back with a tray of shots. I take one of the glasses and drain it in one gulp.

I place a *solis* coin on the counter as payment, and the girl eyes it. "Now you're just confusing me. You're *rich*, too?" she says.

"I thought I'd have some fun, to answer your question." I shrug off her previous comment like it's nothing. I imagine it's something someone working in close quarters with the queen would do. "I wouldn't consider myself rich, but I've got a large sum of money for someone that allows me to interview them for the story I'm writing."

"Story?" The girl looks confused. She cocks her head to one side. "What story could be on the outside of the kingdom? *Inside* Ruri is where the real stuff happens."

"Well, when the board offered me the job, I took it. I needed the alcohol, anyway."

She chuckles. "Boy, do I agree with that." She steals a shot from the tray and downs it. "What's the story you're doing?"

I smile slightly. *Everything is going according to plan.* "It's about the Royal family, actually."

She raises her eyebrows. "The Royal committee has control over all the newspapers, so I'm surprised they'd let you do that. You must have some power over them..." She trails off, waiting for something.

"Eli," I say, holding out my hand. "Eli Jacobs."

The girl shakes it. "Clarissa," she says, "and I'm not telling you my last name. The last time I did that with a reporter, it didn't end well."

I shrug. For what I need, Clarissa's last name is pretty unimportant. "It's not that I have power over the Royal committee. It's that the Royal family is cocky, and they wanted to know what people were saying about them behind their backs."

"You seem so against the Royal family," she notes. "Is there a reason for that, or are you just a spiteful person?"

"Is both an option?"

Clarissa laughs. "What do you want to know?"

"Well, what's the rumors going around about the Royal family?" I say. "This isn't part of the story—I'll make up fake ones to make you look better—but I love having dirt on the ever-so-perfect rich family that does everything right and makes all my decisions for me."

"The rumors?" Clarissa gives me a strange look. "We don't talk much about the Royal family, but I can give you some *facts* about them."

"Please do." To make myself seem less eager, I take another shot.

"Well, they have a son," she says. "*Had,* I guess I should say. He ran away not too long ago, and they still haven't been able to find him. The king and queen are ridiculously strict, but I imagine you already know about those things since you work in such close quarters with them."

I nod. "How long ago did he run away?" I ask innocently.

Clarissa's face twists up into an ugly snarl. "Three years ago. Trust me, *that* year was the kingdom's worst. Those of us that work on the outside of Ruri's borders were cut off completely from anything. I guess the king and queen hoped they would draw the prince back that way, but they never did. He's still missing. Must've gone to another kingdom. Gods know I would've too if this weren't the only source of income I had…but, anyway, I'm getting off track. The king and queen are horrible people. They gave their son ridiculous amounts of homework from his tutors and training tactics from his instructors that he had to complete by the end of the week." She leans forward, lowering her voice. "Some say they would beat him if he didn't."

That gives me a feeling like an ice shard being plunged into my chest. I have plenty of experience with abuse.

"You okay, reporter boy?" Clarissa says, studying my voice closely. "You look pale."

My heart almost stops. I hope she doesn't notice my narrow nose or amount of freckles or eyelashes that are too long to belong to a boy.

"Fine," I say, clearing my throat and taking another shot. "Next rumor."

"Well, I don't really have any more dirt on the Royal family," she says, glancing at the floor. "They keep to themselves most of the time, and the people that I get the dirt from are people that I don't like consulting when others are around. Especially strange reporter boys that are working for the Royal committee." She eyes me suspiciously, like it's just occurred to her that I may not be on her side.

"Do you see me writing anything?" I say, motioning to my notepad, blank on the counter despite the words "outskirts of Ruri."

"In that case, I *may* be able to consult my friends, but for a price." Clarissa points to the pouch of *solis* coins, and I raise my eyebrows.

"Well played," I tell her.

She nods. "Not the first time I've scammed a guy into giving me money."

"You want all of it?" I offer, and her eyes flash greedily.

"Of course," she agrees, her eyes aimed on the pouch.

"You give me the information; I give you the coins." The alcohol is starting to seep into my brain, but I make my eyes focus as well as I can and my speech clear. "Do we have a deal?"

Clarissa's jaw flexes as she considers it.

"I don't have all day," I snap, and I don't, for I know Ben will discover that I'm missing soon enough and that I've stolen some of his friend's money.

"Fine," she says. "The Royal family is growing weaker."

"Weaker?" I say. "What do you mean?"

"Give me the money."

"Give me the information. That's what we agreed to."

She sighs. "Their money's going into other hands. Their guards are either quitting or dead. It's been like this for Emerald, Veridet, Buit, and Marina, too. Like magic, their kingdoms are falling, and they can't do anything to stop it." Clarissa smirks. "Serves them right," she practically spits, and I'm about to hand over the pouch when suddenly a shriek sounds from the dance floor.

I leap up, bringing the *solis* coins with me. I ready my dagger and surge forward, into the crowd, when I spot the commotion.

A man lies dead in the middle of the floor, a dagger through his heart. I notice there's a slip of paper stuck through the blade of the dagger, and I rip it free.

Funnily enough, it's addressed to me.

Sage Jobbs -

You should've listened when the doctor said it was dangerous in this kingdom. You don't have the luck you had before, and in this kingdom there are only people that fight using sheer force, which, unfortunately, you don't have.

Fortunately for me, I am stronger than I ever have been. I also have your little boyfriend on my side, and if you ever wish to have him back, then you will have to choose.

The losing side of this war, or the winning side?

I wish you luck.

Sincerely,

M

I stare at the note for a second, and a second too long—because then people around me start dropping like flies, dead, due to thin daggers with notes attached to them.

CHAPTER 16

ELYSIAN

There's a ringing in my ears.

As it grows louder, I realize it's the sound of screams. My eyes shoot open and when I blink, I see the images of my nightmare reflected in front of me: torches, ghosts, and the taunting smirk of the man I saw when I stepped into Selena's hospital room with Ash, manipulating his face to look like my father's.

"Elysian?" Ameer murmurs from the floor, and I shush him.

"Go back to sleep," I whisper soothingly, and he follows my directions, his eyes drooping.

I stand from the bed, stretching. My muscles are tight from training yesterday and sleep, and I tug a soft robe I find in the closet around my body, tying it and stepping out into the kitchen. I see Ash, and I stop dead.

She's sitting at the counter, looking down at the marble. I wonder if I should approach her or go back to bed, when she turns around and sees me.

No going back now.

"Couldn't sleep?" I ask, just to make conversation, and Ash simply turns away.

I consider going back to bed, but then Ash says, "No. You?"

"Nightmares."

She nods.

I've only had nightmares lately. They're mostly about Merrik and the army he's forming, but some are about her.

I never thought I'd have nightmares about someone I love. Funny.

The nightmares are usually the same: she breaks up with me, I'm publicly humiliated, I die in a hole because of heartbreak. But convincing myself that they aren't real, that they can't affect me, still doesn't stop me from having them, no matter the situation.

I sit next to her at the counter. She glances over at me and we make eye contact for a second, just a second—and I see those beautiful eyes, dark brown flecked with gold specks that make her so special. Ash's eyes are one of the reasons why I fell in love with her.

Now they're just a bitter reminder of the past few days.

We break eye contact, and I stand again, rushing to make coffee. The coffee that I made yesterday morning sits on the counter, forgotten, and I put it in the trash. I would use it, but I just really need something to do right now and making something that will keep me awake and help me not lose my senses is probably the best thing.

I bring out the coffee beans and the brewer. Ash says nothing, but as I start to make the coffee, I can feel her eyes drilling holes into my back. She hasn't stopped looking at me since I stood, and I desperately wish she would.

Just as I'm about to pour myself a cup, the door flies open, and my hand jerks, so hot coffee spills on me.

I gasp in pain, but then turn to see Sage in the doorway, her dagger clutched tightly in her hand, which is covered in blood, and I realize something is terribly wrong.

She doesn't say a word, but Ash and I rush for our weapons, and I elongate mine into a sword by pressing a button on the hilt.

"What happened?" Ash asks Sage, her expression hardening.

We leave Ethan's house as Sage tells us the story: She was at a brothel when four people died – the same way -- with a dagger to the heart. But, each dagger had a note attached to it—one addressed to me, one to Sage, one to Ash, and one to Selena.

"Who killed them?" I ask.

She glances back at me, her eyes showing a bit of sympathy in them. "Merrik."

"That's impossible," Ash says immediately, but Sage shakes her head.

"See for yourself."

We step into a brothel that people are running out of, eager to get home where it's safe. There are a few customers sobbing as they run, and I wonder if they knew one of the victims, if they loved them.

Merrik needs to be stopped. Even if it isn't him that's doing this.

Inside, I see Sage was right. There are four dead bodies on the ground, three of them with thin silver dagger sticking out of their chests. Sage holds the dagger that belongs to the fourth body, I assume.

I walk over to one of the bodies and remove the dagger from their heart. The victim is a woman with bright red hair and stormy gray eyes, and she looks young—my age. My heart aches for the people that knew her, but I can't focus on that. I remove the white piece of paper, flecked with the girl's blood, from the blade of the dagger, my eyes scanning over it.

It says my name on it.

I walk back to Ash and Sage, who are inspecting the rest of the bodies. I hand the note to Ash.

"Read it," I say.

"What?" she says.

"Read it," I repeat. "Read it out loud. I don't think I can."

She gives me a look but starts to read anyway. "'Elysian Viggo,'" she starts, "'I appreciate you coming all this way. It makes it easier for me. Now you're closer to where my niece is. I assume you're familiar with her—Aelia, goddess of the sun? We aren't on the best of terms, but we talk from time to time, unlike Aeolus, my nephew, the god of *your* kingdom. We're on even worse terms now that all of this is going on. He's very protective of the humans that he's blessed, you know.'"

She pauses, and I urge her to keep reading.

Ash takes a deep breath, then continues. "'As for your girlfriend, I think I will dispose of her quickly. Help out the kingdom a bit, you know? And I understand that you two are in a bit of a rough patch currently, so I would be doing *you* a favor too...'" She trails off before shoving the paper back in my hands. "Did you know it was going to say that?" she demands.

I see the anger in her eyes. "What? Of course not!"

"But you would've given it to me either way, right? It would've been a good laugh?"

"Where is this coming from? Of course I wouldn't laugh at *that!* Merrik's a cruel person, Ash, and he's trying to get inside of your mind and make you believe that I'm against you."

"Why'd you ask me to read it, Elysian?" Ash's eyes are hard when she asks me this. "Why? Was it because you knew there was going to be something horrible on there about me, and you couldn't wait to broadcast it to everyone?"

"Ash, you have to believe me—"

"Whatever," she grumbles, leaning down to pull a dagger from one of the bodies. "Don't talk to me for a while, okay?"

My heart drops, and I feel my throat beginning to form a lump as tears threaten to spill from my eyes. I refuse to let her have the satisfaction of seeing me cry, though, so I turn away at the last second, pulling a dagger from the final body. "Okay," I say faintly, giving her the note that's addressed to her. "And, trust me, I haven't read this one."

I leave the brothel and walk back to Ethan's house. The night air is humid and I find that it's quiet. So quiet, in fact, that all I can hear are my own thoughts, repeatedly telling me that she hates me, that she doesn't want me to talk to her, that she doesn't even *believe* me anymore. And though it's a cruel thought, I still wish that the people were screaming, just so I wouldn't be able to hear her words as they replay in my mind.

When I get to the room that I share with Ameer, he's waiting there, sitting on the edge of the bed. I walk in, my arms folded over my chest, and he's about to scold me when he sees my expression.

"Lys?" he says softly. "What—"

I start to sob. The tears leak from my eyes and his eyebrows crease. I'm afraid he's disappointed in me, that he hates me just like Ash does. He doesn't want me to talk to him, doesn't want me to even look at him, probably just wants me to get out.

I'm about to turn toward the door when Ameer stands from the bed, walks over to me, and folds me into his arms, hugging me and whispering into my hair as I sob into his shirt.

Ameer has always been the leader. The good brother, the good king, the best person to support our kingdom. The best person to support me.

He kisses the top of my head, and though I'm sure that I'm soaking his shirt with my tears and snot and that he's disgusted by it, he doesn't let go, not even for a second. I'm glad he's talking, because he's not letting me think those thoughts, not letting me replay what happened in my mind. And he's not asking me if I'm okay—it's more of an unspoken clarification, my cries, and he understands, and he just stands there, hugging me, helping me with just his presence.

"Thank you," I murmur through my tears, and I feel him nod against me, and he leads me to the bed, letting me go so he can bring the covers over me. He pulls the blinds down, making the room darker so I can sleep, and then he straightens.

"I thought—" he says, then starts again. "You left without telling me where you were going. And you came back, and you had a stain on your shirt and I thought you were hurt, that you had blood on you—"

"It's coffee," I say quietly, my tears fading. "I spilled my coffee."

He shushes me. "Get some more sleep. You need it. And if you want me, then just ask. I'll be—"

"Ameer?" I say.

His expression softens. "Yeah, Lys?"

"You can sleep in the bed," I tell him. "I want you to. I don't want you to leave."

He nods, climbing in bed next to me, and for a second I feel like a child. I feel five years old again, hearing the muffled argument my parents are having in the next room, waiting for my big brother to tell me it's all okay, everything will be fine.

I lean my head against his shoulder, noticing the fact that my tears are gone. Ameer smells like himself—like lilac and lemon. He's smelled like that since we were kids, and I always thought that it was because of the shampoo he used. But now I realize that's just what he smells like. Lilac and lemon is my brother, and there's no changing that. I'm thankful for the familiarity of it, and I let my eyes close, let myself start to drift off.

Right as I'm about to fall asleep, I mutter, "Ameer?"

"Yeah, Lys?" he says.

"I love you."

There's a pause, and then he says, "I love you, too."

* * *

When I wake for the second time, Ameer is still next to me, staring up at the ceiling. I feel more refreshed, even though I'm sure I look horrible, and a laugh bubbles out of me at the thought. He turns and notices I'm awake.

"Morning, Lys," he greets. "Or, I guess I should say *afternoon*. It's three o'clock right now."

"And you didn't wake me up?" I ask. I push him away from me, laughing. "You're a horrible brother."

"You'd been tossing and turning the entire night, so I figured I'd let you rest," he says. "And as for the horrible brother part—" He stops. "There's really nothing I can say in response to that."

I laugh again, turning so I'm on my back. The bed is comfortable but warm, and as I sit up, Ameer wraps his arm around my shoulders.

"What happened?" he asks me, and I assume he thinks he'll get a straight answer now that I've calmed down, but I say nothing instead, and he sighs. "Lys—" he starts.

"I'm fine now," I say, cutting him off. "Thank you. Seriously. You helped me. If you want to eat lunch or something you can, but you don't have to stay here with me."

"Yes," he says, "I do. I know you. And I know that if I leave this room, you will start to become self-destructive."

"I already said, Ameer, that I was fine—"

"You lied, though, Lys," he says quietly. His tone isn't accusatory, but he says it like it's a fact. Which it is. But he shouldn't know that. "I'm your brother. I'm not Ash. I'm not you. Let me help you. And if you don't want me to do that, then at least let me stay here with you, like I wasn't able to do when we were younger."

I pause, taking in a breath. And then I hand him the note that was attached to the young woman's body, the note that made Ash tell me not to talk to her.

He takes it from me. "Do you want me to read it?" he asks.

"Read it from 'so I should be doing you a favor, too,'" I say, and he nods.

"'I think she's a big pain to both of us. Excuse me if I'm wrong. But, anyway, that's not why I have addressed this letter to you. I wanted to talk about the war. There is going to be a war happening in a very short period of time, and you must decide which side you wish to fight on. Of course, most of you are stubborn and insistent on staying on the losing side, but I know you are more sensible. You have Cirillo's blood in you, after all. So what'll it be? Me or them?'"

Ameer stops, but he keeps going without me having to tell him to.

"'I'll give you time to decide. On October twenty-fourth, just three days after your little friend's birthday, I will expect my answer. And if I do not get one, then I will consider your answer a no and we will go to war. If you make the right choice to be on my side during this battle, then we go to war, but I will delay it by one day. Think of those you love, Elysian Viggo, before you decide to make your choice. Sincerely, M.'"

A chill runs through my body, and I think it's because I'm nervous, until I see that Ameer's hand has been frozen in a block of ice. I raise an eyebrow at him and he smiles sheepishly.

"Sorry," he says. "I'm not the best at controlling it yet."

"There are other matters on my mind right now," I say, and he loses his smile.

"Right. Of course." He gives me a strange look. "Well, are you going to say yes?"

"Of course not," I reply. "It's Merrik. He sent those letters. I'm not going to say yes, but that means we have only one week to prepare for battle—and miraculously lose our fears."

He swallows. "I need some coffee."

"Forget the coffee," I say, climbing out of bed. "We need to start training. *Now.*"

* * *

When I tell Sage what the note said, her jaw drops.

"You're kidding," she says.

"Unfortunately, I'm not," I say, glancing at the ground.

Ameer is fiddling with his fingers, something we both do when we're nervous. "She has a witness."

She turns toward him, mouth still agape, and then her gaze returns to me. "Merrik wants you to choose which side you're going to be on?"

"Yes," I say carefully, "and he wants me to choose *his* side."

"You're not going to, are you?"

"Of course not." I sigh. "Which means we have to start preparing *yesterday*. So…"

"So what?" Sage asks defensively.

"Where's Ben?"

"Why should I know? It's not like I track Ben's every movement. Maybe if you wanted to find him you should try harder." She crosses her arms defiantly, and when she turns to face the wall, her jaw flexes.

She's uncomfortable. I feel a smirk growing on my face. "I know, Sage," I say. "I just figured, since you roomed with him, that you'd have a little knowledge on his whereabouts."

"Well, I don't." She glances back at me. "Why are you looking at me like that?"

Ameer glances at the floor, but I stare at her with a look on my face until she relents.

Sighing, she says, "I haven't seen him. He's probably with Ethan."

"Well, aren't the weapons and armor and all that in the basement?" I say. "We can go down there and get an early start."

"Milo's working on Selena's wound, though," Sage says with a frown. "She can't fight in the war, so what are we supposed to do with her?"

"Simple," Ameer says, finally glancing up from the floor. "She can't fight."

"We make Milo and Ben Healers, and then we go out and fight," I add.

"That might not work so well." Sage glances at the hallway that leads down to the bedrooms. "Ben's swordplay is amazing."

"But you need more than one Healer to heal a gunshot wound, a stab wound, or anything that's more important than a measly papercut or dehydration," Ash says from the end of the counter.

I turn and glare at her. She glares back.

Ameer notices, and he places a steady hand on my shoulder to calm me down. I glance at him gratefully, and he smiles back.

Sage stares at me, then Ash, her eyes trailing back and forth.

When Ash notices, she snaps, "What?" and Sage quits staring.

"Milo is talented enough to—"

"We don't need more fighters," Ash retorts. "We beat Finn, just the four of us."

"This is different. Merrik is an *entity*. We need all the people we can get."

"You're only defending him because he's your new boyfriend," Ash bites out. "If the roles were reversed, if *you* had died instead of Sorin, do you think he would've moved on this quickly?"

Sage's mouth falls open. I stare at Ash, sure that I'm showing a good amount of disgust and hurt on my face, and then she glances away.

Ameer swallows. "We can start training without them," he says quietly. "And I've seen Ben fight. He's good."

Sage nods. She leaves the room, going into the hallway where the bedrooms are.

"I'm going to get changed," I tell Ameer, and I stand from my seat at the table.

As I'm about to make my way back to the bedroom, Ash grabs my wrist and I jerk it away from her. I'm surprised to see that there's a hint of sadness in her eyes when I do.

"Please, Elysian, can you tell Sage that I didn't mean to—" she starts, but I cut her off.

"You can tell her yourself," I say. I'm angry with her, and it shows in my words, in the harsh tone that I use only with her, that makes my words sound more like an insult than anything else. "Besides, I'm not supposed to be talking to you. Or have you forgotten already?"

She recoils, like my words have stung her. A burst of triumph rises in my chest. She deserves it. She's treated me horribly, so why should I not do the same?

But then she lowers her voice and says softly, "I'm so, so sorry, Elysian."

Now I'm the one who's recoiling, and the sudden burst of triumph I felt has vanished, settling into something hollow, empty.

I turn around and continue my path to the bedroom.

I fish through the dresser pushed to the side of the room. There are some extra clothes in here, clothes that I can use for training. I find a T-shirt that's baggy on me and some sweatpants, and I make my way to the basement, using hidden stairs on Ethan's side of the house.

Since we have no stuntmen, Sage announces that we'll be fighting each other. She explains the rules: the fight is over when someone is on the ground. She's dragged Milo down here so he can heal us if we need it, and she says that we'll start with hand-to-hand combat first, and then progress to sword-fighting.

"Okay, everyone," she says finally. "Two will sit out, and two will fight. I think I want to fight…Elysian."

She smirks and I curse inwardly. I want to fight *Ash*. I want to see her be bested by *me*, her ex, and I want to use fighting as an excuse to forget about earlier, to forget about last night, to forget about everything we had because of how angry she's making me.

She notices my expression and her smirk only grows. I match it with my own as she asks, "Scared?"

Sage is my best friend, and I know she'll go slightly easy on me, but even when she's going easy on someone, she's still a good fighter.

Great.

"Not at all," I say through my smirk, and Sage advances, readying her fists.

CHAPTER 17

SELENA

There's a note folded into my hand.

I stare down at it, growing angrier by the minute. How *dare* he write me a letter after every stupid thing he showed me. He's pathetic.

I throw it on the ground, stomping on it. The black boots I wear leave behind a satisfying mark on the piece of paper.

I let out a scream, muffling it with my palm. Why can't everything just go back to the way it was before? Before I met Milo, before that night at the campfire when Sorin died, before I even signed up for that stupid internship at the castle that prohibited me from going home for *five* years? Then I might be happy. Then Merrik may be tracking down someone else, someone who isn't me, who has no relation to me.

It's a ridiculous hope. What is done is done, and there's no changing that.

I glance down at my sword arm, my right one, with the kingdom's slogan printed on it in bold lettering: All's fair in love and war. It reminds us that when we hold our swords, we will not be shamed. All is appropriate and necessary during battle.

I'm glad I left, but when I did everything spiraled out of control. At least when I was a guard I had someplace safe to stay, good meals, and the ability to adventure places and fight. There was a lot of training, but I always excelled at the physical part of everything. That's what made me so intimidating to the other guards.

Unfortunately, now I don't think I'm that intimidating to anyone here. They're all stronger than me, especially considering the fact that I *died.*

The door opens, and I jump.

"It's me," Milo's voice says, and I turn around slowly, relieved. "I just need some more *soigner* for Elysian's ribs."

"Sage busted her up?" I ask, only half-listening. Elysian hasn't always been my biggest fan and I haven't been hers.

"Yeah," Milo says, rifling through the bag I brought with me. "I didn't know Sage had it in her."

"She probably didn't mean to."

For some reason, my voice is filled with more emotion than I want it to be, and Milo gives me a weird look. He eyes the sleeve of my sweater, rolled up to show the tattoo.

"Hey, Selena, are you okay?" he asks, walking toward me.

"I'm fine," I say in a choked voice, though I don't feel close to crying. I feel fine, so he could stop worrying. He should stop looking at my forearm and turn away from me with his *soigner,* trying to tend to Elysian as fast as possible.

But he doesn't.

He keeps his eyes trained on me. I feel like I did not too many nights ago, when I had the dream that my lungs were on fire. With him this close to me, I feel like my lungs are on fire, like I'm struggling to breathe.

When he reaches out, lacing his fingers through mine, I notice how cold my hands are, and I wonder briefly if I was the same temperature when I was dead, or if I was colder.

"Selena," he says softly, "what's wrong?"

The question, when *he* asks it, doesn't feel like something that I have to answer. He's putting it out there, offering his freakish ability to listen for long periods of time. And I refuse.

He sees it in my eyes. Milo steps away from me, letting his hand drop at his side. I miss his warmth instantly, and the tears that burn at the back of my eyes and the ball that is growing in my throat, restricting my breath, are clear indications of that.

"I'm sorry," I say quietly. "I don't want to talk about it."

He nods. There is no anger in the way he looks at me, only understanding. He understands, and he isn't angry. I'm grateful for it, for him.

He removes the medicine from the bag, tucking it into the pocket of his pants. And then he leaves the room again, and I am left alone with my thoughts.

And I break down.

* * *

Incapable of love.

That's what I told myself.

Incapable of feeling it, sharing it, having anything to do with it. My mother and father drilled that into my mind until it stuck, and then, when I was four, my little brother was born. His name was Sorin. He was a bundle of joy in a basket, and his skin, tan already despite the fact that he had never been in the sun, glowed in the fluorescent lights of the hospital. My parents didn't want me to come to the birth of my brother. They thought I would ruin it, ruin him— break his spirit just by looking at him.

They were wrong.

I stepped into the hospital's nursery, and instantly almost all of the babies started crying. It was like they could sense my presence. They could tell I was there. They knew I was there, knew that I wasn't one of them, that I was never meant to be around them. When I was a baby, in that very nursery, the babies around me would cry all the time, only quieting when I finally left with my parents. I was a silent baby, but those around me weren't, and I realized quickly that it was my fault.

I looked around the room, feeling horrible. Not even babies liked me. But then I saw one baby, lying in a crib, staring at the ceiling. And when the baby saw me and I saw the baby, instead of bursting into tears, he smiled his first ever smile.

I will forever remember the way I felt. He smiled, and it was like my heart melted all the way down to my toes, all the way down to the floor of the nursery. I stared at this baby in awe because he hadn't screamed when he'd seen me, a pale, ghostly girl, but smiled instead.

I knew he was my brother. I knew I was going to love him forever.

And so, when my parents took him home, I stayed far, far away from my brother.

My parents didn't question my actions. They knew the effect I had on babies, and they didn't want *their* baby—a boy, blessed by a goddess—around a child they had been unfortunate enough to deliver—a girl, blessed by a god that most hated, a child of the moon. It wasn't safe. I knew that, of course, but that didn't stop me from glancing over his crib from time to time, just to see him.

My mother caught me one night. I thought she had gone to bed, and Sorin was restless, so I crept over to his crib and comforted him until he was asleep. When I was leaving, I noticed my mother in the doorway. She hadn't watched the entire thing, and her eyes were filled with cold fury. "Don't you ever," she hissed close to my ear, "*ever* come near my child again."

And I obliged. It was hard not to, with the threatening looks she would send me, reminding me that I was completely and totally under her control and judgment. My mother scared me, but not just because of that. She was manipulative—she could easily twist the situation if she wanted to.

So I watched my brother grow from a distance. I watched as he went to a daycare every day that I would ride my bike by to see if he was okay, and I watched as he got valedictorian in his fourth year of going to elementary school. I watched as he learned to talk, to walk, to read, to survive. I watched his expression as I went away. He was crestfallen, despite the fact that we barely even knew each other. I searched for his name in the newspaper that declared rebellious Magics were starting a camp called Camp Serenity, and that my brother had been a part of creating it. I was proud of him, even if I was proud of him from the other side of the kingdom. The other side of the world, it seemed.

I watched that night at the campfire. I watched him with the girl he'd loved for years just hours before his death, laughing and joking and being the boy I hadn't gotten to raise. I was proud of him then, for finding the right girl and being good to her. I was proud of him later, when he tried consoling her as he died. And I was proud of him in his final moments, as he tried his best to be who he was inside—a joking, happy, kind young man.

A sob rips itself from my throat as I sink to the floor. I let the hardwood touch my knees and I bring my hands up to cry into them.

I'm proud of him now, because even in death he's still my little brother.

He's still the boy who didn't cry when I was near him.

He's still the boy I loved more than anything in this world.

Anything, Merrik told me, all those moons ago. I could have anything I wanted if I just called out his name.

I do something unimaginable then.

I open my mouth, making sure I'm quiet enough so that the others don't hear me, and I whisper, "I accept, Merrik."

CHAPTER 18

MILO

"You're sure she's okay?"

Sage is breathing down my neck. She's been worried sick about Elysian from the moment she passed out, even though she was the one who caused it.

I examine the bruises on her ribs before nodding shortly. "She's fine," I say decidedly. "Just a few bruised ribs, nothing life-threatening. She's going to be in pain for a bit, though."

"Oh, gods." Sage covers her mouth in shock, and I put my hand on her shoulder.

"You didn't mean to," I remind her. "Unless...you did?"

"I thought I was going to be gentler," she says. "I've been stressed with everything that's going on—walking like this again, Sorin's birthday, wondering if I can trust Ben and Ethan—and I underestimated my own strength." She frowns at Elysian, unconscious in the room Elysian shares with Ameer.

Speaking of Ameer...

"Hey, Sage, where's Ameer?" I ask.

She shrugs, her focus still on Elysian. "Haven't seen him. Which is kind of weird, considering how he's basically attached to her hip."

"Hm." I glance around the room. All of the rooms we're staying in are sparsely decorated—Ben warned us not to get too attached. The walls are a nice light blue, which is fitting, considering Elysian's theme.

I glance back at the door, telling Sage I'm going to go look for Ameer and that she can stay in here for a bit before she has to leave to let Elysian rest. And then I leave the room.

I run into someone as I'm leaving. Unsurprisingly, it's Ameer. His nails are bitten down to the quick and he looks incredibly nervous. As soon as he sees me he starts to ask questions about Elysian's health, and I repeat what I told Sage to him. He nods before ducking into the room.

For some reason, I don't stop after I've seen Ameer. I continue walking to the room I share with Selena and Ash. I don't believe Selena. She told me that she was okay, but I don't believe her. I have a feeling. And it's not a good one.

When I try to open the door, I realize it's locked. *Selena locked me out?* No, she wouldn't do that.

I jiggle the knob. "Selena!" I say her name, surprised at how vulnerable I sound. "Selena, please, open the door!"

The panic in my chest is growing, along with the beating of my heart in my ears. Everything feels like it's going faster—my blood, my heart, the world—and yet she's taking forever to open this door.

"Please," I plead, and the door doesn't open. I slam into it, using my left shoulder. I have to hit it a couple of times, but the door finally opens, the lock destroyed. "Selena."

Selena Torsney, the strongest girl that I've ever known, is on the floor, sobbing. In front of her is a blur. I can't see them, whoever it is. They speak in superior tones, taunting her, and I want to launch forward and wrap my hands around their neck, but something is holding me in place. I couldn't move even if I tried, and the person knows it. There's a smile on the person's face.

Selena is muttering Sorin's name, I realize with a jolt.

"She can't hear you," the person in front of her says, and I register it's a man.

"Let her go," I growl at the man, but I doubt I look very threatening.

He laughs. "She's mine now. She asked for me. And she didn't ask for you, did she?"

I feel the blood draining out of my cheeks. She *didn't* ask for me. Why? Doesn't she trust me?

"Selena," I whisper, a breath more than a word.

Her name sounds foreign on my tongue, so I say it louder. I'll say it until it feels familiar, I decide.

With a final laugh at how pathetic I must look, the man grabs her arm and vanishes.

And it's only as Sage and Ameer enter the room that I realize I'm screaming Selena's name.

CHAPTER 19

SAGE

I'm pacing the streets outside Ruri again, my cloak wrapped tightly around me. I don't want anyone to discover who I am, and I know we're not staying for much longer, so I want to make sure I get the feel of this cloak before I steal it from Ethan.

I shout Ben's name. He's been gone recently, out night and day, and Milo needs him. He's a wreck. Besides, we've stayed in Ethan's house for too long. We need to leave before Merrik officially catches up to us.

Plus, I needed to get out of that house. My knuckles ache from punching Elysian, and there's just so much tension there. I figured a walk through the streets would calm my nerves.

The sun beats down on me relentlessly, and I wish I could shed this jacket, but I can't. It provides me with a sense of protection, knowing that if anyone just glances at me as they're passing by they won't recognize me. The coat hides my horrible thoughts, the memories of the massacre that took place at the brothel last night, the memories of Sorin. As his birthday edges closer, I find myself plagued with the memory of that night at the campfire, the way his body went limp when the life was finally sucked out of him fully. Milo tried everything, and yet they couldn't save him.

They couldn't save him.

Blue eyes.

Blonde hair.

Dancing with Merrik.

"I am designed, as I was at the dawn of time, at the beginning of your entire world, to be exactly what everyone feared the most. And your fear, lovely Sage, is seeing Sorin again."

My mind travels to the ballroom, where Merrik spun me in that silk emerald dress, and I figured he was just being polite, since he had seen me crying in the carriage. And then he told me those things, and my heart dropped all the way to my high heels.

I'm grateful for it, though. If it weren't for that encounter, I wouldn't have found Ben. He wouldn't have helped us. We wouldn't have found Selena.

I stop suddenly, glancing up at the sky.

"I know I never pray to you, Aelia, but it's because I've never needed to," I mumble. "I know it's selfish to be praying to you at a time like this when I haven't before, but I just want to thank you. Thank you for blessing him. If you hadn't, he wouldn't have come into my life. I hope you're taking good care of him up there. Or is one of your siblings doing it instead? I'm not sure. Just...thank you."

The sun seems to glow a bit brighter, and I smile faintly, pulling the hood low, so it covers my face. Then I bump right into someone.

It's Ben, luckily enough. He grins. "Was that prayer for me?"

I shove him back, caught off guard. He stumbles and almost falls into bushes on one side of a brothel. There's beer bottle shards in that bush, but I'm so angry that I don't care. "You heard that? And where were you? We could've used a doctor when Elysian fractured a rib!"

Ben winces. "Not exactly the reaction I was expecting."

"Well, maybe except more accurately next time." I glare at him, crossing my arms over my chest.

"Sage," he says carefully, "I was going to head back eventually—"

"*Eventually* isn't a time frame, Ben!" I yell. "What were you thinking? Where were you? Are you hurt? Why didn't you come back for us? It was your idea to come here, wasn't it?"

"Don't get mad at me—"

"I have every *right* to be mad at you! Selena's gone! Selena is gone, Ben! What would you like to do about that? What would you like to say? You were supposed to protect her, for the gods' sakes! You're the doctor!"

"How could you not help him? You're the doctor. You're supposed to save him."

I feel myself breaking down before the sobs start. My knees buckle and Ben rushes to catch me. He holds me close to him, and I suddenly realize that there's many eyes on the pair of us, that I completely forgot about the point of wearing this stupid cloak: I'm not supposed to be noticed.

"Sage," Ben says quietly, "I was looking for a way out. That's why *I* was gone. But what do you mean by *Selena* being gone?"

"It's Merrik," I say faintly. "He got inside her head, got her to call for him and take her away. She's gone now because she asked to be."

Ben's face pales, and he almost drops me. "He did?"

"Yes," I say.

"That's impossible."

"We thought so, too, but then it happened."

Ben looks honestly scared. "But that's *not possible*. Merrik shouldn't have any power here. It's the sunshine kingdom—it's safe."

"It's *outside* of the sunshine kingdom," I correct, wiping my tears. "It must still be in his jurisdiction."

He smiles grimly at my joke but then glances off in the direction of the tall, towering castle of Ruri. The sunlight bounces off of it, making it glow.

And I swear, I see Ben swallow.

"The king and queen are horrible people. They gave their son ridiculous amounts of homework from his tutors and training tactics from his instructors that he had to complete by the end of the week. Rumor has it they would beat him if he didn't."

"Ben."

He glances over at me, and I see that his eyes are glossy. "I assume you've figured it out already."

"That you're royalty?" I say. Before he has the chance to respond, I nod and say, "Yeah, I did. What were they like, your parents?"

"They were terrible people," he says, and for some reason he looks slightly relieved. But then his mild expression is back and I assume I've imagined it. "They hated me. So much. They would make me do their dirty work. And when they see me, they're going to go berserk."

"Meaning?"

"My parents are deadly, Sage," he says, glancing at me. His tears are gone, replaced by a sort of silent fury. "They hate me. And if they see me, they will do everything in their power to be rid of me."

* * *

When Ben and I get back to the house, it's rather reluctantly. He decides to leave the clothes he has at Ethan's house, as he knows he can use them eventually, and tells me to meet him outside. Then he leaves the house and waits by the door, whistling a tune that's unfamiliar to me.

I step into the room that Milo shares with Ash and Selena. *Shared* with Selena. Now she's gone, and we have no idea why.

It's empty. Milo chose to take Selena's bag of medicine with him, I realize as I look at the deserted bed. That's good—we may very well need medicine if we're going to train to face an entity.

Ethan's at work. Ben told us this was probably the best time to leave, because he'd stall us with terrible jokes and puns and flattery that doesn't work. Ben looks ghostly, like his soul has been sucked out. It's as if he's dreading the thought of seeing his parents so much that it's eating him up from the inside.

I relish in the quiet of the empty room. Everything's so quiet without Selena. And the sad part is, I actually thought we'd have some peace and quiet after we ran from Room 106 back in August. But Elysian instantly became busy, and the campers were more needy. I understand them. I would try to spend more time with the people who had just been on a death mission if I really cared about them, too.

I sit on the edge of the bed, glancing around. Milo's cleaned, I notice, or maybe Selena did. Sorin was a neat freak, so maybe Selena's the same way. But it doesn't matter. I shouldn't be thinking about this anyway. As if—as if just thinking about the things that relate to her will suddenly make her reappear in front of me.

Besides, I'm not even sure I want her back. I mean, when I thought she was dead, I functioned. I can function without her now, too.

I calm my thoughts, so they reduce to only a faint whisper. I don't want to think about that—not right now, not with everything going on.

Ben. That's a better, closer topic. He's handsome, of course, and he's a doctor. Smart. Scared. Scared of his parents, scared of me. Scared of Merrik. But then again, who *isn't* scared of fear itself?

There's a knock at the door, and Ben walks in.

"Funny," I mutter to myself, and he gives me a strange look, but doesn't say anything.

"We're leaving," he tells me, his voice strong. He bears almost no resemblance to the boy that told me earlier that his parents would try to kill him once we got to the castle. "Are you ready?"

"Ready to meet your parents?" I say, sarcasm in my voice. "Well, I think it's a little soon, but sure. I'm ready."

"Sage," he says quietly. I can tell he's not in the mood for joking.

"You'll be fine, Ben." I stand from the bed and stride over to him. We're just feet apart, and I can feel the heat radiating off of him in waves, similar to the sun. I guess that's to be expected. "You'll be with me—me, Ash, Elysian, Ameer, and Milo. You'll be protected."

"That's not what I'm worried about." His eyes are strangely dark, and I don't like it.

"Then what are you worried about?"

"I'm worried they're going to hurt *you*," he clarifies. "All of you. My parents—they're master manipulators. They can find ways to hurt you that you didn't even know existed. It's freaky."

Master manipulators as parents. Where have I heard that before?

Sorin.

"My mom…wasn't the best person either, when I was little," I say. "She hated who I was, and she took it out on me, even though it wasn't my fault. I never knew my dad. But sometimes I would just wonder, maybe, if he came back, if he would protect me from the wrath that my mother possessed. He never did."

"Uplifting," he says with a grim expression.

"My *point* is," I say sharply, "if a six-year-old got through that with no one, then you'll be able to go through it. It's a test of strength, facing your parents. And not physical strength. You've proved you have that. But now you have to prove that you have mental stability, too."

Ben sets his mouth into a tight line. "I hope you're right."

"Look at it this way," I say. "When have I ever been wrong?"

* * *

As we approach the castle, it seems deserted. I don't see any soldiers, like the ones at the wall, and the bridge is down, meaning we can cross over the moat. I glance around cautiously. The last time I decided everything was fine, I got shot in the leg.

I see a soldier by the side of the castle. He's running toward us, calling out for reinforcements. I draw my dagger and tell the others to do the same. Ben is supposed to be sneaking around the castle and finding another way in by now, but he's still standing next to me, frozen.

"Will they recognize you?" Elysian calls as the guards get closer.

"I don't think so," Ben says meekly, and I urge him to leave with a jerk of my head.

"Ben," I say. "Go. We've got this."

He still stays planted in the same spot, facial expression and legs unmoving.

"Ben," I say, more sternly this time. "You have to go."

The guards are getting closer. One of them is already fighting with Ash, and she grunts as he throws his whole body weight at her. She uses that as an advantage and strikes him at a chink in the armor, where he's the weakest.

"Ben!" I shout, and he starts to move, cutting across the green field that surrounds the castle. He sprints toward the side of the tall, light-colored building, and the corners of my mouth quirk up into a small smile as he runs.

Then the soldier appears.

His sword is against my dagger in a matter of seconds. I call on all the strength in my biceps to make sure my face doesn't get sliced. I grunt as the soldier goes for my side, but I dodge it anyway. I pretend to go for his face, leaving him leaning backward and vulnerable, and I strike at his stomach. He jumps back as soon as my dagger makes contact with the skin, though, so it only leaves a shallow trail across the length of his torso.

I'm glad he's wearing bulletproof gear instead of armor. The dagger I hold in my hand is especially equipped for cutting through bulletproof gear. With armor, it's harder. I suddenly feel a pang of pity for Ash, but then it's gone. She can handle herself just fine.

The soldier winces.

"Unfortunately for you," I murmur under my breath, "you'll wince a lot more if you don't surrender."

He seems to hear it, and he starts to fight even more ferociously, using all his weight to push his sword to my throat. My arms start to shake from the effort it takes to keep him at bay, but finally, Ben's voice calls out to us.

"Guys! I found a passage!"

I twist so the guard almost falls and use my foot to pin his shoulder to the ground. I'm glad, suddenly, that Ben made us wear combat boots—they're strong boots.

"Coming!" I call back. I take the sword from the guard's hands, plunge it into his heart, and start to run toward the direction of Ben's voice.

Elysian is running next to me now. We slow as I spot Ben, jogging toward the large, wooden door that's cracked open ever-so-slightly.

"I wasn't sure if it was still here, but—" He shrugs. "It is."

Ash, Milo, and Ameer are behind us now, I realize. "Let's go inside, then," Ash says, sounding winded. Ben nods and ducks into the castle. Elysian and I follow after him, and everyone else after us.

The inside is definitely not what I expected.

The corridors are long and winding, and there's a sort of scent in the air, like something that's meant to be appetizing but has gone horribly wrong. Sunlight streams through several open windows, but even with the gentle breeze calming the horrid smell, the castle still seems empty, like all that lives there is a ghost.

"I grew up here," Ben says unpleasantly, his nose crinkled as he looks around at the castle. He's saying it quietly, so only I can hear him.

I nod solemnly and turn to talk to the others.

"I guess there's not anything else we can do," Elysian is saying. "We have to follow the smell."

* * *

The smell leads to a small kitchen. There's something burning on the stove—a turkey, it seems—and the cook that's supposed to be watching over it is leaning back in a chair, snoring.

I send my friends a look over my shoulder. It says, *Do you think they're using this turkey?*

Ash shakes her head slightly. *Probably not,* she seems to say.

Take it, Elysian pipes in, nodding vigorously.

I nod with her, picking up a towel from the rack above one of the counters and pulling the turkey off of the oven. I blow at it, but with a flick of her fingers Ash has the flame reduced to…well, ash.

We sneak back out of the kitchen, making our way briskly through the empty halls.

"Are your parents home, Ben?" I ask him quietly.

"Fortunately, no," he says. "They're in a meeting."

I nod, and we continue down the hallway without another word.

When we find an empty corridor, Elysian leans back against it. I notice that there's a gash in Ameer's forehead, and Milo rifles through the bag holding Selena's medicine before bringing out the *soigner* and applying it to the wound. I guess the *soigner* works faster than Milo's healing, especially when he doesn't have any medical equipment.

Ben and I pick off the acceptable parts of the turkey and distribute them evenly. Elysian gnaws at it—I can tell she's not hungry, just needs something to do.

"I'm sorry," I say carefully. "About your ribs."

"Oh, it's okay," she says with a distracted smile. "I'll be fine, you know? Not a big deal."

"I got carried away."

"You were thinking about other things," she adds. "I get it. It's fine."

I nod, letting it sit for a moment. Then, I say, "I really *am* sorry."

"Sage. It's *fine*. I'm fine. Everything's fine. My health is actually the least of my worries right now, and I'd prefer that it be the least of yours, too."

I swallow and look away. Everything's tense right now, and the silence is nearly suffocating.

"Are you thinking about Ash?" I say quietly, so only Elysian can hear me.

Almost unwillingly, she turns and glances at Ash, sitting a little farther down the wall. "I think about her all the time," she tells me, matching my tone. "I want things to go back to the way they *were*. Before we got into that stupid argument that ruined everything."

"You know, you're both stubborn. She's not going to admit that she was wrong. She's not going to beg you to get back together. That's just not who Ash is."

Elysian gives me a scalding look. "Your point?"

"*You* have to do it, Lys, even if you believe you aren't in the wrong," I continue. "I understand you're *both* stubborn, but come on. This is your first relationship, your first time trying it out. I see the way you look at each other. She *wants you back*, Elysian. So you have to make sure you get her back."

She stares at me, then groans. "You're right," she mutters, leaning her head back against the stone. "Gods, why does this thing have to be so frustrating?"

I shrug, about to laugh, when I hear the sound of footsteps. I jump to my feet along with Elysian and push her so her back is flat up against the wall.

The footsteps stop. There's two people, it seems, talking in hushed conversation. One is a woman, and the other is a man with a squeaky voice so high that I almost confuse it for a woman's.

"I'm telling you, Uriah," the woman says in an agitated tone. "You are seeing things!"

"I'm not!" the man, Uriah, protests. "Someone stole my turkey! It was cooking, and I fell asleep for just a second, and when I woke up, it was gone!"

"There are no intruders in the castle," the woman says. "My guards would have alerted me. And as for you, I might as well fire you for leaving a burning stove unattended.

The footsteps begin to recede, and I hear Uriah start to say, "It wasn't left unattended! I was there, I just fell asleep! I swear it, Your Majesty!"

Once the footsteps fade completely, I let out a sigh and step forward.

"Was that the queen?" I ask Ben, and he nods shortly.

"Yes, it was," he says. "But if she's getting suspicious and thinking that there are intruders in the castle, then we need to work even quicker."

"So, what's your plan?" Ash asks.

"I'm glad you asked." Ben grins.

CHAPTER 20

ASH

I wake up before the sun rises, wiping drool from the corner of my mouth.

"Good morning."

Elysian's voice makes me freeze.

"It's only three in the morning, of course, but it's still *morning*, right?" She shrugs. "Time is an odd thing."

I glance at her. Her hair is tied into a loose braid, as she doesn't have a hair tie, and her blue sweatshirt has a dark stain on it—blood, I realize, from our fight with the guards. Still, she's gorgeous.

No, I shouldn't be thinking that right now. She told me to stay away from her, and that's what I did, and now she's talking to me. She's talking to me, and I don't understand *why*.

Still gorgeous, though.

"Morning," I grumble in response, turning so I'm facing Milo, asleep next to me. He sleeps so peacefully that I can almost forget the eye bags that hang under his dark brown eyes, the sadness that so clearly possesses him.

"Ash, please."

"Go away, Elysian. I'm trying to sleep."

"I made you this."

My eyes snap open, almost against my will, and in her palm is a flimsy circle of straw. "I didn't have the best materials," she says, using her free hand to rub the back of her neck, "but consider it a peace offering. As long as you have this bracelet with you, I'll know we're on good terms."

I sit up, using my elbows to support me. "Why are you doing this, Elysian?"

"What do you mean?"

"Why are you trying to make me feel better? I thought you told me not to talk to you."

"But…I'm trying to form a truce now," she tells me slowly.

"I understand that, but *why?*"

"I…"

I wait for her response, but then she shrugs helplessly and I turn on my side again. What's the point in listening to her if she has nothing to say?

"Good night, Elysian."

I close my eyes, willing myself to fall asleep, but then Elysian's whisper interrupts the silence. "I don't want us to be like this."

"Too bad," I grumble. "It's going to be like this for a while, Elysian. You're busy—I get it."

"You're not…*understanding.*"

"I understand plenty well. You don't want to be with me. That's fine."

"I want to be with you, Ash!" she whisper-shouts. "I want to be with you more than I've ever wanted anything. And *you* broke up with *me*, remember? Not the other way around. *You* said you didn't need help, *you* said we should be apart from each other. I never wanted that."

"Elysian—"

"Please," she whispers, her eyes glossy. "Please. Let me…let me give you this friendship bracelet. We don't have to be anything more than friends, if that's what you want, but just…let me know that you don't hate me. Okay?"

I swallow, avoiding eye contact with her. Usually I'm blunt and straightforward, but I find now that I am dreading looking into her eyes. I don't want to see the hurt in them—the hurt that *I* caused.

"Okay."

I reach out and take the bracelet from her hand, putting it into the pocket of my jeans. She watches me, a light, broken smile gracing her features, and my heart aches, yelling at me to reach out and kiss her, to tell her that I want to be with her too.

Don't, my mind protests. *She needs this. It's—it's what's best for her.*

I refrain, scooting closer to the wall.

"Thank you," she says quietly. "Thank you."

* * *

The sun comes out rather quickly, considering the fact that I on;y get three more hours of sleep before someone shakes me awake, whispering my name softly.

My eyes shoot open, and my hand clenches around the hilt of my sword, but I realize it's Milo and I relax.

"Is it time?" I whisper to him.

"Yes," he whispers back, nodding, the echo of a smile in his eyes.

I bring myself to my feet and shake myself fully awake. Sage is already whispering furtively with Elysian, her eyebrows creased as she reviews the plan that we've already been over.

"Are you excited to be the bait?" I ask him, and he smiles grimly.

"Well, considering I'm the most likable out of all of us, if I die, I'll be the one that you mourn the most for," he says, shrugging, "so, no."

"How rude of you." I smack his arm. "I'm *totally* the most likable."

His eyes dance for the first time in days, and I smile. *I recognize this Milo.* "Whatever you want to tell yourself."

We walk over to where Elysian and Sage are standing.

"I found the perfect thing for you to wear," Sage announces, grinning, holding up a bright yellow outfit.

Milo groans. "And you're sure *this* is going to get me noticed?"

Ameer comes up behind us. I can tell because the frame of his tall, lanky body casts a shadow upon Elysian. Their heights are so different to the point that it's ridiculous.

"Are you kidding?" he asks, eyeing the outfit.

Milo sighs. "Yeah, you're right."

"So you know the plan?" Sage asks nervously. She's the one who makes sure everything is perfect—when it's not, she panics.

"I pretend to be the kingdom's messenger and inform the queen that there are intruders in the kingdom," he says. "I'll lead her out of the castle with a search party. Once she's gone, the five of you will sneak into the training room and train there until their search is completed."

"Which will take a while, because the kingdom is large," Ben pipes in. "Once you've got the queen prancing about, then you can head back here. She won't know what hit her."

"I feel like that was said with malicious intent," Milo says as he glances at Ben sideways.

"No malicious intent," Ben tells Milo easily, but his eyes flick over to Sage before he says anything.

"Go change," Sage says, thrusting the clothes forward at Milo's chest. He scurries off to another corridor to get dressed, and we stand there against the cold stone walls, waiting for him.

"I still don't understand why he's doing this instead of me," I say. "I don't *need* the training. And, besides, I know how to fend for myself. Milo doesn't. He tries to avoid physical contact at all costs."

"Destruction is not the only way of getting things done," Ben says sharply. "The queen appreciates wit, as do I. If you burn down every home in the kingdom, what's left of it other than remains and anger? Plus, Milo has his power. If the queen figures out the fact that we're not supposed to be here and that he's actually an intruder, he can use it and then escape."

He's right, I remind myself bitterly. Destruction *isn't* the only answer, and I've been living my life for years thinking that it is.

Milo returns to the corridor and I clear my throat, trying to stifle a laugh. He looks like a walking eyesore in the yellow suit, the color matching with the tapestries that dangle from the walls of the castle.

"Wow," I say, my mouth curling into a disgusted expression. "You look… Wow."

"Isn't it?" Milo says with a grin. I smile back.

Milo is my soulmate. A platonic soulmate, of course, but he is the one that I am connected to, rooted to, and I feel it deep in my bones. He's the person I love, and it will always stay that way.

"The queen should be in the throne room right about now," Ben says. "I can tell by the direction of the sun."

"How do you know the queen's schedule?" Elysian asks, her eyes narrowing.

But all Ben says is, "She's a woman of routine."

Sage clears her throat. "Okay, so, Milo, you'll head to the throne room and tell the queen that there are intruders in the kingdom. You leave the castle to search and we sneak down to the basement to start training."

Milo nods. "I know, Sage. Stop worrying. Everything will be okay."

Don't make promises you can't keep, I want to chide, but I refrain from doing so, because it seems to console Sage. She hugs him once, then pulls away. Elysian hugs him next. Then Ameer and Ben pat him on the back, giving their luck.

I step up to Milo and wrap my arms around his neck. I've always loved the fact that he's slightly taller than me—it makes hugging him that much easier.

"Don't get yourself killed," I whisper in his ear.

"I won't," he whispers back as I pull away.

Maybe I'm being dramatic, but I feel a sense of emptyness as soon as he says goodbye and runs to the throne room at the end of the hall. Milo is leaving, and I'm not sure if he'll live.

It's like my heart is refusing to beat.

"He'll be okay," Elysian says to me, and I smile at her gratefully, and I realize what I'm doing. I take a step away from her and flatten myself against the corridor walls as footsteps begin to approach—more this time than the last time.

"I told that cook he was crazy." The queen's voice fills the corridor. Her voice is a sharp sound, like the jagged edge of glass, slicing through the air. "Perhaps he was right after all."

No one says anything in response. I know enough about royalty to understand that you *never* disagree with a queen, not if you like your life.

Once a large door slams in the distance, Ben waits a few beats before motioning for us to follow him down several long, twisting hallways.

"Here it is," he says as my legs are beginning to ache.

The staircase that leads to the basement is old and dusty and dark. It smells of sewage, as if it hasn't been touched in a while.

"Gross," Elysian mutters, and I silently agree with her.

"It's the only thing we have," Ben remarks, "but if you'd like to risk capture by finding something else, then be my guest."

We hold our tongues and walk down the winding staircase.

The training room is cleaner than I expect.

Punching bags and mats are on the floor and hanging from the ceiling. There's boxing gloves in one corner of the room, hanging on a hook, and in the other corner is a rack of dumbbells. A weapons cart is next to the rack.

The room is painted a bright shade of red, probably to aggravate the person training even further. Despite the feel of the room, a clock ticks slowly on the wall above the punching bag.

Sage turns toward the punching bags. "Are these leather?"

"Just like the boxing gloves." He grins proudly. "Have a go if you'd like."

Sage smiles, walking over to where the boxing gloves hang from the hooks on the wall. She puts them on and advances toward the punching bag, jabbing it right in the middle. The bag barely moves, which usually discourages normal people but makes Sage beam.

"This is the best quality I've seen," she says, her eyes sparkling.

"You've used a punching bag before?" I ask, only half-caring.

Her eyes dart over to Elysian. As far as I know, Elysian is the only one who knows about Sage's past, and I'm guessing the punching bag is a part of that.

"Forget it," I mutter, studying the room even more carefully. I pick up one of the dumbbells and set it back down again.

"Just a question, Mr. Know-It-All," I say to Ben. "Do you have any fireproof fabric here?"

Elysian glances at me. She knows about my mother, as she had a dream about it, and while we haven't talked about it more than once, I'm sure it's a very vivid memory for her. It's a vivid memory for *me*, after all.

"Unfortunately, no," he says. "The queen doesn't believe in restricting power."

What if there's a power that she has to restrict? I want to ask, but I don't, in fear that Ben will realize the true extent of my power. I simply nod silently.

"You know a lot about the queen, don't you?" Ameer says.

"Yes, I guess I do," Ben responds with a shrug. I can see the hint of fear that flickers in his eyes once Ameer mentions it, though, and I crease my eyebrows in confusion. "It's polite," he says, "in Ruri, at least, to know a lot about the Royals. Do your subjects not do that in Buit?"

Ameer glances down at the floor, uncomfortable. "No," he says quietly. "No, they don't. They barely even knew I existed, and they all hated my father, so…"

"Oh." Ben looks uncomfortable now.

"It doesn't matter," I say, interrupting. "As long as the queen is gone, we can start training, right? So, what's the plan?"

Ben nods and leads us over to the mats. "Okay," he says, dishing out weapons, "we'll start with basic sword-fighting, which I'm sure all of you know how to do. Then we'll move on to physical fighting, and then manipulation."

"Manipulation?" Elysian says, sounding dumb-founded. "What, you mean we're going to *manipulate* an entity into leaving us alone?"

"Wits, like I said before, are very powerful." That's all Ben says, and he hands me a weapon, letting me and Sage step onto the mats first.

Right before Ben says go, I swear I hear a faint "Good luck" from Elysian. But when I look back, her face is stone and unreadable, and I realize I must have imagined it.

I find a good grip on my sword, and Ben calls, "Go."

CHAPTER 21

MILO

The doors to the throne room loom ahead of me like a dark shadow, an indication of what could happen when I step through them.

I knock, waiting until the queen's shrill voice calls, "Come in!"

The ridiculous outfit that I'm wearing is incredibly tight, and it's hard to walk. Or maybe it's just the utter fear that I feel when I see the queen sitting on her throne, legs crossed, looking more than threatening.

She has bright blonde hair and blue eyes that somehow feel cold when she looks at me, despite her kingdom's cheerful appearance.

I look around at the throne room. I see all kinds of different furniture—chests and weapons hanging from the walls, tapestries depicting the sun rising over the horizon. But what really catches my eye is the pile of money in the corner. Some of the coins on the top of the pile are gold, and some are green. Ruri and Veridet coins.

"Who are you?" she demands.

"I am your informant, Queen Aria," I tell her. I remember reading about the sunshine kingdom a few years ago—about Queen Aria and King Blaise, and about their extraordinary power when it comes to manipulating sunlight. "I have noticed that there are intruders in the kingdom."

"Intruders?" The queen seems to sit up straighter. "What do you mean, *intruders?*"

"It seems that there are people in the kingdom who are not meant to be there, my queen," I clarify, trying to keep any expression other than solemn from crossing my face. "We do not have their names on any of the files in the great...Royal...filing room."

You just blew that, says a tiny voice that I silence bitterly.

But the queen eyes me thoughtfully, like she didn't hear me saying random words that probably have no reference to any room in this castle at all.

"If you lie, then I must kill you." The queen stares at me, scrutinizing me, her blue eyes hard and calculating. I feel like I'm about to wither under her intense gaze.

Then she lets up, only slightly, straightening in her throne. "Lead me to these intruders," she commands, and I nod, because talking seems wrong. One of the guards at her side helps her down from her massive throne, and then we walk out of the front doors, one soldier at the front, me in the middle, and the queen and guard behind me.

The doors fly open, and the blazing sunlight almost blinds me, but I ignore it. The guard at the front whistles, and a horse comes striding forward, its mane white and reflective of the sunlight. I squint in order to watch as the queen sits upon the back of the horse.

The other guard calls for a horse of his own, and a horse for me, too. Two more white mares come trotting toward us. I hop on the back of one of them and point them in the direction of the 'intruders' and the queen takes the lead.

I'm more nervous than I thought I would be. Nerves tingle in my palms and legs as I ride the horse, gesturing to unfamiliar houses, saying things like, "They were spotted here," even though I have no idea where they were spotted, considering the fact that they don't exist.

Riding on the back of a horse gives me an opportunity to look around at the houses. There are several stone houses, but there're also plenty made of wood. They're all decent sizes, and some of the doors are open, giving us free entertainment. Some doors, though, slam closed instantly upon seeing us riding through the streets.

"Are we getting any closer to these intruders?" the queen asks after I have given her complicated instructions on how to get to a creek that the intruders were supposedly at. "I swear to every god, if you are simply leading me on—"

"Why would you think that, dear queen?" I ask.

I guess I've done something I'm not supposed to, because the queen clenches her jaw and whips her head around to look at me and the guard gives me a mildly surprised look. "Do not *ever* interrupt me, boy!" she yells, her voice shrill.

A pang of fear hits my chest, and I shrink back against my horse. "Of course not, my queen," I say meekly.

"Take me to these intruders," the queen says, her voice like blades cutting into my skin, "or I will kill you."

For extra emphasis, the guard unsheathes his sword, and it glints in the sunlight.

Aelia, help me, I pray silently, and then I nod, motioning for them to follow me.

CHAPTER 22

ELYSIAN

After training, Ben sneaks up to the kitchen and grabs us more food. He comes back with his hands full of granola bars and other packaged snacks, which we dig into eagerly.

"Never, in my twenty years of life, would I have guessed that *Sage* could beat me in sword fighting," Ash says, grinning through a mouthful of granola.

"Sage is a very violent person," Ameer says thoughtfully, and instead of glaring at him, Sage laughs.

"I guess I am." She shrugs. "How do you think Elysian bruised her ribs?"

I laugh along with her. So far, training has been going fine. I won against Ameer, which is to be expected, since he doesn't have the experience that I do. But I lost—*again*—to Sage.

"You're a psycho," I say, which only makes Sage laugh harder. I'm glad for it. Ever since Sorin died, she hasn't smiled that much—hasn't really found anything funny, I guess. He was always telling jokes and making her laugh, and he can't do that anymore.

The funeral is in a few days, on his birthday. Ben told us about it. It's going to be a quiet ceremony, and he's going to bury things that are made out of paper to honor him. I think it's a nice gesture, but Ash pointed out that we should wait—wait until Selena gets back, if she ever does.

But the closer the ceremony gets, the closer the deadline Merrik gave me gets. Exactly one week from today, I will be forced to choose—my friends or him. And if I choose my friends, then we go to war.

If Merrik ruins everything—if he kills my family, my friends, my campers—then I will kill him. And I will make him suffer, in whatever way you *can* make something more powerful than gods suffer.

This is so confusing. We can't fear anything, but no one fears *nothing*. We have to show him that we're strong, but there's no way that we can be stronger than him and people that aren't even alive. He's making everything difficult, and I hate it. I hate it so much.

"Lys?" Ameer says, touching my arm. "You okay?"

I nod, flashing a smile at him. "Just thinking."

Of course Ameer knows what I'm thinking about. He read the letter to me, for the gods' sakes. He understands how big of a deal this is, and he understands what it's doing to me.

He places his hand on top of mine reassuringly. *It'll be okay*, he seems to tell me.

Will it? Will it really?

Instead of saying that out loud, I nod again, silently thanking him. He squeezes my hand in response, and I rest my head on his shoulder.

I feel eyes on me and lift my own from our hands. Ash is staring at me curiously, like she can't figure out what she's thinking about me.

I divert my eyes as soon as ours lock. Those gold-speckled eyes still haven't changed, which is both a blessing and a curse. They're one of the things that make her so beautiful, but they're also one of the things that reminds me of our argument and the way they sparkled with emotion after I said we should take a break.

But it's not my fault that we're like this. *She* broke up with *me.* Doesn't that mean something?

It might. Do I really care, though?

No, I don't.

"Milo should be getting back soon," Ash says to us.

Ben nods.

"How long are we going to be staying here?" I ask. We don't have anywhere to stay, and we're using this training room while putting our friend's life on the line. "Soon we're going to run out of houses and excuses."

"Yeah," Sage says, "and *his* birthday is getting close, and I really don't want to spend a day of celebration trapped here, waiting until the queen figures out we're here and kills us."

Without meaning to, I glance at Ash again. She spent her twentieth birthday on our death quest. It was the day after Sorin died, too. I can only imagine how terrible she felt if Sage is feeling like this when it's not even *her* birthday.

But at the same time, I'm too tired to care.

This exhaustion, though, is an exhaustion that resonates deep in my bones—it's the kind of tired that someone feels not in their eyes or arms or muscles, but the kind of tired that someone feels deep in their soul.

Despite the fact that I know it won't help me, not really, I let my eyes close and my body relax next to Ameer. And then I fall asleep.

* * *

Merrik visits me in my dream. He appears as my father, a permanent nasty expression on his face.

"Elysian," he says, smiling. Somehow it makes him look even more ugly and mean. "I assume you've noticed that the decision you must make is approaching."

I clench my jaw. "How is it, Merrik, that even in my dreams you find ways to terrorize me?"

"I work in many wonderful ways," he muses. "How unfortunate that you have not noticed it yet. Your girlfriend has."

"Ash isn't my girlfriend," I say, defending myself, though I'm not entirely sure why.

"Though I suppose she *has* been through more than you," he continues, ignoring my previous comment. "I mean, killing her mother at the ripe age of seven... And where were you at seven? In the comfort of your castle."

"I was not in the comfort of my castle at seven!" I'm growing angrier, and he can sense that, because he laughs. I feel a little bubble of fear rise in my chest: is that really what they think of me? That I'm spoiled, that I haven't gone through as much as they have, that I don't deserve to be there with them? "If *anyone's* spoiled, it's my brother. He just sat there as my father dragged me away—barely lifted a finger—didn't even *try* to help me—"

I glance at him sideways, then start laughing dryly.

"Oh, I see," I say. "You're trying to turn me against him. Against all of them. So that way, I choose your team. Isn't that what you did with Selena, after all?"

Merrik's smile widens. "Selena, Selena. No. Unfortunately, I didn't get the opportunity to charm her into joining me. She did it herself. And, oh, how her boyfriend was devastated."

I glare at him. "You ruined lives."

"*She* ruined lives," he corrects. "Free will is a thing, remember? I did not call on her; she called on me."

"I don't believe that," I snarl. "You're a liar. Selena would never betray us. She would never betray *Milo*."

"Would you like to see her?" Merrik asks. "Because it seems to me, and I see her in person every single day, that she is having the time of her life. Or, her second one."

"I am never going to choose you." I continue to glare at him. "No matter how many offhanded bribes you throw at me, I will not choose you. You understand that, don't you? Or are you too idiotic? Can you get that through your skull?"

"Would you like to see her?" Merrik repeats, ignoring me. "Would you like to see Selena, see how happy she is, since you obviously care so much about her well-being?"

Before I can refuse, Selena's face is in front of me, and she's laughing. There's a goblet in her hand that's made of glass, and when she sees me, it drops to the floor and shatters on impact.

I don't care about that, though. I see Selena and all other thoughts float away. Her dark hair is pinned away from her face, showing off her features. She's wearing nothing more than a simple tank top and jeans, despite the cold weather. But what really stops me is the happiness that lingers in her fading smile, the glint in her gray eyes. She looks happier now with *Merrik* and his army than she's ever looked with us.

"Elysian," she says, surprised. "I—Hi."

"Hi?" I demand. *"Hi?* Is that *really* all you have to say, Selena? I can't believe you."

"Okay, I'm a little confused right now," Selena tells me, chuckling nervously.

"*Confused?* Of course, you'd say that. Did you know, Selena, that Milo has been a wreck ever since you left? Did you know that the man you've decided to work for is a heartless monster who is only using you to get what he wants?"

"W—You mean *Merrik?* Oh, no, he's not heartless at all. He gave me the opportunity for freedom." She says it like the *thing* showing me this is the greatest thing ever. "Did you know that I get to visit Sorin whenever I want? Usually he's happy to see me, but I think he's a little angry with me right now. Though he *was* the fun one. I really thought he'd approve of me partying and having fun, didn't you?"

She flashes a grin at me, expecting me to agree.

To her obvious surprise, I shake my head slowly, resigned.

"No, I didn't think he would. I still don't," I say quietly. Sorin is a touchy subject—*especially* now. "I think he has a *right* to be angry at you. I think you abandoned us, and I think you are a coward."

"A coward?" she breathes, astonished. At what, I'm not sure. My bluntness, maybe, or maybe how red my face is getting.

"A coward."

"I was a Royal guard for years—"

"That doesn't make someone brave," I tell her sharply. "You betrayed us. You left us to join Merrik's forces, just because you crumbled under the pressure. Because it was too much for you. Well, guess *what*, Selena? Every single *day* is too much for me, but it's not like I'm desperate to make things easy for me. I get you had it hard, but we needed you. Now more than ever. And you let us down. So, yes, I think you're a coward."

For a second, she seems to come back to her senses. "Is he okay?" she asks me quietly. "Milo. Is he okay?"

"He will be," I say.

She nods, satisfied, and blinks again. "Bye, Elysian," Selena tells me.

I see Merrik as soon as she's gone. I try to talk, but he cuts me off with a flutter of his fingers.

"Bye, Elysian," he echoes in a lower tone, and then he's gone too, and I awake as a spluttering mess.

"Lys!" Ameer says in alarm. "Are you okay?"

"Milo," I say. "I need to see Milo."

* * *

Milo has always been considered the most responsible of both Camp Serenity and Camp Havoc, the sanest. Now, I'm not sure where people got that idea, considering the fact that he's now off with the crazy queen of Ruri by himself, practically leading them both to his death.

I push those thoughts aside as I wait anxiously. I desperately need to talk to him, and my horrible attempts at trying to make myself laugh are pitiful.

"It'll be okay," Ash tells me as she sits next to me on a bench. She hasn't been talking to me much yet, but I can see the straw bracelet I made her hanging out of her jeans pocket, which means we still have a mutual agreement not to kill each other. "I've been telling myself that ever since he left."

"Huh," I say in response. "Has it worked?"

"Not at all, but I wanted to try it on you to see if it would." She glances at me sideways. "Do you feel reassured right now?"

"Reassured?" I ask, and she nods. "Not at all."

Ash shrugs. "Worth a shot."

"It's actually making me wonder how you can stand it, him being away for so long," I tell her, "not knowing what's happening to him."

"Oh, I can't." She looks away. "All I think about is him, *especially* now. He's my best friend, and I love him, and he knows that him being away from me for an extended period of time will drive me crazy. He's known it since we met. I'm sure there's a psychological explanation behind it, but I don't care enough to get it investigated."

"How *did* you meet?" I say, then add, "You and Milo."

"We met because I was an idiot," Ash tells me.

"Tell me something I don't know."

"Haha, very funny. Do you *want* me to keep telling you this story or not?"

"Yes," I say quickly.

Ash smiles smugly, a hint of superiority creeping into her expression. "His father was a baker," she tells me, and I resist the urge to tell her that I already know that. "I would pass this little bakery that they owned every day when I went to collect the newspaper for my father. I remember looking through the windows of their bakery and seeing the three of them—Milo, his mom, his dad—together, sharing stories and laughing at breakfast time, and I remember how jealous I was. I would wait for hours on end to see that family laugh with each other, because I never had that, even when my mother was alive. She was *not* the nicest person, especially when it came to me. So I would watch this family, and I would get so jealous of the little boy in there that had parents that didn't fight and food that didn't go to waste and love that was always replenished at the end of the day. And I decided I wanted to be a part of that family, too. So I did something really stupid.

"The next day, when I was on my way to pick up the newspaper, instead of crossing the street like I was meant to in order to get to the newsstand, I hid behind the bakery building and snuck around to where they kept their trash cans. I fished for decent food *in their trash*. And I would eat it and peek through windows until the sun started to go down, and Mother would yell at me, but it was okay because I got to see the happy family that lived in the bakery.

"And then one day, after a week of trying this, Milo spotted me. He saw me, and he told his parents that he was going to take out the trash, but he was really coming to meet me. He stopped me as I tried to run away and I was impressed with how strong he was, even at a young age. He asked me what I was doing there, and I said I had gotten lost on my way to the newsstand. I could tell he didn't really believe me, but he went along with it because he was trusting and friendly and *Milo*. He offered to take me to the newsstand, but I told him I could see where it was now, and I thanked him.

"The day after that, I was determined not to stop at the bakery, but Milo came out to talk to me just as I was crossing the street. I tried to walk away, because I was embarrassed, but then he told me he meant no harm—he just wanted to tell me that I was welcome at his bakery for meals whenever I wanted. He had already checked with his parents, and they said it was okay. They felt bad for me, I guess. So I went to dinner, and it was wonderful. And I went every day after that.

"So when we were choosing what Camp Havoc was going to do to make money, I remembered the kindness that he had shown me the day we met when I was going to get the newspaper, and I told him I wanted to start selling newspapers."

I stare at her for a minute, letting her soak in the happiness of her memory. "That's sweet," I say finally.

"Yeah, yeah, Milo's amazing." She says it teasingly, but I note that there isn't much sarcasm in it—at least, not in the usual amount.

She goes silent, and I don't do anything to keep the conversation going either, so we sit there quietly, waiting until Milo gets back.

If Milo gets back, a voice reminds me.

I take a deep breath and the voice disappears. Milo is going to live. He's going to live, and he's going to help me.

He's going to help me decide what I should do.

On one hand, there's the fate of the world. On the other hand, there's my friends and family. Friends that have become family, and friends that have become even more.

"Do you have any paper?" I ask Ash, an idea sparking in my mind.

"I have this." She holds out a napkin from Ethan's house.

"Does anyone else have paper?" I call to Sage, Ben, and Ameer, who are practicing sword-fighting and the physical elements of battle.

Sage walks over to me, dropping her dagger, and hands me a crumpled piece of paper and a pen.

"Where did you get this?" I ask her, bewildered.

"I snagged it before we left the hospital." Sage shrugs. "I figured we'd need it eventually."

"How'd you keep it in your sweatpants pocket?" Ash says.

"Vines," Sage answers shortly, and then she turns around walking back over to the others.

Ash glances at me. "Do I want to know how that works?"

"No," I say quickly.

She nods, an understanding look on her face. I know Ash has had her fair share of strange magic over the past several years. I doubt anything magic-related surprises her anymore.

I begin to write.

Dear Anne Kheefe,

If you're reading this, then it got to you safely. This message may be intercepted—who knows the ways of the greedy?

I'll keep it short and simple.

A war is coming. A war that you need to prepare for. It will be a brutal war, and it will knock out most of the forces we have. But we need them.

I'm safe for now. I've been moving around quite a bit. If you're worried about Max, I unfortunately have no idea where he is, but I trust that he is protected in the hands of the other campers.

Stay unnoticed, and everything will turn out fine in the end.

With love,

Elysian

I'm lying to her. That last line is a blatant lie, more a wish than anything else, but she doesn't need to know that.

Gods, I hope everything will be okay.

Gasps shake me out of my thoughts.

There's a sword on the ground, frozen in a block of ice. Ameer stands before it, staring down at it, his eyes full of fear.

Everyone else's mouths are hanging open. I guess, over the course of the past few days, they forgot that Ameer has the ability to manipulate ice.

"Woah!" Ben says. "Have you done that before?"

He looks fascinated, starry-eyed, like Ameer is something he can gawk at. It makes protectiveness overwhelm me.

"Is it any of your business?" I demand sharply.

"If we want to win this war, then, yes, it is my business," he shoots back.

"Y-yeah," Ameer manages. "I've—I've done it before."

"That's incredible." All the harshness has left Ben's voice. "Can you control liquid water, too, or just ice? Has this power been something you've known about? How do you feel about it? Confident enough to use it in battle? What about in the war? Do you plan to use it in the war?"

Ameer starts to answer his questions, but then there's footsteps coming from the stairwell.

Ash reaches out and pushes me against the wall. Her strong arm keeps me pinned there, and I can hear her breathing as everyone goes silent and ducks behind various pieces of equipment.

Then Milo appears.

And all he says is, "We have to go. *Now.*"

CHAPTER 23

AMEER

As soon as Milo says something, everyone jumps into action. I'm the last one to sprint up the stairs, and my lungs are burning by the time we get outside. There's shouting and jeering, and I watch as horses race toward us, their hooves making loud, thundering sounds as they hit the cobblestone.

"What did you do?" I ask him as we sprint away from the castle.

"What did *I* do?" He snorts. "More like what the insane queen did."

"Insane?" Ash says. She's running beside Milo. I slow my pace as my legs start to ache and quickly fall to the back of the group.

"Ameer!" Elysian shouts. "Run!"

"I'm *trying*!" I call back.

"Use your power!" Ben yells. "Use it to help you!"

Help me? a tiny voice in the back of my mind says. But then what he's saying registers with me, and I will the ground to ice over when I walk on it.

Surprisingly, the ground obliges. I almost slip a few times, but then I find my balance and realize one thing: I'm in my element. I'm using my power. And so I have nothing to be scared of.

"I feel like I'm walking on water right now!" I call out to the group, hearing the unmistakable happiness in my voice.

"Well, it's frozen water, so you are!" Sage responds.

I laugh in delight as I glance down at my feet, hopping from ice shard to ice shard, perfectly in tune with the flow of things. I have never been this coordinated—especially not on ice. I was horrible at dances and dreadful at simply walking. One time, I broke my leg going horseback riding. I don't remember how exactly, but I remember that there was a lot of screaming on my end, and that my father couldn't even be bothered to come to the castle's infirmary with me, despite the fact that it was only a few feet away from his office.

Sometimes I miss my father horribly. Other times, I remember all the things that he did to me—telling Finn to kidnap me, leaving Elysian on the streets after Mother left, going after Ash and her family, hiring Finn, hiring Ash's mother to kill Ash, using Malikah, my stepmother, for fame until he gained some of his own and killed her, blaming it on the Magics. He was an evil man, and I do not have any sympathy for him. I have sympathy and grief, though, for the man he was when Elysian was five and I was six—the sweet, kind, caring man who would buy us ice cream after we fell off our horses, the man who loved our mother more than he loved life itself, the man who put his children and his wife and his family before everything else, who was not moved by guilt and greed and the insatiable hunger for power. I miss *that* man horribly. I wish I would've spent more time with him.

But he's been gone a very long time.

The shouting behind us has faded as we ran, and Milo, at the front of the group, has slowed, leaning against a tree to catch his breath. I notice we're in a slightly shaded area and decide that I've used enough of my power for one day, finding a tree of my own to rest against.

"We need a new plan," Sage says to the air. "This one has failed horribly. Ben, do we still need somewhere to stay?"

"I—yes." Ben looks a little startled by the instant plan-making, and I just shrug at him when we lock eyes. He should know by now that this is how Sage works. The gears in her brain are always turning; she's always thinking, always planning. It's something I noticed back at Camp Serenity, when she taught classes on battle strategy. "I don't know anyone from Veridet too well, and that's the next kingdom over...."

"Okay, so the first thing we find is somewhere to stay." Sage is pacing back and forth, creating a trail in the mud. "Does anyone have any suggestions?"

"Well, are we close enough to Buit that we could go back?" Ash says thoughtfully.

"Into the horrible weather?" Sage says, scowling. "Yeah, like that's a good idea."

"Right now, Sage, it's our *only* idea," Milo says. He's always defended Ash. It's something I've admired for a while—their friendship. "Unless you have a better one, of course."

"I think Sage is right," I offer, sending an apologetic look to Ash. "I mean, we need the sunlight. Back in Buit, it gets dark earlier. It would be dangerous. But there's always more than one kingdom."

"What, you mean we should travel to Veridet?" Elysian glances at me from her own tree.

"Well, we're going to fight in a war against Merrik and his forces, right?" I say. "Veridet is a very flat land. It has a lot of fields and not that many mountains. They're known for selling crops. Plus, it's a very violent kingdom. I'm sure they'd be willing to offer up a few warriors in exchange for some money."

"Where are we going to get money?" Sage asks. Even though she sounds skeptical, I can tell my plan is growing on her.

"I..." Milo starts, then changes his sentence. "While I was in the throne room, I saw a pile of money in the corner. Then we left, and I didn't get the chance to snag any. But then, once I was coming back, I made a beeline for the money and grabbed as much as I could." He motions to one of his pants pockets. "It's in there."

Relief wells in my chest. *This may work.*

"So, Veridet is an option," Sage says, scowling as she glances up at the relentless sun. "But if we have reinforcements, isn't that a long way to go to get to a battle?"

"Not really." I shrug. "Veridet is also very large. If the reinforcements are coming from Buit, they can go around Ruri and travel into Veridet on foot, if they wish. But there's also horses and wagons and all kinds of things."

"How long would it take if they were to travel to Veridet the way you suggest?" she questions, her eyes narrowing.

"It would take them around a day if they didn't stop," I say. "If they did stop, it would take them a little over twenty-six hours."

"Twenty-six hours of non-stop fighting?" Ash snorts. "Wouldn't that be a show."

"Indeed," Sage grumbles. "I suppose we'll have to come up with another plan."

"But war isn't all about fighting, is it?" Elysian says, coming to my aid. "In a war, there's wits and strength. There will be battle, yes, but it won't be nonstop. Even ghosts get tired sometimes."

"Yeah, and there's another thing," Milo says, turning to Ben. "How do you suppose that we defeat ghosts when they're see-through and don't have physical bodies?"

"Um…" Ben glances around, probably looking for someone to help him. "Kill them with kindness?"

Ash peels herself off of a tree. "That sounds like an inspirational poster, not a plan."

"Well, if the ghosts benefit off of Merrik, then all we have to do is defeat him, right?" Elysian says. "They're 'alive' because of him. If

we defeat him by using our training, then the ghosts will disappear."
She looks over at Ben expectantly. "Right?"

He looks relieved not to have all the questioning eyes on him.
"Right."

"We'll figure it out," I say, trying to sound as encouraging as I
can. "So…Milo, what happened?"

"Ooh, story," Ash says, clapping her hands together as Milo
takes a deep breath.

"The queen and her guards followed me into the village. I
pointed out where I thought the fake culprits were, and then we'd
look around for a while. At one point, I heard them whispering about
my execution. But, of course, it wasn't anything I haven't dealt with
before. We continued on, but I could tell the guards were getting
restless, and the queen kept talking about the sun being in her eyes.
They desperately wanted to stop riding—I know that since *I* wanted
to stop riding, too—but I had to make my excuses believable. We
stopped for lunch, and then the guards said they were going to kill
me while we were eating. I brushed it off and we started riding again.
But then I felt a sword in my back and realized they weren't joking—
they were actually trying to kill me."

"Well, you're not dead, so you must've done *something*," Sage
snaps. "Get on with it, will you? We have a tight schedule here."

"I'm telling it, Sage," Milo says calmly. "So I led them back to
the castle."

"You did *what?*" It obviously isn't what Sage was expecting, because her jaw flies open, earning a slight smile from Milo.

"I led them back to the castle. They were going to see us escaping anyway, and by then, they had already figured out that I wasn't the real messenger—*that,* I'm sure of. I led them back to the castle, rushed down the stairs to find you where Ben said you would be, and then we ran. It's as simple as that." He shrugs.

"Well..." Elysian hesitates, thinking. "...you didn't *lie,* so I guess it's not that bad. I mean, you did what you told them you were going to. You led them to the intruders."

"Exactly," he says, grinning.

"You *led them to the castle?*" Sage still seems shocked. "Are you *insane?* Do you know how risky that is? They're going to know who we are now. This messes everything up. Oh, gods, this cannot be happening. They're going to kill us!"

"Come on, Sage," Ash says, smiling along with Milo, "where's your sense of adventure?"

"It seems that I left it back at the campfire!" Sage yells angrily.

Campfire? My gaze travels from everyone's shocked faces to Ben's confused one and Elysian's sympathetic one. When she catches my eyes, she mouths something about death, and I get it. That's where her boyfriend died.

"Veridet is a good idea," Ben says, clearing his throat.

"We should go before it gets dark," Elysian agrees, her voice low.

The rest of us nod, and we begin to walk in the direction of the large stone wall, protecting the borders of both Ruri and Veridet, thousands of feet of silence looming ahead.

* * *

By the time we get to the wall, my breathing is coming in short spurts, and still no one has spoken.

I glance over at my sister. She's somehow not out of breath. This makes me think about her training every day at the camp she built—the camp she *had* to build, because of my father.

I remove my eyes from her and stare at the back of Ash's head. I remember when I met Ash—she was so independent, yet not. She was trapped with Finn. She was going to marry him. He was going to force her to marry him.

I remember the horrible way my father and Finn treated her that night—like she was nothing more than a pretty face. I'm glad she proved them wrong. I'm glad and I'm proud. But I'm also sorry.

I see the way her shoulders droop and the way guilt and sadness takes over her eyes when no one's looking. I see the tiredness in her posture, in her words, the loose set of her jaw that betrays the tension in her shoulders. I feel bad for her, honestly, and I know that if she just has my sister to support her everything would be better.

But they must work this out themselves. In order to strengthen their relationship, they have to admit they were wrong.

"Just like in Ruri, there should be a few brothels or taverns as far away from the castle as they can be while still within the kingdom borders," Ben says, and when Elysian gives him a weird look, he clarifies his words. "It's seen as offensive. But I'm sure some of the tavern or brothel owners have a shed that they can spare."

"We're sleeping in a shed?" I say slowly, making sure that I've heard him correctly.

"You've slept in worse," Elysian whispers to me, and I shudder as memories of the cell that Finn trapped me in resurface.

"You're right," I whisper back.

"Okay, then," Ash says. "Let's go to the sheds."

CHAPTER 24

SAGE

As darkness settles over the kingdom of Veridet, I actually miss the relentless sun of Ruri.

I notice Ben shivering in his T-shirt and smile smugly. I *told* him not to put on a T-shirt, and look who's right.

"Sir," Ben says, towering over the tavern owner yet trying to look smaller so he's pitied, "please, can't we just have a place to stay for a few nights?"

The tavern owner's squashed face turns down into a frown. "Where are you kids from that your parents can't take care of you?" he asks.

"My parents died when I was very young," I tell the owner, which isn't really a lie. My parents *did* die, at the very least. "And his parents are…"

"Missing," Ben fills in.

"And those kids behind you?" He nods to our friends.

"They will be of no trouble to you," I say, keeping eye contact with him.

"Are their parents dead, too?" the tavern owner asks.

"They are."

"So you're on a field trip?" He raises his eyebrows, starting to laugh at his own joke. "The orphanage owners let you out?"

"Yes, sir." I'm hoping to intimidate him. Luckily enough, he glances back at me, sees Ash, and slinks away from us.

"Okay, okay," he says, "but only for a few nights."

I flash him a smile, letting the murderous look leave my eyes. "Thank you, sir."

As it turns out, the tavern owner has two sheds behind his building. I assume one is for supplies and the other is for guests. I make my way toward the one of supplies, but stop when I notice Ben following me.

"What are you doing here?" I ask him.

"I'm sleeping here," he tells me, crossing his arms over his chest defiantly.

"Oh, no, you aren't," I tell him, matching his stare with one of my own. "*I'm* sleeping here."

"Are we seriously doing this again?"

"Well, it's not like I want to."

"And you think I do? Sage—" He groans, cutting himself off. "Someone else is going to have to stay with us, you know."

"You think we need a chaperone?" I joke, though my tone is completely flat.

He mutters something that sounds strangely like "Most likely," but then he clears his throat and marches forward, almost beating me to the door of the shed. I don't know what he's doing, but I don't like it. He's messing with my brain, getting me angry and irritated.

I stand in front of the door, blocking it from him with my body. I'm tall enough that my head almost reaches the top of the doorway.

"Sage," he says, annoyed. "Move."

"I don't understand why you can't just go to the other shed. I'll room with Elysian and Ameer, and you can room with Ash and Milo. And, besides, I touched the door before you did."

I know I'm being childish, but I don't care. I don't want to put myself through rooming with him again. I hated it—hated that I couldn't be comfortable in my own space. But it was also kind of nice, the way that he was always warm, the way that his shirts smelled, the way that he would always lay on the side of the room with the window, so I didn't have to wake up and be blinded by the sun. In this shed, though, there's no windows, none of Ben's shirts, and he'll probably be freezing, considering the temperature outside.

"You know as well as I do that Ash would kill me in my sleep if she got the chance," Ben says shortly. "And it's not likely that Elysian and Ash would leave each other's sides, since they're trying to make amends."

I clench my jaw, angry, but a tiny voice at the back of my mind asks, *How does he know that?*

"So, Milo, then," I say. "Milo will stay with us."

"I thought we didn't need a chaperone."

I ignore him. "But it's likely that *he's* not going to leave Ash's side, either so that means…"

"We're by ourselves," Ben grumbles. "Move, Sage. I want to get inside before we freeze to death out here."

I twist the knob and throw the door open, stomping inside and maneuvering the supplies so they won't get in my way. "Don't get in my way."

"Whatever you say," he taunts. He still has Selena's bag slung over his shoulder, and he sets it in the corner, pulling out a large blanket. "Get me those scissors." He points to a pair of gardening scissors to the right of me.

"Are you going to kill me with them?"

"Tempting, but no." Ben takes the scissors from me. "I'm going to cut this blanket into two parts. That way, we can each have half to use overnight."

I nod, resisting the urge to tell him that I have slept in much worse conditions without luxuries such as a blanket.

Once he manages to cut the blanket in half, he hands me a part of it, and I find a space on the floor that isn't too dirty. I set the blanket down and roll myself in it, like a caterpillar inside a cocoon. The events of the day weigh heavily on my eyelids as they begin to droop, and I fall asleep.

* * *

I wake up the sounds of screaming.

For a second, I'm worried that we're being ambushed, but a quick look over at Ben assures me that he's just having a nightmare. I try to tell myself that it's okay, that he's okay, but there's a cold familiarity in the pit of my stomach as I remember the nightmares I had, and the way I felt when no one was there to comfort me.

I unfold myself from my cocoon and crawl over to Ben's spot on the floor. I grab his shoulder and shake, and his eyes shoot open immediately. He reaches out to hit me, but then his arms fall back to his sides when he sees who I am.

"Sage," he breathes. "Sage—did I wake you up?"

I nod. "It's okay, though, Ben, it's okay." My voice is soft, matching his tone.

He murmurs my name as his arms wrap around my waist, pulling me close to him. I let him, relaxing in his grip, firm but not uncomfortable. I was wrong—he has as much body heat as he did in Ruri, even despite the temperature. I urge a vine to come up and take my blanket to me, and I wrap it around the two of us as Ben continues to say my name.

"Shh," I say. "It's okay, Ben. It was just a nightmare."

He opens his eyes and stares straight into mine, holding eye contact. I feel a little self-conscious but not enough that I back down. "Thank you," he whispers, and I nod.

"You're welcome," I reply.

Ben leans forward and buries his head in the crook between my neck and my chin. I hug him, pulling him closer to me, welcoming his warmth.

"Ben, I—" I start, but then I hear his soft, rhythmic breathing and know that he's asleep.

What was I going to say? I ask myself. *Ben, I'm sorry. Ben, I still don't like you. Ben, I want you to know that this is so weird for me. Ben, I* know *that this is weird, but I don't care. Ben, I...*

I don't know. But I mull over the possibilities of what it was that I wanted to tell Ben about myself until my eyes close again and everything fades to black.

* * *

I wake up for the second time, this time frantic. I don't really remember where I am, or why Ben is hugging me, or why we're sleeping in the same space *again*, but then the events of the hours before fill my mind and I feel a blush settle on my cheeks.

I scramble away from him, taking my blanket with me. He groans but doesn't wake, and I step outside after lacing up my shoes and find Elysian already awake, pacing in front of the other shed.

"Morning," I murmur, rubbing my eyes.

She glances over at me and smiles, walking to meet me. "Well, well, well. You and Ben are sharing a room again."

"It's not really that much of a room. It's a shed."

"Same thing."

"Are they?"

I notice the bags under her eyes, the way she picks at her nails. "Are you okay, Lys?"

"Everything's just..." She shakes her head. "Everything's weird, Sage. You know? It's all out of order."

I know exactly what you mean. "Out of order?"

"Back in July, that quest was...different. My brother wasn't with us—he was actually the person we wanted to save—Selena was with us for most of it, Milo was happier, Ash was more...vibrant, and Sorin... Well, you get it."

"I know. It's strange." I stare at her, wanting to hug her. "When's your deadline for Merrik again?"

"Six days," she tells me automatically, and I resist the urge to hit myself as I realize that she's been thinking over it for a while.

"Elysian," I say softly, and then I'm hugging her, wrapping my arms around her as she starts to sob. She's been carrying this huge weight on her shoulders and I haven't even stopped for two seconds to make sure that she isn't crumbling under the pressure.

Above us, the clouds start to churn, in tune with Elysian's emotions. Just like the day that Ash broke up with her, the weather is unruly, unsettled, trying to cope with the sadness and pressure that she feels.

"Elysian," I say again, letting her collapse against me. There's a gap in between the sheds, and I lead her to them, setting her against the wall. She sobs and sobs and I try my best to just be there for her, because I know that's all I can do.

"I need to choose him," she gasps. "In order to delay the war, I have to choose him."

"No, Elysian, no, you don't," I say. "We can fight this war. We're ready."

"No, we're not!" she says. "Anne isn't here yet and everything is falling apart..."

"Believe me, Lys. We can fight. You don't have to put yourself through some kind of personal hell, because we can fight."

"Merrik is so strong—"

"We can beat him," I insist, growing angrier now.

"Sage..." Elysian whispers. "I don't know what to do."

Her tears are slowly beginning to dry. "It's not going to be easy," I say.

"I want to delay the war," she tells me. "I want to give us more *time*. But I'd never be on the same side as *him*."

"Lys—"

"We've already lost Selena." She gazes up at me, her sky-blue eyes huge. "I...I don't know what I'd do if I was forced to leave you."

"Elysian. You do know that you can ask for help, don't you?"

"That's rich coming from you, Miss I-Can-Do-Everything-On-My-Own." She chuckles, wiping her eyes.

I laugh with her, then say, "Seriously. I'll always be here for you."

She nods and sniffles. "Do you think they'll wake soon?" Elysian asks nervously, glancing at the cabin.

"Considering the meltdown you just had, I'm sure it's probable," I tell her.

She winces. "I really don't want Ameer to see me like this."

"You mean Ash?"

Elysian glances over at me and glares. "I mean *Ameer*," she says, her voice as hard as steel.

I raise my eyebrows, amused, and Elysian looks away.

"And *you* want Ben to see just how angry you can get?" Her voice is tight, her teeth clenched.

I whip around so I'm facing her. *"What?"*

"I'm just saying, you seem to care a lot about what he thinks of you." Elysian makes eye contact with me and shrugs, but there's tension in her shoulders. Obviously she's hurt by what I've said.

"Don't try to pin this on me," I tell her, scowling, but she just shrugs again, and as she turns her head I see the faintest smile on her lips.

Fine. Two can play at that game.

"I have to admit, it would affect me a little," I say. "But if I had an angry ex, then it would hurt more. I would be very hurt. Maybe almost *publicly* hurt."

"Don't."

"Hey, what's the point of only doing it to one? Why not the other?"

"Because the *other* can make lightning strike you and make it look like an accident."

"Oh, yeah? Well, I could make a sinkhole appear right under your feet, and there'd be nothing you could do about it."

"Fine."

"Fine."

I turn on my heel and stalk back toward the shed, slamming the door behind me. Ben props himself up onto his elbows, and I stare in embarrassment and shock as I realize *he isn't wearing a shirt.*

Then I scowl. *Why am I thinking about this?* "Put a shirt on," I tell him, and he groans and sits up, burying his head in his blanket.

"Good morning to you, too," he says, his voice muffled.

I clench my jaw at his sarcasm but the images of last night—the sounds of his screams—flash through my mind, and I relax, wondering if I should say anything about it. I ultimately decide against it. If Ben wants to say something about it, then he will.

"Hey, Sage, about what happened last night..." he starts, and I wince. *Okay, so he definitely does want to say something.*

"What about it?"

"I just wanted you to know that I'm grateful. Sometimes I have nightmares and…Oh, well, you don't care. But I just want to thank you for helping me."

I feel a flush settle on my cheeks, and I hold back a snarky retort. Instead, I manage a weak, "You're welcome."

He glances over at me, seeming satisfied, but then he notices my expression. "Is…everything okay?"

"Yep—yeah, everything's perfectly fine. Nothing to worry about. I just—I need some air."

"Weren't you just out there?"

"Yeah, but it's really stuffy in here, and the air is just so cold out there, so I needed a break."

He doesn't say anything for a long moment. Then, "Okay. I'll go with you."

"What?"

"I'll go outside with you, to get some air," Ben clarifies. "It *is* stuffy in here, and I promise I'll put on a shirt. I just…need to find mine…."

"No, it's okay. You don't have to come with me."

"I *want* to. Seriously, it's no big deal. Right?"

"Right," I squeak.

I swear I see Ben smile from the corner of my eye.

∗ ∗ ∗

"See those hills over there?" Ben asks me, pointing to a large range of them.

"They're hard to miss," I tell him.

"We should hike them."

"Climb the hills? With no gear or safety equipment or *anything*? Yeah, sure, because that's a good idea."

"Come on, Sage. These are the only non-flat landforms for miles, and we both need something to do."

"No."

Ben glances over at me. "You're grumpy this morning."

"Well, I would've had a better sleep if *someone* weren't screaming their head off."

He leans closer to me, dropping my voice to a low whisper. "I know that's not the reason, Sage."

A shiver runs down my spine, but I try to ignore it. "Oh, yeah? And what *is* the reason, since you know everything?"

"I don't know yet, but I plan to find out."

And with one more glance at me, he starts in the direction of the hills.

∗ ∗ ∗

"Good gods, I hate you," I yell to Ben, who's laughing as we scale up the steep side of the first hill, the trail in front of us growing in length and height.

"You never had to follow me," he calls back, and I'm surprised he does, because he's laughing too hard.

I shove him as soon as I'm within shoving distance. "Oh, shut up," I grumble.

"You think they'll be mad at you for leaving?"

"Leaving with a strange man that is definitely frowned upon in their rulebook."

"Strange man? But you know me."

"And yet that doesn't make you any less strange."

He glances back at me, a glint in his eyes, and starts to run along the trail. I follow after him, though reluctantly, because I would *really* hate to be by myself on a hill, lost and confused.

"Ben!" I scream, wanting to hit myself for the way real fear envelopes my tone. "Ben, don't you dare leave me here! Ben!"

He continues to run in front of me, and I curse.

"You suck!" I yell. He laughs, and it rings in my ears.

I finally catch up with him at a flat area near the top of the hill. I shiver as the cold air, even colder from where we stand, hits me.

"I hate you so much," I tell him as I approach.

He's grinning broadly. "Do you? Well, I suppose that puts you in the same boat as the girl who told me I suck earlier—have you met her? I think you'd get along well."

His eyes, a deep, flawless brown, are alight with happiness and sarcasm. His cheeks are red from the adrenaline and the cold, and when he reaches out to grab my hand, his skin is warm.

I glance to the right of me, where the hilltop ends. The sun is still in its early-morning position, and the light blue sky and crisp air complements its pale yellow shade perfectly.

"It's beautiful," he breathes, staring at the same view.

"It would be more beautiful if I weren't scared I was going to fall off that ledge," I tell him, and he laughs.

"You're scared of heights?" He grins.

"There's no reason to look so cheerful about it. I've been scared of heights ever since I was little."

"Any reason why?"

I shrug, but my mind fills with memories of the way my mother used my fear against me every chance she got. "Not a reason I remember well."

He glances over at me, and his smile fades a little, but then it reappears, just as broad. "Well, don't worry. I'm scared of snakes."

"Snakes?"

"Snakes."

"Like there's any reason for you to be."

"You know the ones with venom? Those are the ones that I'm scared of. But I'll probably never be attacked by a snake. And as for your fear of heights, don't worry about that. If you fall, I'll catch you."

I look over at him. It seems like a weirdly vulnerable statement, and I'm honestly surprised that he's said it. Based on his display last night, when he talked to me like I was the most childish person ever to live, I'm not too sure he likes me too much.

"Ben, I—"

I'm about to say something, but then my voice fails, and I'm unable to say what I want, just like last night. I still don't know what I would've said.

But it doesn't matter. It doesn't matter, because Ben seems to know exactly what I'm saying, because he's kissing me.

He's kissing me, and there's fireworks in my stomach that are exploding, all common sense leaving my mind as his warm hand touches the side of my neck and pulls me closer to him. I don't pull away, and I don't resist, but I'm so confused. It seemed like he hated me.

And I don't care.

I don't care. I don't care that the wind has begun to blow harder, or that people are definitely going to connect the dots when our lips are swollen and we look like we've been through some kind of disaster, or that I have other things to care about right now than the feel of Ben's lips against mine and the way that my heart seems to beat a million times a second.

And I realize I've begun to not care so much that I barely hear yelling until Ben pulls away from me, and, without saying anything, without even giving me a moment to react, he starts back down the trail.

Rather reluctantly, knowing that there's nothing I can do, I follow after him toward the sound of the screams.

*　*　*

When Ben and I finally meet the others back at the tavern, my dagger is unsheathed. There's the sound of metal on metal, of grunts and blood splatter, and I wince.

Already we're destroying things, and we haven't even been here for a day.

I run to join the battle. As I run, I notice the familiar face of the tavern owner, his eyebrows shot up in surprise, his lip quivering with fear. When he spots me, he points and glares and says, "It's all your—"

But I'll never know what is all mine, because someone cloaked in armor causes his head to roll on the ground, separated from his body.

I stare at the gory scene for a moment, utterly horrified.

The murderer of the tavern owner walks toward me, their bloody sword raised threateningly. I duck as they deliver a killing blow, straightening and slamming my dagger against their helmet so hard that the vibrations run through my arm. The armored person crumples to the ground, silent and unmoving.

I find that I have to duck again as an icicle comes hurtling toward where I stand. I glance behind me, and I see someone else in armor who was planning to attack me, their blood staining the dead grass.

When I look forward, Ameer grins at me.

"Elysian!" I call out for my best friend, hoping that she at least has some answers as to why we're being attacked right now.

She appears at my side instantly. "What is it?" she asks, using her sword to fight off two armored soldiers in front of her.

I cut one of them down, and she takes care of the other. Using my precise knife-throwing skills, I aim my dagger at a moving soldier and throw. The dagger hits the soldier right in the gap between their armor, and the soldier crumples.

"What happened?" I ask her, running to retrieve my dagger. Elysian runs after me, and I stab another soldier as they try to surprise me by attacking when I bend over.

"I don't know," she tells me honestly. "I had gone inside right when it happened. People in armor started stabbing the wood of the sheds. There was thudding and then yelling, to alert us, probably, and then we started fighting."

"And you don't know why they're here?"

"Excuse me for not asking while they were trying to cut my face off," she tells me angrily. "We could've used you and Ben here earlier, you know, while you were off wherever you were. There were a lot more, but we managed to get them down to only a few hundred."

"There were *more* than a few hundred?" I ask her.

"Yes," she says. "They might be working with Merrik. He seems to always know where we are. But he also seems to be a very organized...*thing*. He never does anything without reason. All of these notes are just so we know that he's coming, that this war is inevitable."

"But he is also a very *bold* entity," I say. "The soldiers just showed up here, no explanation or reason? I don't believe that. I believe, if they're working with Merrik, that there's something we're missing. Something that's coming."

As if on cue, the soldiers start to retreat. I glance over at Milo, who is cursing and bleeding, and my eyes widen.

"This is only the beginning of what is to become of you when the war starts," the soldiers say in unison. I want to start toward Milo and try to help him the best I can, but I can't move. It's like I'm paralyzed. "We are stronger, faster, better. You shall learn soon enough."

And with that, the soldiers vanish.

Elysian and I sprint in Milo's direction and crouch next to him. I grab his hand and tell him to squeeze if it hurts. He nearly cuts off my circulation, and I ask him *where* it hurts.

"My...c-chest," he manages, and Elysian's dagger slices through the fabric of Milo's shirt and peels it away. It comes off sticky with blood.

Fear courses through my veins as I finally see the wound.

"Oh, my gods," Elysian breathes, and she curses. "Ben!" she yells, and Ben rushes over to us and bends down next to Milo.

There's a thin knife sticking out of Milo's chest.

"Oh—" Ben's about to curse, but then he cuts himself off. "I'll be back with the *soigner*. Stay here, and make sure you *do not pull the knife out*. That knife is literally the only thing keeping him alive."

Milo whimpers.

I drop his hand just for a second so I can rip off a piece of his already-torn shirt. I ball it up and grab his hand again. He clutches mine instantly.

"Bite down on this," I say, "whenever you want to scream."

He nods, his breathing shaky and uneven. "It...hurts..."

"I know, but it won't hurt in a little bit. You'll be better."

Elysian, who has been intently inspecting the wound, asks, "Milo, can you try to heal yourself?"

"I need…to remove the—knife in order to…try…" He puts the ball of fabric into his mouth and screams into it while holding my hand like his life depends on it, which it very well might.

I glance around at us. Ben still has not returned from the shed we stayed in, where Selena's bag containing the *soigner* is, and for a minute I can't see Ash or Ameer. But then I find Ash, pale and looking sick, several hundred feet away.

"Are we supposed to—?" I say, but it doesn't matter.

Elysian tells him that it's going to hurt, and he tenses as she pulls the knife out of his chest. He grabs my hand so tightly that it startles me, and he screams into the bundle of cloth. He starts to pant, controlling all of his power and strength onto healing himself. Blood begins to spill from his wound, and I curse several times as I try to block it with my hands.

Milo's breath is short and choppy, and his energy is being drained, but the wound is slowly starting to close, the blood clotting. It leaves a very jagged scar where the blade was. He continues to scream as the wound fully closes, and I remove my hands from it, which are now coated in red.

"Milo," I breathe, "you're okay." He leans back, and I take the cloth from his mouth, dropping it onto the grass.

He doesn't say anything in response, and his eyes droop and he falls asleep, exhausted.

I share a knowing glance with Elysian as Ben emerges from the shed. He sees the scene and his eyes widen.

"What the – ?" he demands. "I told you not to remove the knife—is he dead? Did he die?"

I clench my jaw, but when I speak, my voice is soft. "He saved himself. He healed *himself.*"

"But…that's impossible." Ben finally meets us at Milo's unconscious body and bends down, still looking at me and Elysian. "He was *dying.* I thought—he was dying. You're telling me he's still alive?"

"That's right," Elysian says.

Ben sees the blood on our hands, Milo's blood, and curses, though I don't understand why. He starts to apply *soigner* to Milo's body. "Well, you've done all you can, so you should leave now."

He says it almost angrily, and I feel my heart sinking in my chest, but I oblige. I stand from the scene and storm away from Ben, thinking about the feel of his lips on mine.

Ben, I am falling in love with you.

And I hate it.

CHAPTER 25

ASH

I take a long drag of my cigarette.

My heart is still pounding. Milo almost dying scared the crap out of me. I decided that I most definitely needed a break, and I found a pack of cigarettes in the tavern, so here I am.

I know that they're not good for me, but I don't care. How can I, when cigarettes are the only things that make me calm down?

I'm sitting behind a rock, staring up at the sun, high in the sky. It's freezing still, and I'm sure I look like an absolute idiot, sitting here in the middle of nowhere while smoking and moping, but I don't care.

I don't *care*.

My best friend almost died. That's not something I can get over too easily.

I hear footsteps and turn around, noticing Elysian. My heartbeat slows a bit, and I lower my cigarette, knowing that she hates it when I smoke.

She sits across from me, leaning against the rock. "Hey."

"Hey," I respond without expression.

"Are you okay?" she asks me.

"Am *I* okay?"

"Yeah."

"Why wouldn't I be?"

"Oh, you know. The…thing with Milo."

"Not your fault," I mutter, shrugging. "You told him to heal himself. I have to thank you."

"No, you don't," she says.

"Yes, I do," I insist. "If it weren't for you, my best friend wouldn't be alive right now."

I play with the ring on my right pointer finger, twisting it. It's still rather new, so I'm not completely used to it, but I'm starting to become more comfortable with it.

Elysian eyes the ring. "Where'd you get that?"

It has a sleek silver band and Latin words engraved in it. I glance down at it. "I found it."

"Where?"

"In the tavern," I say. "It was sitting on the bar, and I was looking for something to do, so…"

"You stole it?"

"It was made for me," I tell her quietly. "It was made for me because it has my initials on the other side."

I take the ring off and hand it to her. She spins it in between her thumb and pointer finger, and when she spots the A.K. carved into the other side of the silver, her eyebrows raise slightly in surprise.

Finally, she hands it back to me. "Okay. Then I guess the stealing is justified."

"It better be, because there's no way I'm returning this thing," I grumble, and Elysian laughs.

"How is it you do that?" she asks suddenly.

"Do what?" I say, still inspecting the ring.

"Have a joke on hand constantly."

"Oh, I guess—"

"I mean, it's interesting. You think you'd be fully out of jokes, considering Milo almost just died."

She winces upon seeing my face.

"But I guess you don't want to talk about that, either."

I take another drag of my cigarette. "It's okay. You didn't mean it." I raise an eyebrow in her direction. "At least, I don't think you meant it."

"I didn't," she says quickly.

I twist the ring on my finger, suddenly uncomfortable. Elysian is sitting in front of me, fixing me with that blue-eyed stare of hers, and for some reason I can't find it within me to be mad at or upset with her.

She reaches out for my hand, and I flinch away from her. A tremor appears in her jaw, but she relents, returning her hand to her side.

"I know," she says softly, dropping her voice to a whisper, "that you don't trust me. Not in the way you used to. I know that it's my fault, too—that your hatred for me would not be hatred if I had trusted you and not overreacted. And I'm sorry. I am truly sorry."

I inhale through my cigarette and exhale a puff of smoke. Her nose curls but she says nothing.

"It's my fault, too," I say. "It's my fault that we fought, that we grew apart. If I hadn't been so controlling, then maybe—"

"Ash." Her voice is barely a breath. "It's okay. Trust me, it's all right. The gods know I've had my faults, too, especially when it comes to you." Elysian pauses. "It's okay. I forgive you. Do you forgive me?"

This time, when she reaches out for me, I don't flinch away from her. I let her grab my hand, let her touch my ring, let myself get caught up in the endless blue of her eyes, in the adoring and determined look in them. I let myself start to love her again.

But I'm not really sure I ever stopped.

She brings my hand to her lips and kisses my knuckles. "Do you still have the straw bracelet?"

I reach into my jean pocket and bring out the straw bracelet she made me, falling apart. I don't care. I've kept it safe—almost unconsciously—from the moment she gave it to me.

She laughs lightly, her voice still low. I don't speak, because I'm afraid that I'll shatter this—this truce that we've formed, this relationship that we're starting to build again, this moment that we're having.

No, I don't speak. But I lean forward, and I kiss her.

She responds almost instantly, using her other hand to put it on the side of my face and touch the length of my cheekbone. I put one of my arms around her neck and pull her toward me, and I let her hold my other hand, fiddle with my ring.

I wonder, distantly, what a ring might look like on her finger one day, and if I'll ever get to see it. All I know is that I want to be there to see it, want to be the one who puts the ring on her finger. I want to be the *one*.

And she breaks away from me and then I'm hugging her, holding onto her like she's the last piece of sanity that I have. The smell of her—rain, vanilla, the metallic smell of blood, Milo's blood—mixed with the lingering cigarette smoke in the air is miraculously comforting. I hold onto her like my life depends on it and I'm struggling not to cry. But I let myself cry.

I let myself cry, because the weight of the day has fallen on my shoulders, too much for me to carry. I try to wipe the tears from my eyes, but she stops me, giving me a nod of assurance that tells me it's okay.

It's okay to cry.

And I love her even more.

* * *

When I open my eyes, I realize night has fallen over Veridet, and I grimace. Elysian is below me, her head on my chest, and I realize that we must've fallen asleep, even though I have no recollection of it. I don't want to wake her, but my neck aches and everything hurts and I'm pretty sure sleeping against a rock, no matter how used to it we are by now, is not good for you.

I don't wish to wake her, though. She looks so peaceful when she sleeps—a sense of calm seems to settle over her every time she escapes to a world that is not this one, the one that is not filled with bloodshed and lies and bruises and fighting and the endless possibility of death looming above us, waiting to corrupt us.

As lightly as I can, I press a kiss to the top of her head. I catch a glance of the silver band of my ring as I do, and it makes me stop dead.

I let my eyes close as I remember the desperate way Finn was willing to make me his bride. Who's to say that he doesn't feel that way now, that Merrik isn't going to help him get exactly what he wants?

I imagine, for a minute, that the band on my finger is a wedding band, that I am married to the man who I hate so much. Fear clutches my heart at this thought, and my eyes fly open.

I find Elysian looking at me.

"Ash." She looks incredibly tired. "What's the matter? Is something wrong?"

And I remember where I am, and that the band is my own, and not Finn's, not a promise of love that I will never really believe in. I smile lightly.

"Nothing's the matter, Lys," I say softly. "Nothing at all."

I wait until her eyes are closed again and she's fully asleep, based on the steady rhythm of her breathing, before I slip one arm under her head and the other under her knee joints. She doesn't stir. Her waking would probably make things easier, but I like carrying her. It's a weird feeling.

I try my best to carry her back to the sheds without my legs failing, and it's a struggle, but I do. I set her softly on the makeshift bed next to her brother, and almost instantly, her brother's hand reaches out and grabs her. It's a sight, a feeling, that I've always wanted as an only child, but something that I have never gotten. After me, my parents refused to have more children. *"You were plenty," Father would say.*

I exit the shed and pull my pack of cigarettes out of my pocket, using a lighter I find in my other pocket to light it. I love the way that the flames dance across the end of it, the way smoking makes me feel completely in control, even though I am the farthest thing from it.

"Hey," says a familiar voice.

Sage's voice.

"What are you doing up?" I ask, not even sparing her a glance.

I see her shrug from my peripheral vision. She looks rather rumpled—and I'm saying this in the nicest way possible. Her hair is mussed, her clothes coated in the dirt that she had to kneel on when she was healing Milo. Her hands still have his blood on them.

"I could ask you the same thing," she says. "Can I have one?"

This time, I look at her. She's motioning to the cigarette in my hand. I feel my eyebrows raise slightly in surprise. "You smoke?"

"Never!" she tells me, chuckling humorlessly. "But it's been a long day, and I really need something to take my mind off of it."

I let out a puff of smoke and reluctantly reach for the pack in my pocket. I hand her one of the cigarettes and light it for her. "Inhale slowly," I tell her. "You're going to choke your first time, but don't panic. It happens to everyone."

She puts it in her mouth and takes a slow drag. Almost immediately, she starts coughing. She takes the cigarette out of her mouth as her eyes start to water, but then she recovers her breath and nods subtly. She places the cigarette back in her mouth and inhales again. This time, she only coughs for a few seconds before regaining her composure.

"Good?" I ask her.

She nods again. "It's okay. Tastes weird."

"I didn't mean that," I say, laughing. "I mean, what's it feel like? Good?"

She closes her eyes, throwing her head back. "Good."

"So, what's up?"

"What?"

"Why was it a long day?"

Sage shrugs again. "I just… Earlier today, Ben kissed me. We were on top of a mountain, and we were just talking, and then he leaned forward and kissed me. And I liked it? At least, I think I did. It wasn't weird or anything like that, and he wasn't a bad kisser. And we didn't have any time to feel embarrassed or awkward because then the soldiers invaded. But, I mean, I'm still getting over Sorin's death. His *funeral* is in a few days. It's just insane, you know? And then I started thinking about how disappointed he'd be in me if he knew, and that he would feel so betrayed, and it would be my fault, along with Ben's, and I just couldn't bear it. I would go into the tavern and get a drink, but all the bottles were smashed when it was invaded, and I'm not desperate enough to start licking alcohol off the floor."

I blink at her. "He *kissed* you?"

"Yeah." Sage straightens and opens her eyes, just to fix me with a glare. "Why?"

"Nothing, it's just…" I smirk. "I knew he liked you. And I'm pretty sure Milo knew, too. Gods, he's going to be so clueless when he wakes up."

She throws her cigarette on the ground and stomps on it, sighing. "Yeah, I guess."

I stare at her. "Sage."

"What is it?"

"Sage, look at me."

She looks up at me, matching my stare. She's still the same girl who I had to team up two months ago—still the same hardheaded, stubborn, loyal Sage Jobbs Elysian loves as a sister. But there's something in her gaze; something unsettling, something unnerving, something incredibly broken.

She swipes angrily at her eyes as tears start to pool in them. "I just…I feel so helpless without him. Everything's about him. Everything reminds me of him. And now Ben's kissed me, and it complicates everything."

I find myself stepping toward her. I don't reach out, but I stand there, in front of her, saying nothing, trying to communicate the understanding that we have. Trying to tell her that she isn't the only one who's grieving, not the only one who is so confused because *what is even happening?* I want her to know that, and it doesn't take hugging or sobbing or anything other than the look I'm giving her for her to understand.

Sage sniffs. Realization dawns in her eyes, and she nods slightly.

"I get it," I tell her. "I understand."

Her shoulders relax. With a final nod in my direction, she spins on her heel and walks in the direction of the shed she shares with Ben. I sigh finally, extinguishing my cigarette and dropping it. Then I make my way to the shed.

I open the door, letting the moonlight shine on Elysian's sleeping figure.

I make my way to my own makeshift bed and lay down, staring at the ceiling for a little bit, thoughts running through my mind like wildfire. Finally, sleep catches hold of me, pulling me under.

And I see Elysian's face as I'm falling asleep.

CHAPTER 26

AMEER

I can't sleep.

I hold Elysian's hand, trying to cope with the fact that Milo almost died today and I was off somewhere else, hallucinating. All of this Merrik business has been freaking me out lately, especially now that Selena's been…taken.

I close my eyes tightly, but when I open them again, I'm not in the shed. The floor has caved in under me, and I'm infinitely falling, screaming as I do. Adam, the boy from the ball, is taunting me, and I wince, wanting everything to go away.

When I wake up from that horrible nightmare, I decide enough is enough. I remove my hand from Elysian's clutch, boost myself to my feet, grab my sword that's sitting by the doorframe, and exit the shed.

I walk into the forest that surrounds the tavern until I can barely see it anymore. The only light provided is the light that comes from the blinding moon. I yell Adam's name until my voice is nearly gone.

Finally, a person materializes in front of me, and I'm so upset that I nearly stab them right then.

The boy leaning against one of the many trees has an amused expression on his face. *Adam.*

"Oh, sure, this time you're confident," I snarl at him.

He laughs. "And you're very blunt. Angry, Ameer?" He leans forward, holding eye contact.

My jaw clenches, and I feel heat climbing up my neck. I let my hand drop to my side. "You ruined my life," I tell him. "All of you, the entire ghost crew."

He tilts his head to one side, still maintaining his amused look. "Is that so?"

"You little—"

"Now, now, Prince Ameer, I never thought it was in you to use such foul language."

"I didn't even say anythin—"

"But that's right. You're the king now, aren't you, with dear old Dad dead?"

I suck in a breath.

"What did you call me for?" Adam asks me suddenly, and my breath catches.

"I want you to give me answers."

"The answers I gave you before weren't good enough?"

"No." My expression hardens. "I want to know what you want from me—what you want from all of us."

He sighs. "It's not that simple."

"No. Really?" Sarcasm drips from my tongue.

Adam rolls his eyes. "It may not be something you want to know."

"Trust me, I want to know."

"Fine."

He steps so close to me that I can see the calluses built into his hands. "Illusions," he tells me when he catches me looking.

"The calluses are illusions?"

"Well, not really." He runs one hand through his hair. "This is what I looked like when I was alive, but not anymore. Now, I'm just a soul."

"That sounds...dreadfully sad."

"Oh, trust me, it's not. When you're a soul, you can do whatever you want. You can steal or kill or do something absolutely horrible and blame it on the humans. Plus, scaring them and watching their faces go white is enjoyable." He grins at me, and I notice vaguely that I'm an inch taller than him, even though he seems so much bigger than me.

"All of you are ghosts?"

"Pretty much." Adam shrugs.

"Because you can't be wounded if you're already dead."

"Yes."

"But my sister can be wounded. *I* can be wounded." I fix him with a harsh stare. "So why do you want us?"

"No, your sister isn't untouchable," he says finally. "But she's powerful. More powerful than anything I've seen in centuries—" Adams cuts himself off, starting again thoughtfully. "Maybe it's because of Aeolus, maybe it's because of her ancestry. That's what Merrik is trying to figure out. It threatens him so he wants her on his side."

"Like Selena." Then I glance up at him. "That *is* why he wanted Selena, right? Why she's been taken?"

"Personally..." Adam lowers his voice, as if he's telling me a secret, despite the fact that no one else is around. "I think he took her as an example. You know, to say that even the strongest soldiers have a weakness."

His eyes have left my face, and when they return, a new kind of meaning lies in them, and an indecipherable emotion starts running through my mind.

"Thank you," I say, though I don't know exactly what I'm thanking him for. I still have so many questions left to ask— questions that have now left my mind entirely.

"You're welcome," he says, his voice still low.

We stand there for a minute, until finally I regain my senses and take a large step back, nearly bumping into a tree.

"Well, uh, thank you for the information," I say awkwardly, only too conscious of my flaming cheeks. "I'll—um—just try not to kill us, okay?"

A smile lifts the corners of his lips. "Okay." He seems slightly amused, even as I run, nearly tripping in my haste to get away.

But, when I turn around, he isn't there, and I wonder if maybe—just maybe—Merrik is trying to make an example out of more than one of us.

* * *

I wake in the morning with my back aching.

I'm on my side next to Elysian, and I watch the peaceful way she looks when she sleeps for a few moments before turning so I'm on my back.

The ceiling of the shed is plain wood, but for some reason it brings me comfort. It reminds me of the meeting room at Camp Serenity—my "cabin." I wonder wistfully if I will finally have my own cabin with my own decorations, if I will finally stop having to worry about people walking in on me sleeping, expecting a place for them to talk about business.

But, of course, that is a ridiculous fantasy. If I come back from this alive, the crown will be forced upon me. I will be king of Buit, Elysian the princess alongside me, and there is absolutely nothing I can do about it.

I groan internally and prop myself up on my elbows. There are grass stains on the knees of my pants, though I'm not sure how they got there. Everyone else in the shed is sleeping peacefully—everyone,

I notice, except for Ash. Her make-shift bed is deserted, the mess of bedding obviously untouched.

I push myself up fully onto my feet and, as carefully and quietly as I can, I exit the shed.

"Hey," says a hushed voice, almost directly next to my ear. I jump, and a patch of grass directly in front of me freezes instantly.

Ben laughs. "You'll have to figure that out before we start fighting."

I laugh nervously. "Yeah, I guess I will."

"It gets easier, you know," he tells me. "Dealing with magic. It becomes more of a part of you than anything else."

"Isn't it already a part of you?"

"Well, yes."

"So shouldn't it be easy to manage?"

He chuckles dryly. "Oh, you'd be surprised."

I fall silent and Ben does the same as we watch the skyline. Suddenly, almost as if he'll burst at the seams if he doesn't say anything, he declares, "I kissed Sage."

I recoil in surprise "What?"

"I kissed Sage," Ben repeats, though I know exactly what he said. "I kissed her on top of those hills right there, and then she…she kissed me back. And I have no idea what to do now. I mean, imagine *you* kiss the girl of your dreams. How would you respond?"

I open my mouth, but no words come out. Finally, I shrug. "I guess…I don't know."

"Oh, come on. You've got to at least have a game plan."

"A game plan?"

"Yeah. A what-happens-if-she-likes-you-back plan."

"I don't." I notice that I'm tense. "I've never really thought about it. Sorry to disappoint."

"Okay, so you don't have a game plan. But surely you have some advice for me? On the Sage situation," he adds quickly, blushing furiously at the pure mention of the girl.

An emotion fills me, but it isn't romantic at all. It's a fierce protectiveness, a protectiveness due to Sage almost seeming like another one of my little sisters.

"I think you should stay away from her," I say, bitter suddenly. "She's grieving, very clearly, too, and you just swoop in and confuse her. Kissing her isn't doing you any favors, you know. Sage probably doesn't even care about you."

His face contorts at my last statement. "Oh, and you know what and who she likes now?"

"I'm sorry," I say, chuckling humorlessly and holding up my hands, "but the last time I checked, you were arranging a funeral for her dead ex-boyfriend, who, may I remind you, has been dead for *two months*. That's it. And now you're just suddenly so interested in her?"

His jaw flexes as I watch him, and I notice the hint of fear that appears in his eyes when I mention him using Sage. I don't really mean what I'm saying, but it's too late. *Can't take it back now,* I think indignantly. "I'm trying to give her space," he says quietly. "I'm trying my hardest, Ameer, but the more I try, the more I notice her, and the more I fall in love with her. I—I can't—" He cuts himself off and turns away. "I understand you care about her. I understand that she's close to you, like a sister. But I swear to you, I would never, ever do anything to hurt Sage. I swear it on my life."

I glance over at him, raising an eyebrow.

He nods furiously. "I'm serious. I'm falling in love with her, Ameer. I don't know why now or why life-altering or endangering things always seem to bring people together, but it most definitely is bringing me closer to Sage. I'll promise you everything, Ameer, if it means you believe me when I say I am telling you the truth. Now, if you don't want to help me, that's okay. But I'm telling you now— nothing will stand between me and Sage. *Nothing.*" And without another word, he spins on his heel and heads toward the shed that he's sharing with Sage.

I silently curse myself. What am I doing, the soon-to-be king of Buit, letting people tell me what to do and giving me orders, letting them step all over me?

What am I doing, indeed.

CHAPTER 27

ELYSIAN

Ash is holding my hand.

A few days have passed since Milo nearly died and we made up, and we both relish in it now.

We're looking at the ceiling of the shed. She's moved to Ameer's spot on the floor, closest to mine, so that she can stay close to me and touch me. I feel the cool silver of her ring against my hand and I wonder how I let myself drift away from her.

I'm grinning like a dork in this shed, almost completely alone with her except for Milo, who snores on the other side of the room. She looks over at me and breaks into a grin of her own.

"Weirdo," she whispers to me.

"Nerd," I whisper back.

She begins to laugh—her gorgeous, completely real, almost completely silent laugh. I laugh with her, and it takes at least a minute for us to calm down. I'm guessing we're simply hanging desperately onto little things that make us happy and laugh, and we are both each other's best comfort.

I wipe a tear from my eye. Ash actually has to shove her fist into her mouth to keep from laughing too loud and waking Milo. It's not that funny, and we know it. But the moment is still nice, and we're giddy because of the fact that we're back together, all happiness and no more tension.

The sky is clear outside, the sunshine bright. I'm assuming today we'll have one of the warmest days we've had all October, thanks to my cheerful mood.

"Hi," I whisper to her, just because I can. Before yesterday, words would be ignored, backs turned at even a glance. Before yesterday, before the soldiers attacked and Milo almost died and we realized just how little time we have, I would never get to greet her without her glaring at me.

Now she smiles at me when I say it, and I feel a shiver go through me with her smile. It's gorgeous, just like everything about her—just like her laugh and her style and the way she looks when she cries and her voice. "Hi." She leans closer to me, and I bury my face in her neck. She smells like she always does, like smoke and the outdoors—like *Ash*.

I glance down at the ring on her finger. It has her initials on it, almost like it was made for her—almost like fate.

Fate. What a funny word.

"When we get back, we should have another ball," I whisper suddenly. "We should have another one so that I can ask you out properly, and you can say yes and we can go together."

"Why is it that you're implying *you* are the one asking *me?*"

"Because we both know you're a coward," I say simply, and Ash starts to laugh.

But with all the light feelings, there's still one of my words that hangs in the air like a disease.

When. *When* we get back.

If we get back, I want to say instead, but I don't. I keep it like that because I need to keep it like that—I need something to be so set in stone, like the fact that the sky is blue and the month is October, little things like that. I need the *when* instead of the *if,* because I don't know. I don't know if I'm going to survive or not and it scares me. It scares me so bad.

"Where are you?" Ash asks me, and I glance over at her.

"I'm with you."

She looks a little unsure of that but lets it go, turning on her side to talk to me. I do the same.

"When we get back to the camps, I'll most definitely go to a ball with you," she tells me quietly.

I nod, but once again I'm thinking about something else. I'm thinking about the camps, the campers. Are they all right? Have they returned yet to Camp Serenity? Did Anne get my letter?

There's a knock at the door, and I jump to my feet. Ash stares at me curiously but says nothing. I swing the door open, nearly forgetting that Milo's asleep.

Sage is standing in the doorway. In her hand she holds a piece of paper that I recognize as the paper I wrote my letter on. It's perfect timing, but my heart drops. What if whoever got that letter just sent it right back? What if they read it?

Almost as if I'm telling it to, the letter jumps into my hands.

"This just flew in here," Sage says, whispering and stepping into the shed. "Literally."

I turn the paper over and see Anne's looped handwriting, reading the message scrawled on there obviously very quickly, as if she was in a rush when she wrote it. My stomach flips at this thought.

Elysian -

They're starting to invade already. The camps are destroyed. The soldiers are here.

We are headed your way. You mustn't do anything rash until we find you.

- Anne

I stare at the note in shock. *The camps are destroyed. The soldiers are here.*

How can that be? The camps are safe. They're protected by magic that hasn't failed for years.

I feel a bubble of fear rise up in my chest, as well as sadness for the home I've left behind.

"Elysian?" Sage says from behind me. I turn around. Upon seeing my expression, Ash props herself up onto her elbows. "What is it?"

I try to speak, try to tell them that we need to go, that we should've immediately after the attack, but I can't talk. The grief for the camp that I gave my soul to is overwhelming, tightening around my throat like a rope.

Ash stands up and walks toward me. I notice vaguely the fact that she's a few inches taller than me. Her face is lined with concern, and when she grabs my face and glances into my eyes I feel like falling apart. But I don't, because I can't. I simply *can't.*

"Elysian, what happened?"

I can't speak, except for a few words: "We need to go."

I'm sure I look so stupid right now—shaking and sweating over a few sentences. But Ash and Sage don't seem to care. Ash pulls me toward her and tells Sage to wake Milo, and then we're out the door and searching for Ben and Ameer.

My brother is by my side in seconds, a silent but comforting presence. He doesn't pry or ask questions, which I'm thankful for, because I'm sure that if he did I would break down crying.

Ben appears next to us soon, too, and Sage is yelling at him to give Milo as much strength as he can with the spare *soigner* in his bag. Ben nods and brings out the jar of *soigner.* Not wanting to see

Milo's scar again, I stare straight ahead. The wind picks up around us, whistling in my ears.

A question manages to echo in my mind, somehow making itself louder than the jumbled curses and weak plans to rebuild: how am I supposed to be a leader of now-ruined Camp Serenity, of *Buit*, when I fall apart at the first sign of trouble?

But this is different, I remind myself. This is my home.

Is it that different, though? a tiny voice whispers in my mind. *How are you meant to be a leader, meant to be anything, when you fail so easily?*

I wince at the thought. The voice vanishes, and shouts fill my ears instead—shouts that are coming from the others around me as we start to run toward the Veridet castle.

"Are you okay?" Ameer yells over the roaring winds.

"Fine," I say. "What makes you say that?"

He motions to the harsh weather around us, and I wince. I often resent my power because my feelings are constantly on display.

"Did something happen?" Ameer asks.

I shake my head. "Nothing."

He gives me a look that says he doesn't believe me, but he drops the subject and focuses on running away. If the soldiers are coming, if the soldiers have already invaded Camp Serenity, then that means they'll find our location soon enough, and we need to be prepared.

The winds die down eventually, but my thoughts are still swirling around in my head like a tornado. I'm trying to grasp at them, at least one of them, and yet I come up empty handed every time. The recurring thoughts, though, seem to be failure, Camp Serenity, and war.

I take deep, shaky breaths as we soon find ourselves in the middle of a prairie. There's barely any trees for several miles. I glance around and vaguely remember that Veridet is the kingdom of flat land.

"Elysian, what did that note say?" Ash says as soon as she's next to me. She's not pushy, but I can see the desperation in her eyes that tells me she needs to know that I'm okay, that our campers are safe. I'm assuming that if Merrik's soldiers were able to get into Camp Serenity, they were able to get into Camp Havoc, too.

"The soldiers attacked Camp Serenity," I tell her, forcing my voice not to shake. "I wrote to Anne, the supervisor, a couple days ago, saying that she and the back-up needed to be ready in case of an attack. But I wasn't expecting...I mean, I didn't *want...*"

She wraps me into a hug. The others stare at us, stunned. They must not know that we're back together. "Did she say anything about the campers?"

I pull the note out of my pocket and hand it to her silently. Her eyes skim over it, and I see her mouth slowly fall open as she reads.

"Destroyed?" she says quietly. "The camps are destroyed?"

Even though she's whispering, the others still hear her. Sage's face falls, Milo winces like he's in pain, Ameer wipes away tears that have appeared in his eyes, and Ben looks guilty.

"So that means no Camp Serenity, no Camp Havoc?" Sage says.

"I don't know," I say pathetically. "I don't know."

"So Anne's soldiers are heading here to Veridet," Ash says. "Or...did you tell them to head to Veridet in the note you wrote?"

"I don't think so." I glance around, then lower my eyes to the ground. *Gods, this is horrible.* "I told her that we needed them, but I didn't tell them where we were heading."

"They'll figure it out eventually," Sage says, trying her best to sound confident. "When we were fleeing after the ball, we went east. I saw a few campers watching us before they started to run in the opposite direction. Since then, we've stayed east, so I assume it won't be that hard to find us. Plus, Veridet is the home of war, due to all the land for fighting." She motions around at the vast prairie around us.

My shoulders sag in relief. If my campers find us, if Anne and her followers find us, then we could have an advantage in this war.

"They're smart," Ameer adds, "your campers. They'll find you. You're their leader."

I tense at what he says. The word *leader* is not one that I want to hear right now, but he doesn't know that. He can't know that.

Ash lets out a groan from next to me. She runs her hand through her hair, and somehow a burst of fire flies through the air before hitting the prairie land. It starts to blaze through the grass toward us, and her eyes widen.

Ameer turns around and squints at the spot she fired at. Almost instantly, the fire stops, coated with a layer of ice that melts immediately after.

"Did you…mean to do that?" I ask him cautiously.

He looks confused, like he's not sure what just happened. "I…think so?" he says, and it sounds like a question.

I shake my head, and Ash mumbles an apology for almost getting us all killed.

"What do we do now?" Ben asks.

"We…" Sage pauses, thinking about it. "We look for another place to stay until either our soldiers catch up to us or Merrik's do."

It doesn't seem like a good plan, but it's the best we have, so we all nod collectively and set off for another tavern to stay at, maybe a house with a generous host.

An hour later, we've had no such luck. My feet are killing me, and the sun, even though the temperature is near freezing, is blaring on our backs. Eventually, we find a mostly clear patch of land that doesn't seem like it belongs to a farmer or someone—or something— else, and we sit down.

Ash is on my right and Ameer is on my left. I grab my brother's hand and Ash places hers on my knee, as if to reassure me that she's there.

It's meant to cheer me up, but at this point, I don't think *anything* can cheer me up.

"We have to have a plan, don't we?" Ameer wonders aloud. "I mean, we can't just walk into this blindly, can we?"

I look over at him. "Oh, yeah, because we totally had a plan when we were trying to save you," I say sarcastically.

His eyes widen, his eyebrows shooting up to his hairline. "You *didn't?* And you still tried to save me anyway?"

"Ash was the only one who remembered she even met you at one point," I tell him. "And we had a deadline. Ten days doesn't exactly provide any time to sit down and brainstorm."

He shrugs and nods.

"We'll just have to go along with what Merrik throws at us," Sage says.

Ben, who is applying more *soigner* to the scar on Milo's chest, grins from where he sits. "Sounds great."

"It *sounds* like we're going to die," Ameer says. "And, honestly, I'm not that big a fan of dying."

Sage sighs and rolls her eyes. "Trust us, Ameer. You trust us, don't you?"

His eyes close, and I let out a strangled, exhausted laugh as I realize he has to think about it. I don't blame him. I mean, the only ones that he's really familiar with are me and Ash—that's it. He has no family besides me, no friends besides Ash.

I reach out and grab his hand. He squeezes back almost immediately, but he opens his eyes slowly and reluctantly replies, "Sure."

"Then you should trust that we'll destroy Merrik and win this war." She speaks with determination and a hint of anger, as if she's appalled that Ameer doesn't believe we'll make it out alive. I want to remind her that we just barely got by the last quest we went on, but I don't.

As the sun hits the middle of the sky, I glance up and suddenly remember something.

"Today," I say aloud. "Today is the twenty-first."

Sage turns even paler. Ben straightens and Ash clears her throat and looks away.

"I'm going to go..." Ben pauses, thinking about his words, "...set up."

"Okay," Sage says quietly. And I realize when I catch her eye that she's known the entire time that it was the twenty-first, but she hasn't said anything, and that makes it so much worse.

"I'll go help him," Ameer says, clearing his throat and standing from his spot next to me.

"Me, too," Ash adds, and she follows after him in the direction Ben left.

Milo's asleep, his face turned toward the sky. I stand and walk over to him, sitting down beside him. I twist my fingers in his hair and smile at him. He's the sweetest person I know. He saved Ash when she was younger. He's one of my best friends.

"Sage," I direct my attention to her, quietly, as to not disturb Milo. "I know you know."

This is all I have to say before the tears start running down her face. She's silent when she cries, and she angrily swipes away the streams of tears. "I hate this, all of it. Why'd he have to die, Elysian? Everything was going so great, and then he died. And he's never coming back."

I don't say anything. I'm not sure I have the strength for it. Sorin was one of my best friends, too. He was my family.

She looks away from me.

"Everything happens for a reason," I tell her finally. "If Sorin hadn't died, do you really think you would've continued on that quest? It was his memory, his final wish that caused you to save Ameer. You did because it was what he wanted."

She closes her eyes and tenses her jaw.

"If Sorin didn't die, we wouldn't have made relationships with those we love," I say. "If he didn't die, I probably would've never fallen for Ash. Our camps would still be rivals. His death, though sad, brought us together, in one way or another."

She lets out a breath and opens her eyes, turning her gaze back to me. "Gods, I hate it when you're right."

I laugh for a second, then return to being solemn. "Sage, I'm going with you—"

"I can't ask you to come, Lys."

"You're not asking me. I'm going," I say. "He was my best friend, too, you know." I watch as she considers it as if she has any influence in this.

There's a shout that sounds like "We're ready!" from somewhere to my right, and I stand, gently waking Milo. I know he'd want to be up for this.

"Let's go," Sage says, and then we walk, all three of us, toward the funeral grounds.

CHAPTER 28

SAGE

Everyone is expecting me to be sad when I see where they stand, in front of a patch of land that has been marked as Sorin's gravesite with a stick. I can tell they think this because of the careful way they look at me, like I'll break if they give me the wrong look. I hate it so much.

I'm not fragile, not weak. I'm angry. Angry at the guard who shot him, angry at everyone for acting like I'm something that can shatter at the first mention of him. I'm angry at the king for causing us to go and find Ameer in the first place and angry at myself for resenting him for so long, for not spending the time I had with him wisely enough. I'm just *angry*.

Ben tries to hold my hand, but I keep my arms held firmly at my sides until he decides that there's no use in trying and lets his hand fall.

No one says anything. It's silent. The birds that haven't migrated yet have even decided to stop chirping from overhead.

I review the memories that I have with Sorin in my mind: saving him from being shot, telling him I wouldn't bring him somewhere that would help him if I had the option, arguing with him over his mom and then hugging him, arguing with him after Ash got kidnapped, kissing him by the edge of that cliff, telling him I'd fallen in love with him in that forest, that night at the campfire. Most of them are good, but some of them I wouldn't wish on my worst enemy.

I remember that portrait I have hanging in my cabin of him and me in December when we were around fourteen, standing in the snow and smiling. I never really understood why he still had it whenever I went in there and saw it for the first time after he died, but now I do. He'd been in love with me since we were children, and I was too stupid and young to notice.

I wish I had noticed sooner. Then, maybe, by some miraculous turn of events, I could've convinced him not to come along on our quest.

I feel the anger in my chest turn boiling. It's struggling against my heart, trying to force itself out. I don't let it though. I don't let it until people start to walk away and I'm left alone. Once I'm sure everyone is gone, I shout and stomp around the stick. I hate him so much for leaving me. I'm the angriest at *him*, because he shouldn't have gone without a warning. And I know I'm being irrational, but I don't care. I don't care. I'm angry, so angry, being consumed by anger, and I haven't realized it until right now. I shout until my throat hurts and then I realize I'm crying. I notice the tears running down my cheeks and I drop to my knees and put my face in my hands. I feel arms around my shoulders and I wonder for a second, a thrilling second, if this is Sorin's ghost come to comfort me, and then I recognize that smell of vanilla, meaning it's not Sorin, but for some odd reason I'm not too disappointed.

"Shh," he whispers into my ear, and it sends a shiver down my spine. "It's okay, Sage, it's okay. I'm so sorry."

I'm saying his name, saying his name frantically like it's the only thing keeping me holding on. *Ben*, I'm saying, over and over and over again because that's what is keeping me here with him—that's what's keeping me from passing out right here.

He's holding me and his arms are strong and solid. His skin is still warm despite the cold, and I let him hold me and I let him comfort me until I can finally pull myself together.

And then I kiss him.

I kiss Ben. I kiss him like we're the last two people on planet Earth; I kiss him like he's oxygen and I desperately need a breath of air. I kiss him and he's caught off guard, still reeling when I bring my hands up to grasp his neck and pull him closer to me. I know I'm not in my right mind and that when I come back to my senses he may hate me. I know that and I kiss him anyway.

My mouth is hard on his, but he still touches me gently, which makes me even angrier. Doesn't he understand that I'm not going to break?

"Sage," he gasps out. "I know you're upset, but—"

I cut him off. "Please, Ben," I say.

Instead of doing what I want, he pushes me away from him and stands up. "Sage, you're upset and angry. Trust me, you don't want to do this."

I'm breathing heavily. *"Stop doing this."*

He stares at me like I've gone crazy, and I probably have. I know what I've done is wrong, and I still want to do it anyway. "Doing what?"

"Leading me on." I stand and wipe my mouth angrily. "You kiss me and then run away. I kiss you and you tell me I don't want this when you have no *idea* what I want. And you should stop treating me like I'm going to break every single time you touch me. I'm *fine!*"

He stares at me for a second and then tilts his head. "Are you drunk?"

"Gods, no!" I yell. "I'm trying to talk to you and tell you how I feel and you're disregarding it, asking me if I'm *drunk—*" I stop myself before I can continue and glare at him with blazing eyes. "Go."

"What?"

"Go. Leave me alone."

He looks upset about it, but Ben turns on his heel and starts to walk away from me.

And then I do what I said I wouldn't.

I watch him leaving, remembering the feel of his lips against mine, and then I break.

* * *

By the time I gather enough strength to walk over to where the others sit, the sun has begun to set. My skin is bright red, but I don't care. I may not look put together, but I've already had a total meltdown in front of Ben, so it doesn't really matter.

"Sage, where were you?" Elysian asks me quietly. I send her a look that says not to talk about it, and then my eyes dart over to Ben. She nods like she understands.

Ben looks unbothered by the earlier events. He tends to Milo's wound, speaking with him animatedly. He looks perfectly fine. I wish I could say the same about me, but I know that I look like a deranged mess.

He turns his head for a millisecond and catches sight of me. Ben pales slightly and turns back to Milo, but now he seems distracted.

I glance at the floor before sitting down next to Ameer. He looks from me to Ben and raises an eyebrow, like he knows about what happened. After all, if Ben heard my meltdown, then why wouldn't he have heard it, too?

"Have you gotten any other letters from Anne, Elysian?" I ask her.

Elysian's shoulders sag. "Nothing," she tells me solemnly. "Just that letter about the soldiers invading the camps."

I twist my face into a sour expression. That one letter about the soldiers was horrifying, and after it I've been really hoping for some good news.

"We need to wait until the others get here, then?"

"Hey, I thought we were just going to 'wing it,'" Ameer says.

"Yeah, but I've changed my mind," I say, harsher than I mean to, because he flinches away from me.

Something spoils inside me when I see the look Elysian is giving me.

"Sorry," I say quietly, but I'm not sure he hears me.

I'm exhausted, and Elysian must sense it, because her eyebrows start to soften and she touches Ameer's forearm reassuringly, as if to let him know that I didn't mean it. I'm grateful for it. I've never been the best with people.

"So we wait until the others get here, and then we find Merrik and demand that he fight us," Milo says.

I glance unconsciously at Elysian when I remember that her choice must be made in only three days, that she must decide if she wants to delay the war or stand with us.

I know what she will pick, but it's still nerve-wracking. It means the war is coming a lot sooner than we'd anticipated.

"What if they don't get here in time?" Ameer asks quietly, timid due to my outburst.

"We have to trust that they will," Elysian says. "If they don't get here before the 24th, then we must make some…drastic decisions. But they will, so long as we believe it. There's nothing to worry about." She says this last part mostly to Ameer, but it reassures me anyway, because I can't detect anything that proves she doesn't believe what she's saying.

But there's something she says that catches my attention.

"If they don't get here before the twenty-fourth, then we must make some…drastic decisions," she said, and then brushed it off like it was nothing. Could that mean she's considering betraying us if things get bad, like Selena did?

I push the thought away. Elysian would never do that. She'd never even consider it.

Never.

"Exactly," I confirm, but there's a voice in my mind that tells me I'm mostly reassuring myself and not the others. "Plus, doesn't Anne own a whole bunch of different wagons and things like that?"

Elysian nods. "And horses. They'll get here in time. There's no point in worrying."

Ben has apparently applied the right amount of *soigner*, because he leans back on his palms and does his absolute best to avoid eye contact with me.

I keep trying to catch his eye as he surveys the group, but he doesn't look at me—doesn't even look in my direction. I guess I can't expect him to, but I'm so confused. When he kissed me, didn't he realize that it would change everything?

I continue to stare at him until I know that he senses my gaze. I want him to look at me. I need him to look at me. I need to apologize, admit something, anything. I just need him to look at me.

And then finally he turns his head. He makes eye contact, even, but his eyes are empty and unreadable. Ben doesn't say anything, but just a few seconds of me staring straight at him is enough for me to turn away.

I wonder what's happened to him. He always has that glint in his eyes—even when he's angry at me.

I'm suddenly exhausted, so I decide to take a long name. I lean so I'm resting on my back, face toward the sky, and I close my eyes.

Quicker than I expected, before I even get a chance to overthink, sleep overwhelms me and I'm caught in a world between fiction and reality, between my heart's deepest desires and the infinitely disappointing truth.

* * *

I wake up in the dead of the night, unsurprisingly, but I wake up because someone is frantically shaking me awake, whispering my name over and over again, which is more surprising.

The person shaking me awake is Ameer, and he looks as pale as a sheet.

I shoot up into a sitting position as soon as I see his face, fearing that something has happened to Elysian.

Ameer's expression turns serious, like he knows exactly what I'm thinking.

I stand, bracing my hand around my dagger. "Has something happened to one of the others?" I whisper urgently, glancing around to take a headcount. And it's exactly as I feared—Elysian's gone.

"I—I woke up and she was just—just *gone*," Ameer tells me. "I don't know what happened to her, and I haven't tried to look for her yet—"

"Okay," I say slowly, processing and making a plan. I start to walk to the left of the group, so that we don't wake the others. Ameer trails after me. "The first thing we have to do is try to find her. She could be anywhere."

"Do you think wolves got to her or—or something else?" Ameer asks me anxiously.

"Wolves normally like to spend their time in heavily covered areas, meaning they wouldn't be in a space as open as this," I say, reciting facts to reassure myself. "That's usually true for all predators, so I don't think an animal took her."

He looks relieved, but his hands are still shaking, though not as violently. "Okay, good."

"If we find nothing—and I'm not saying we will—then we report next to the others and get them to help us. We won't give up until we've found her, right?"

He nods. "But…you're saying we should split up?"

"Yes, that's what I'm saying. It would make everything go faster, and we would have more of a chance at finding her.…" I trail off as I notice the way he's looking at me, like a wounded dog. "Or we could go together."

He looks notably more cheerful after I say this, and when I start off across the plains, Ameer follows after me.

We walk together for a while, until I finally see a trail of blood, and Elysian, passed out just a few hundred feet away.

I start to run toward her and crouch down once I'm close enough. There's a gash on the left side of her face from her temple to her jaw. The blood around it is still wet, an indication that the incident happened not too long ago. She has her hand in a fist, wrapped around the hilt of her dagger, so I begin to loosen her grip. I notice that the blade of the dagger has a note attached to it.

The Magic Crew, it says in messy handwriting.

I hear you've encouraged more people to join our party. I thought this event would be invitation only, but that's okay. If you insist on breaking the rules, then I suppose I can, too.

With love,

M

I stare at the note for a second in shock. How did he know where we were? And if he wanted to get a message to us, he didn't have to attack Elysian.

I swallow a lump that has formed in my throat.

If you insist on breaking the rules, then I suppose I can, too.

Something tells me that is most definitely a threat.

"We have to get her back to the others," Ameer says, and I nod, but I can't fully process his words. All that I can think of, all that I can process right now is the fact that Merrik hurt Elysian *while she was armed.* That means none of us are safe.

That means Merrik can attack any of us and there will be nothing we can do about it.

I remember the blood dripping down her face, and with my dagger I slice off the hem of my shirt and wound it together, making it thicker. Then I stick it against her face to stop the blood flow. "Tell them where we are, Ameer," I order sharply. "We're a quarter mile east of them. Tell them that."

He nods quickly and rushes off in the direction we came. I curse repeatedly under my breath, trying my best to stop the cut from bleeding. While I search for any other wounds and wait for Ameer to get back, my mind wanders to Ben, and if our relationship will be the same now that we've fought. Of course, we've fought before, but everything is different now.

Everything.

I shake my head, trying to be rid of those thoughts, but the memories of his lips against mine and the way every interaction doesn't seem like nearly enough keep resurfacing, to the point of my annoyance. What is it about this boy that makes me think about him all the time? Sorin's funeral was just a few hours ago, for the gods' sakes.

He looks almost exactly like him, if it weren't for his deep brown eyes.

Those brown eyes are the bane of my existence.

I could drown myself in them, and the gods know I would. But I *cannot* be thinking about that right now, not with my best friend bleeding below me.

My thoughts are scattered. I'm frantically reaching out for something rational to think about and coming back empty-handed.

What should I do to make her warmer? is a thought that passes through my mind. *Where's her sweatshirt?* is another one.

Wincing at the mere thought of the cold, I tug my shirt over my head and lift her limp arms to put it on her. Even in her unconscious state, she seems to be shivering.

I have to say, now that I'm just in a tank top, I agree with her.

There are suddenly footsteps pounding on the ground, muddy from the melted snow. I whip around and see Ameer with Ben, and I feel the color being immediately sucked out of my face.

Ameer raises his eyebrows for a second and then quickly looks away. Ben doesn't seem to notice.

"What happened to her?" he asks, his voice taking on that serious tone he gets when he's acting like a doctor.

"Why are you here?" I say, desperately trying to hide the giddiness from my voice.

"I was the only one awake when Ameer came to get someone," Ben tells me quickly. He finally seems to notice that my shirt is off and he blushes profusely, pulling my shirt off of Elysian and handing it back to me. "Put your shirt on, Sage."

It reminds me vividly of the day of our first kiss. I resist a smile at the memory and grudgingly do as he says.

I watch as Ben places careful fingers on Elysian's face in the exact spot that I've kept the cloth. At the sight of the hem of my shirt, Ben tenses a bit but then relaxes when he realizes he has a job to do. I stare at his calloused hands as one comes up to cup the side of her face and the other is used to heal her. He's murmuring words under his breath, though I don't remember Milo ever doing anything like that before.

Finally, he removes his hand from Elysian's face and leans back, looking relieved. I watch in wonder as the wound on the side of her face closes magically.

"We better get her back," Ben says softly. He's not looking at her, though, I realize when I look up finally. For the third time in these past twenty-four hours, he's staring at *me*.

"Take her back, Ameer," I tell him, keeping my eyes trained on Ben's. "We'll catch up with you later."

He glances between us, uncovering his eyes. He looks relieved now that I have my shirt on, and he obliges quickly, picking up his sister almost effortlessly and carrying her back in the direction of our makeshift camp.

"What was that?" Ben says quietly, but I can tell he wants to raise his voice.

"What was what?" I ask him, honestly confused.

"I come over here and Elysian's unconscious and you're only wearing your—" He stops himself, blushing again. "I was surprised and confused, and I got no more than five words from you."

"Well, what did you expect?" I retort. "My best friend was freezing and losing blood—I had to help her somehow, I had to do *something*. She was shivering, and it was the first thing I thought of. I was waiting for you and then—my gods—I start *thinking* about you like you don't already confuse me enough, and—" I give him a withering stare after cutting myself off, but he doesn't back down or look affected at all. He's staring at me, his mouth open slightly.

Finally, he says, "You thought about me?"

It's a question, but it comes out like a statement. I drop my voice from a shout to a whisper so that I'm matching his tone. "I thought about you," I say.

"Why?"

"That's exactly what I'm trying to figure out."

He shakes his head, like he doesn't believe me. "Please, Sage, believe me, I wanted to kiss you earlier today, but I figured you didn't deserve being so confused after all of this—" He breaks off and closes his eyes tightly, as if he's in pain.

"Ben, please, don't do this," I whisper. "Don't do this now."

"If I don't tell you now, I never will," he gasps out. "Sage, I—"

I pull him toward me and kiss him. It's not impatient like it was earlier—it's slow and soft and like we have all the time in the world. He responds almost instantly, and he's kissing me back, elation filling my heart. When we break apart, the tension is gone from his face.

"You were saying?" I ask quietly, surprised to see that he has a strange expression forming on his face.

It seems like our roles have been swapped, because then he says, "Go."

And though my heart is screaming at me not to, my legs start moving and then I'm running away from him without looking back.

CHAPTER 29

MILO

I'm running my fingers over the scar on my chest when the pounding of footsteps on the plain makes me fully wake up.

I sit up and groan as pain ripples through me. My joints are still incredibly sore, and I guess that's to be expected after I saved myself from death, but I hate that I can't do things as swiftly as I used to. I wonder if this was what Sage felt like when she got shot.

Where *is* Sage, speaking of?

"Milo," Ameer says as he comes into view. He's holding Elysian, I realize, and my heart drops into my stomach.

"Is she injured?" I ask him anxiously, propping myself onto my elbows.

"She was," Ameer tells me. "Ben got there just in time, though, and helped her. There was a huge gash on the side of her face, and he used some of that healing magic that you guys do—"

"Ben?" I say, sounding more arrogant than I expect to. "Why didn't you wake me instead?"

He looks taken aback. I guess he wasn't expecting me to get angry. "I figured you needed as much as rest as you could get, but it doesn't matter, does it? She's okay now—she's healed."

"She should've been healed by me," I say indignantly.

"Why is that?"

"Because *I'm* her friend. She doesn't even know who Ben is. What if he were to hurt her even more?"

"Then I would've gotten *you*, Milo." He sets Elysian down on the ground gently and then jumps back up to continue our conversation. "But I didn't really think that you would be in the right condition to heal anyone. I mean, you should barely be able to heal yourself. So, really, what good would you have done?"

That stings, even though I know he's right. I'm stuttering wildly now, trying to reach into my mind for an explanation for this protectiveness that I'm suddenly feeling. "I—"

Sage comes running back, her cheeks flaming, her hair flying behind her. "She's okay," she tells me as soon as she sees me.

"I know, but I still don't understand what happened," I say, wanting desperately to change the subject.

Sage takes the bait and launches into her story. "Ameer woke me up and we walked to the prairie where Elysian was. She was bleeding, so I cut off the hem of my shirt to stop it. Ameer went and got Ben. When they got back, Ben healed her gash, and then Ameer carried her back here and…here we are."

I nod, but I notice that when she says Ben's name it's as if it leaves a bitter taste in her mouth. I'm about to ask why they didn't come and get me instead of Ben again, but I refrain when I see Ash waking. I know that if she wakes up and learns something's happened to Elysian, she'll set something on fire. I crawl over to her and pull her head into my lap, starting to run my fingers through her hair. It's something that always put her to sleep when we were kids, and it seems like it still works when she grunts and begins to snore. To make sure that she doesn't wake again and also out of habit, I continue the movements.

"Where's Ben, though?" I ask, my eyebrows creasing.

"He...he asked me to leave, and so I left. I have no idea where he is now," Sage says.

"You left him alone in a place where we have no idea where we are?" Ameer asks slowly, like he can't believe it.

Sage crosses her arms over her chest defiantly. "I made it back here okay. I don't see why *he* can't, too."

"He's not like you, Sage," I say quietly, so as not to wake Ash. She pales slightly, but then busies herself with the now-frayed end of her shirt.

"He has an incredible sense of direction. Plus, *he* told *me* to leave. Trust me, if it had gone my way—" She breaks off suddenly, like she's said something she wasn't supposed to.

Instead of asking anything, Ameer and I ignore her outburst. He leans down and sits next to his sister.

"Should we risk getting sleep?" I ask.

Ameer shrugs. "It doesn't seem like a bad idea, but who knows what could happen while we sleep?" He suddenly seems to remember who he's talking to, because he startles and then says, "But you should sleep, since you need the rest."

"We all need the rest," Sage says, finally snapping out of her thoughts. "I'm wide awake, though, so it doesn't matter. You all should go to bed, and I'll watch and make sure that there are no other attacks." Her hand hovers to her side, where she's keeping her dagger.

"Sage, please," I say, "it's okay. You need to sleep."

She sighs and glances up at the starry sky.

I do the same. A voice whispers in my mind with a few different constellations: *Andromeda, Taurus, Sirius, Scorpius.* I recognize the voice after a second as Selena's, listing the constellations to me whenever we went after Ash, Elysian, Sage, and Sorin in August. I never really wondered how she stayed awake even in the dead of night, but she was a master at making me fall asleep. She had this smooth, silky voice that she would use, and I would be a goner, in more ways than one.

"The stars are pretty," Ameer says, and I smile. It's weird to think that, when we get back to Buit, Ameer will be the king.

"Yes, Ameer," Sage says, almost wistfully. "The stars are very pretty."

My smile grows at the way Sage just plays along, but there is still the weight of Elysian being injured and Ben out somewhere by himself looming in the back of my mind.

Sleep sounds nice.

* * *

The next time I wake up, I'm in considerably less pain. Ash is still below me, but she's awake, staring up at the morning sky. Ameer is asleep, and Sage looks half-dead where she stands, keeping guard. I feel more rested than I ever have, and I push away memories of my dream—thoughts of Selena and the nights that I would hold her hand, the first kiss we had before she was taken by Merrik.

"Good morning," Ash says quietly, so as not to wake the others. I notice that her voice is hoarse, her face tear-stained. That must mean Sage told her about Elysian.

As if she knows what I'm thinking, Ash's eyes trail to Elysian, unconscious on the ground. There's a scar the length of her head on the left side of her face, where she was cut by Merrik.

"Morning," I murmur sleepily. I'm sitting up now, so Ash has to look up at me through her eyelashes.

"Merrik got to her," she tells me softly. "He slashed that gash into her face. Ben healed her, but now she has a scar."

I can't think of anything comforting to say, so instead I respond, "Yeah."

352

"You already knew," Ash accuses. "Why didn't you wake me?"

"You needed all the rest you could get," I say. "Plus, if you had woken up and discovered that Elysian was seriously injured, you would've burned something. Am I right?"

She pauses, as if she actually has to think about it. Eventually, she says, "I would've burned the world down if I learned Elysian was in trouble."

"And that would've been very inconvenient for us, don't you think?"

She smiles slightly.

"Sage," I call out, though softly, so that Ameer and Elysian can sleep. "Go to sleep. It's okay. I'll wake you if I notice anything."

She sends a grateful look my way and collapses, falling asleep instantly.

"That was nice of you," Ash tells me.

"I'm generally considered a nice person." I shift uncomfortably. "Plus, I figured someone else should get to sleep. I've been doing enough of it recently."

"If you're blaming yourself for getting stabbed, then you're an idiot," Ash says, though she sounds very tired. "It was Merrik's fault, not yours."

"I know that," I say quietly.

"Gods, I wish I had my cigarettes right now," she says, letting her eyes fall closed.

"You don't have them?"

"I lost them back at that tavern when Sage asked for one—" She cuts herself off and looks suddenly guilty, which is unusual. Ash normally never says anything she doesn't mean to.

"Sage smoked?" My eyebrows meet. "When?"

"After…after Ben kissed her." Ash winces.

My eyes widen. "Ben *kissed* her? Why am I so in the dark about all of this?"

"Probably because people don't trust you enough."

I glance at her, offended. "I'll have you know that Elysian came to me back in August and asked about 'friendship' with you. She seemed really worried, too, which shows that she trusted me."

Ash grabs my hand and laces our fingers together. "I was kidding, Milo."

"Oh. Well. Obviously."

One corner of her mouth tilts up in a partial smile. "I love you. You know that, right?"

I smile gently at her. "Of course I know that."

"Okay," she says quietly. "I just wanted to make sure."

"Ash, of course I know you love me. And I love you."

"Good." She leans against me, and I wrap my arms around her, cherishing this moment for its tranquility. I'm thankful for it, because I know that nothing will probably ever be this peaceful again.

* * *

I'm breathing heavily, running through the grasslands of Veridet. Birds screech overhead. I look back and forth, feeling my heart beat a million times a minute in my chest.

I've stopped running by now, but my breaths are still coming out short and choppy. I'm surprised to find that there is no pain in my chest or any of my joints. I look down as if to check that my scar is still there, when I notice that I'm wearing clothes spotted with blood—a white button-up, stained red, and black dress pants obviously darker in some places.

I wonder if it's my blood, but I can't think about that for long, because a bird flies down and cuts my shoulder with its sharp beak.

I look back at the bird. *Apparently the blood* is *mine.*

More birds start to shower around me, picking at me with their beaks and talons. I try to run farther away from them, but they continue to peck me until there are several bleeding wounds on my body—too many to count.

I'm about to cry out, but then the birds all squawk collectively, almost rupturing my ear drums, and they fly away from me.

I look down at the cuts I have, which are rapidly closing. "How—" I start, but then someone cuts me off.

"Milo," she breathes, and I stop dead.

"Selena?"

I glance back up, and there she stands. Her dark hair is loose, framing her face. It's longer now—past her shoulders. Her skin is pale but her gray eyes are vibrant and she looks happier than I've ever seen her. She's wearing jeans and a gray sweater that matches her eyes.

At the sight of her, I want to collapse. But then anger overwhelms those feelings and destroys them.

"What are you doing here?" I ask her, my voice dangerously quiet.

"Well, considering the fact that *here* is your dream, I suppose I don't exactly know what I'm doing," she says conversationally, like her being in my dream is something that happens often. "Do you dream about me, Milo?"

"Selena." I stare at her. There's no way she can be talking to me like everything's fine when she abandoned me. "I have no desire to talk to you."

She looks hurt at that, but that vulnerable look is quickly replaced by a look of charm and confidence—the look she had on when I met her the first time. "You're saying that like I *asked* to be here. I don't know why I'm here. All I know is that I showed up here whenever you fell asleep."

"But *why?*" I say, looking up at the sky. I try to look through the clouds at the gods, but I know that's impossible.

"The gods must be just playing a joke on us," Selena says dryly.

I snort. "Clearly."

"Milo—" she starts, trying to step toward me, but I take a step back.

"Don't touch me," I tell her fiercely. "Don't you think you've done enough harm already?"

She looks like I've slapped her. "I didn't mean to," she tells me quietly. "He manipulated me. He told me I could forget, but I can't forget you."

"Really?" I say. "Because it's been pretty easy for me."

"The battle is getting closer and closer," she says suddenly. "In a few days, you and I will be facing each other on opposite sides. Doesn't that scare you?"

"Why would it?"

"I guess I should stop asking at this point." She looks dismayed by my responses, but I don't care. "It's obvious that you don't care about me at all. But trust me, Milo Belittle, I miss you more than you know. I regret my choice, and I am dreading the day that we must fight."

I stare at her, wanting to tell her something, wanting to have the last word, but I can't. I have nothing to say.

So I clench my jaw and stare at her until her eyes dim. "Goodbye, Milo," she tells me softly, and then she's gone.

And I'm awake.

Ash is in my face, standing over me, and she looks incredibly concerned.

"Milo, are you okay?" she says to me. "You were talking in your sleep. Something about Selena."

Goosebumps rise along my arms. Ash seems to notice.

"If something's going on, I should know about it," she says quietly, dropping her voice. "I could help you. I'm your best friend. I *should* be able to help you."

I stare at her, my expression turning grim. I feel thankful for her endless support, but also guilty, because I can't tell her about my dream.

"I don't think this is something you can help me with, Ash," I say, watching her face fall. "It's a matter of my life or hers."

CHAPTER 30

SAGE

Ben finally shows up again a day later with a bag of food that most likely he's collected from a farmer somewhere. Everyone starts to dig in, Ash taking the biggest portion, but I focus on Ben and the horrible way he looks rather than the food. His eyes are tired, his hair and clothes muddy, and he looks like he's been to hell and back. I don't say anything to him because I can't. Because if I say something then this cycle will start again and I'll be ripped to shreds *again.*

As the days begin to go faster, the sun rising and falling quicker than usual at the new arrival of winter, I can't help but look at Elysian. She's jittery, obviously noting how much time we're losing with the time changes.

It's early on the twenty-third when Ben comes to me and tells me that he's sorry.

I glance up at him with a bewildered expression, wondering if I heard him right. "What did you say?"

He looks frustrated with me, his jaw clenched and face turning red slowly. "I said...that I was sorry."

I blink at him. "You're sorry?"

"Are you really going to make me say it again?"

"No, sorry," I say. "But…you're meaning to tell me that *you*, one of the most stubborn people I have ever met, are apologizing without any kind of a bribe?" I raise an eyebrow at him, and he grunts.

Then he nods, slowly, and I feel a laugh bubble out of me.

"Well?"

"Well, what?"

"Are you going to accept my apology or not, Jobbs?" he asks.

His use of my last name strikes me as odd for a second, as I don't think I've ever told him what it is, but it doesn't matter. It was probably mentioned by another one of my friends in another conversation. "Fine, Abott," I say. "I accept your apology." Quietly, I add, "And I'm sorry, too, for being so crappy."

He nods, smiling. "I accept your apology," Ben responds.

"I guess we're even, then," I say, grinning. Ben lets out a laugh and runs his tongue along his bottom row of teeth.

"Even?" he says. "No, I think you're worse than me."

"You *think*," I point out, but he won't let it go. He's teasing me, but there's a way he pushes that makes my stomach twist in a weird way.

"I know we're past this, but I'm not the one who kissed you when I was sobbing, am I?" He keeps his eyebrow raised as he talks, and it makes him look…unattractive, like he's sneering at me.

"Sure you're not," I say, and my argumentative instinct kicks in. "But am I the one who kissed you on top of a mountain and then ran away? Am I the one who pushed you away after that, telling you what you wanted? Am I the one who initiated this pointless argument in the first place?"

He stares at me for a second, and it's like something dies within him, because his shoulders sag and his face loses that sneer. "I guess we *are* even, then." He says it lightly, like he's trying to lighten the mood.

As he's leaving, I reach out and grab his arm. He stops instantly, glancing back at me, the anger gone from his stance but the tension definitely still there. "Ben," I say, whispering it almost. I stand, still holding onto his arm, and I trace his cheekbone gently with my thumb, as if he'll break. A little voice reminds me how ironic this is, but I don't listen to it. I don't care enough to.

"Ben, what is it?" I ask him. He seems wound up tight enough to cut through metal.

He glances over at me, but he is lost in another world—the images of somewhere so far away that I couldn't reach it even if I tried are echoing in his eyes.

"Tell me what happened to you, and I can help," I say softly, but at this Ben flinches, as if I've hit him.

"Don't say that," he gasps out, and I drop my hand so it's at my side. "Don't say that," he repeats, and his voice is ragged and it's almost like he's desperate, like he needs me to know that I can't say anything close to that again.

"Don't say *what?*"

"Don't say you can help me." Ben looks sad now. He forces his gaze to the ground as he speaks to me. "Don't say it's that easy."

My eyebrows meet, and I find myself shaking my head. "It isn't?"

He shakes his head and lets out a puff of air. "You're not that stupid, Sage. You know that—"

But I never get to find out what I know, because an arrow lands right in the gap between us. I glance down at it and it's like the gears finally turn in my head—I'm looking around frantically, pulling my dagger from its sheath and bracing it and myself for battle.

Ben yanks the arrow from the ground. "Sage, what day is it?"

"It's the twenty-third," I say. "But if it's Merrik's army that just started attacking, it's not supposed to be. We were supposed to have another day—"

"One thing you'll learn about Merrik," he tells me, his mouth forming a hard line as his reflexes kick in, "is that he does what he wants when he wants to do it."

He's bounding toward the others and I'm following him. Our friends are already standing and armed, looking around for where the arrow came from. My cheeks start to flame at the thought of them seeing the arrow, meaning they saw parts of our conversation.

"Where'd that come from?" Ash asks, and I feel even more embarrassed. Ash doesn't particularly care about feelings other than Elysian's, but it's embarrassing to think about the teasing that will ensue when we get out of here.

If we get out of here.

"It came from that way." Ben points at the horizon, and I nod in confirmation.

But I suppose we don't really need to point that out, because the sound of thundering footsteps rises from the air. Dust starts to form into clouds, and I squint so that I can still see through it.

I see Elysian out of my peripheral vision, and she's biting her nails nervously. I know she thinks this whole thing is her fault, but she never could have anticipated that Merrik and his army would come early.

And then I remember: Anne and our other alliances aren't here yet. I don't think they're even *close*.

Oh, gods.

"How are we supposed to fend off an entire army when we don't even have reinforcements?" Ameer says, voicing my thoughts.

Ben pales at this, but then he swallows. "We're going to have to hold our ground. Remember, if we're not scared of Merrik, then he has no *real* power."

"He's an entity," Ash says glumly, looking over at the dust that's becoming thicker as his army nears us. "He always has real power."

Ben clenches his jaw but doesn't say anything. The army gets even closer. I raise a finger and a vine grows next to me. A bubble of anxiety eases within me, because if nothing else, at least my powers have stayed consistent.

I adjust the grip around my dagger, reviewing all the ways that I can kill someone with just my dagger. I tell myself that I'll be fine—this is what I've been training all my life for, after all. For battle, for war, for the chance to prove myself to my long-deceased mother, even though I know there is not even the smallest chance that she's watching me right now. For my chance to prove myself to everyone.

Merrik's army is still coming toward us, and I can see the cruel face of the boy with blonde hair and blue eyes in the ballroom. The minute I notice him, his words come rushing back to me—*"I have done some things to your little...group—camp—whatever you call it. Not things you'd approve of."*

My mouth falls open. How did I not notice sooner?

But then there's someone in front of me, slashing out in a wide arc with their sword. I duck just as their blade comes hurtling toward me, and they come close enough to give me a haircut.

I dodge their blows and try to hit them with some of my own, but each time I 'pierce' the skin my dagger comes back bloodless. It seems as though the ghosts are impossible to wound and defeat. They're getting stronger from our attempts as we get weaker.

I glance around for any sign of the blonde hair that Merrik has taken on as a disguise, but there's nothing. I'm distracted from my search, so the ghost's sword grazes my forehead, leaving a cut that stings instantly. I'm about to try my best to hit it back, but then the ghost vanishes, falling back, and I look around to see if I'm the only one that this is happening to.

Time has slowed, and I see my friends fighting each of their own ghosts. Elysian is slashing at the ghost's translucent feet to distract it, and she disarms it with the flat of her blade. Ash is a naturally great sword fighter, and she has muscles. As she meets the ghost's strike with one of her own, the ghost drops its sword, as if the contact between the two metals has burned it. Ameer is using his ice to freeze the ghost's blade, which startles the ghost enough to drop its weapon. Ameer looks victorious before another ghost replaces the one that he just beat. Ben is struggling, but finally decides he's going to use solar power to beat the ghost and reflects the energy off of his blade, so that it hits the ghost's eyes and renders it temporarily blind. It stumbles back, and Ben snatches the sword from its hand. Milo looks like he's in pain, but the ghost is fighting with the same vigor as all the other ghosts. It obviously doesn't care that he's injured.

I creep around Milo and his ghost to see the face of his enemy, when my eyes catch on Selena's gray ones.

They widen, but she's just as slow as the rest of them. I wonder why everything seems so gradual when I hear something from behind me.

"Surprised?" says a familiar, taunting voice.

I whip around and come face to face with Merrik. "Why are you doing this?"

"I figured I'd give you a chance to study the battle, one that you are very clearly going to lose," he muses, that smile still on his face.

My fists clench. "Why so sure?"

He laughs. "What a good joke, my dear Sage," he says. "Please, take a look around. In what universe would you win this?"

"My friends are all good fighters, and you want a fair fight. You want to brag that you won without any cheats, because your army is so amazing and can't be defeated." I smirk. "So you won't cheat, and you won't use your magic. Those facts will make this whole thing so much easier."

"You act as if you know me," he notes. "It's peculiar, considering you barely know your own friends." I give him a look, and his smile turns sour. "Tell me, Sage, dear, did you ever notice that every single one of you in this line of *warriors* fears someone that they also love?"

I stop smiling instantly. "What did you say?"

"Oh, yes, it's true." Merrik is grinning cruelly now. Before he speaks, he motions from me to himself—or, at least, the image that he's formed. "You see your ex-boyfriend, the one that died tragically in your arms. Milo sees his best friend, that fire girl, dying in agony. Why he would see that when there are plenty of other good gory things to see beats me, but to each their own."

I desperately want to say something, but I don't. The truth is I have no idea how far Merrik is willing to go, but I don't want to test it. So I clench my jaw and steady my gaze.

"The prince sees his sister as a scared seven-year-old, by herself with a black eye," Merrik continues. "Elysian sees her father. Ash sees her mother. And Selena, though I know I shouldn't call her one of your *group* anymore, sees your little boyfriend all grown up without her."

I'm silent for a second. Then, I say, "And what about Ben?"

It's Merrik's turn to stop. "What did you say, girl?"

"What does Ben see?"

"He is not in your group."

"Why not? He's traveled with us this entire time, helped us train, told us about you and all the things you can do—"

I may be imagining it, but I swear Merrik blanches. "He told you about the things I can do?"

"Beats me how he knows anything about that kind of stuff," I say, shrugging though inside I'm grinning like a maniac because *I finally found something that affects him*, "but to each their own."

"Don't twist my words." Merrik actually looks panicked, which surprises me. "This is a topic that concerns nothing of you. Or has the relationship you've made up in your head poisoned the view of what's real more than I guessed?"

I recoil at his harsh words. "What is your *deal*?" I demand, my voice rising. "Why do you hate Ben so much? What do you want from us? Why declare war, why get Selena on your side, why do all that you've done? Just to target us?"

He shakes his head. "You have no idea, do you?" He's snarling at me by this point, baring his teeth like a wild animal. "Your friends, especially the fire girl and the wind girl, hold power that everyone in the heavens above wants their hands on. Do you think Aeolus or Adar planned that their creations would be as powerful as they are now? Do you think they ever *dreamed* it? The wind girl causes tornadoes with her sneeze. The fire girl set her mother aflame without even meaning to. They are more powerful than anything you've ever fantasized about. And everyone wants them, including myself."

"So, what? You're planning on kidnapping them and selling them?"

Merrik laughs mirthlessly. "You really are stupid, aren't you?" he says. I continue to stay silent so that I don't do something I'll regret. "Money does not matter to entities. Blood is more valuable than anything in this world. I kill them, I get their blood, and then I can become just as powerful as them."

"But you're already all-powerful," I say, disgusted with the thought of someone killing my friends just to harvest their blood. "What more could you need?"

"I may be an entity, but I would have ten times the power with the blood of Adar and Aeolus in my veins," he tells me, his gaze maniac. "More powerful, even, than my brother, Sawn. I would be the best, and everyone would have to bow down to *me*. Not to him. He's never deserved the throne of entities, you see, never deserved the attention of millions of mortals, and yet he's gotten it." His voice is bitter as he talks about his brother, and I shake my head in disbelief over this entire war caused because of familial rivalry.

"If he doesn't deserve to be worshiped, then *you* certainly don't."

Merrik holds his hands up and glances around, smiling derangedly. "My followers are here, but I cannot spot his. Do you see them?"

I open my mouth to answer, but something in my mind tells me not to, that Merrik's brother will prove him wrong. All I have to do is believe that he will follow through.

"Now, if we're done here, I suppose I should let you return to the battle," Merrik says softly, though there is nothing calm or kind in his voice. "Oh, and, Sage?" he says. "Try not to die. I would really like to kill you myself."

He snaps his fingers, and the battle resumes. I sprint over to my spot, where another ghost has spawned. I leap into battle, loving the way it makes my joints burn and my bones ache, living off the way it steals the breath from my lungs and inspires a hunger that only fighting can satisfy.

I realize what to do now, upon watching the others fight. I know it will drain me even more, but the anger I have remaining from the talk with Merrik builds up inside of me, telling me that using up my power will be well worth it in the end. So I urge a vine to come up and wrap around the blade of this ghost's sword. The vine yanks the sword down to the ground as it retreats, and I move to pick up the sword so I can be armed in both of my hands, but the sword vanishes as soon as the ghost does. I realize the magic here: these swords are bound to these ghosts, and as soon as they are defeated, one separated from the other, both vanish.

I smile wickedly.

This battle may be more entertaining than I thought.

CHAPTER 31

ELYSIAN

The wound on the side of my face is throbbing, and it hurts. A lot.

But I have to power through this. Otherwise, we lose and all of the suffering and pain and training that we've gone through has been for nothing.

All of it will have been for nothing.

The *thing* that I'm fighting is translucent, and I can't scar it, but I can disarm it. So that's what I did to the last five things—ghosts, I think?—that have approached me. It's actually kind of sad, the way they just disappear into thin air the moment I steal their weapon. But then I remind myself of the reason why I even have to disarm them in the first place, and anger replaces the pity.

After I disarm the sixth ghost, my arm starts to ache, throbbing in unison with the side of my face. There's a cut on my arm, I notice, but I don't have much time to focus on it, because there's another ghost coming at me with its sword raised and I have to fight back.

I take a chance at dying to look at Ash, who's standing next to me. The sun hits her just perfectly, so that her eyes glow with the intensity of war and make her look like some kind of warrior goddess.

She glances at me after I look at her, and our eyes meet. I try for a reassuring expression, but the way the corners of her mouth tilt up in a small, anxious smile lets me know I look like everything but reassuring.

Finally, the ghost falls back. I'm readying myself for another battle when I notice that all the ghosts have vanished or surrendered.

Then I spot Merrik in the middle of them.

Anger and despair and frustration release themselves as I shout. "Come over here and face us yourself, you coward!"

I'm angry and frustrated at Merrik for starting this in the first place, despairing over all of the injuries and the hardships I've been forced to endure. To my surprise, Merrik obliges, walking toward us.

Despite how reckless and brave I acted when I yelled out to him, I have to inch toward Ash in order to feel comfortable. I lace my fingers in hers, and she squeezes my hand like she knows what I'm thinking. Her grip on my hand becomes slick, and I don't know if it's because of sweat or blood or something else, but I don't care.

Merrik continues walking. The sun hits his face, and I tense. I know it's Merrik and not my father, but the resemblance is uncanny. I sense Ash is having the same problem, because she holds onto my hand tighter than before.

"How brave," he says, his eyes cutting into me fiercely. "How utterly *stupid.*"

"Shut up," Ameer calls from the middle of the line we unintentionally formed. "Don't call my sister stupid, you—"

"Hush," Merrik orders, and though he seems to struggle against it, Ameer still closes his mouth. "I hope you all understand that it was not my *intention* to inspire war or fighting."

Ash snorts at his words. "You certainly inspire something."

He sends her a glare so harsh that it makes even *me* recoil. "If you had just done as I asked, by giving me your blood and letting me kill you"—he's talking to me and Ash now, and his lip curls in a snarl as he does—"then we wouldn't be here."

"Why didn't you kill us?" I ask suddenly.

Merrik's eyes travel from Ash to me. "What did you say?"

"You had plenty of opportunities to kill us," I say, not bothering to repeat my question. "We were unguarded in the prairie land. The tavern owner we stayed with wouldn't notice if you crept in and killed us while we slept. You even got close to killing me a couple nights ago, and yet you didn't. Why? Why wait? If you wanted our blood so badly, then why did you not use the opportunities you were given to do it?"

Merrik looks around, chuckling. "You don't understand, do you?" he bites out. "When you are Blessed as newborns, it is the job of the god who Blessed you to protect you while you are in your element. Your friend's boyfriend died because it was nighttime, and he was no longer protected. As for you, wind girl, I could never kill

373

you, because the winter wind was always, even in the kingdom of sunlight, blowing. And for the ritual to work, I had to kill you both together. I would not be able to harness both powers while one was still in use. But tell me, girl, do you notice the wind blowing around you today? Do you feel it in your heart, in your mind?"

I feel my heart drop into my stomach. I haven't used my power at all today—haven't tried to. And I realize that Ash hasn't either. She seems to notice it, too, and tries to summon a ball of fire to her hand. It doesn't work, and she pales.

"What did you do, Merrik?" she demands.

He's grinning widely, evilly, and it makes me want to slap the smile from his face. "Fires can't start if there's no wind to urge them."

My eyes widen. How did I not realize there was something going on earlier? "What do you want?"

"Let me kill you," he says, looking absolutely giddy as he approaches me and Ash. "Let me kill you, let me have your blood. I'll let your friends go, and you'll never have to worry about them."

"No!" Sage says. "Whatever he says, don't listen to him! Nothing is as valuable as you two—"

"Shut up," Merrik snaps, turning ugly. It looks strange to see my father's face twisted in such a way. "Shut up, you *idiot*—"

"What does she mean, nothing is as valuable as us?" I ask cautiously.

"Don't tell me you've never noticed the power you hold," Merrik says, sounding incredulous. "You two are like *gods*. And I want it. I want it all. I'll do anything, just so long as you let me kill you."

I glance at Ash. I don't care if I die, as I knew from the day my father dropped me off in that alley that I was going to die young and prepared for it, but I care if *she* dies. Ash cannot die. If she died, I don't know how I would be able to stand it.

She looks like she's thinking the same about me. She looks back at me, and I see something in her eye that makes me want to fall apart.

It's hopelessness, I realize. She knows that if we don't agree to this, it'll mean war, but if we do, it'll mean we'll lose each other forever. I don't think I've ever seen Ash hopeless.

"No," I say, for the both of us. Merrik looks as if he's caught off guard by my response.

"No?" he echoes. "What do you mean, no? You realize this means all of you will die now, instead of just the two of you?"

"That's only if you win, Merrik," I say, smiling.

Ash's back straightens, and she fixes him with a glare. I notice she's almost taller than him. "Summon Finn," she tells him, her voice hard, and I glance over at her, my eyebrows furrowing.

Merrik notices my surprise, and he grins. "Gladly."

A ghost comes forward, his face twisted in an angry expression that immediately turns to one of surprise when he sees me and Ash.

"Ashlyn," Finn says, and his voice sounds muffled, like he's underwater.

Ash clenches her jaw. "I have nothing to say to you, Finn, other than this," she says, and leans forward so that they are inches apart. "I want you to keep your eyes open for all of this. I want you to watch as your entire world crumbles. I want you to see the look of utter hatred I give you as soon as this is over. And I want you to see your own *body* fall away from you, to see the deepest parts of hell as you fall into them."

She stands up straight as soon as her speech is over, and I notice Finn's eyes are wide, as if he's afraid of her. Of what he'll see as he keeps his eyes open.

Merrik takes a step back. "So we fight," he says, summing up our entire conversation. "We fight, and I get your blood either way."

"Or we win and you are banished, with your army, to burn in hell forever," I say.

"Sounds like pretty good odds," Ash says.

And then we step toward Merrik.

✻ ✻ ✻

He doesn't summon his ghosts. He simply stares at us, a light, cocky grin on his face like he *knows* he's going to win. I throw my dagger, knowing it will come back to me, but Merrik dodges it and catches it, blade first. He throws it back to me, and I manage to duck just in time as it sails toward me.

Sage tries to sneak behind him, but he uses his legs, without even looking at her, to sweep her feet out from under her. She collapses but scrambles back to her feet, keeping considerable distance this time.

I try to use my power to cause a distraction, when I remember bitterly that I can't. But the others can.

"Ben, use your solar power!" I call out, and Ben nods silently. He flexes his hand, and the light from the sun seems like it shines right into Merrik's eyes, because he winces. It must not be strong enough, though, for he regains his composure quickly—too quickly.

It's not working, whispers a voice in my mind.

Another, stronger one, though I'm sure it's not my own, whispers back, *Everything will end up the way it should.*

Ameer tries using his ice, but it's like Merrik anticipates everything we do before we even do it. Finally, we're too tired to continue. Merrik looks victorious as he steps forward, raising his sword so he can slit our throats. I grip Ash's hand like my life depends on it, which it very well may, but then the voice in my mind says, *Now. Now, Elysian Viggo, daughter of Aeolus. Call us now.*

Who are you? I ask the voice in my mind.

Call us, it responds, and I close my eyes and let out a deep breath.

I call on you, I say. *Come to me. Help me.*

There's a whooshing sound in my ears, and everyone else seems to hear it, too, because Merrik looks around frantically as we search for where the sound is coming from.

White figures appear in front of Merrik. There's more than one—it seems like there's hundreds—and I back up, still holding Ash's hand.

You called, daughter of Aeolus, says one of the white figures. Despite the sensation of its voice being in my mind, it's still very clear, and everyone else seems as though they can hear it too.

Merrik looks terrified.

"*You* did this?" Ash asks, craning her neck to see me.

I'm about to tell her that I don't know, when the white figure answers for me.

We respond to Aeolus, our creator, and his descendants, it says. *And we have a particular disliking for the entity that stands before you.*

"And who are you?" I ask again, hoping it answers this time.

"The ghosts of Room 106," Merrik gasps out, and I feel my mouth fall open.

That's right, says the voice. *We are the spirits that have haunted the dungeons of Room 106 since Jackson Ramirez Buit, also a descendant of Aeolus, founded the kingdom. We are the protectors of your friends, the protectors of you, Elysian Viggo. We are the reason you survived in your youth without your parents. We are the reason why you defeated Finn Brocker successfully.*

Memories of the years I spent on the streets, narrowly missing each attempt at my death flash through my mind. I remember wondering how I kept surviving, but I never researched anything past that.

"I—" I cut myself off. "Thank you."

We do not need, nor desire, your thanks. The white figures turn away from me, facing Merrik. *Though we do hope you are quite finished.*

"Arielle, please," Merrik begs. "I know you're in there. I'm sorry. I didn't mean to curse you, I just—"

There are no excuses for the things you have done, Merrik, entity of fear and destruction, the voice says coldly. *Now you will pay in blood.*

And without another word, Merrik's head falls back. He flies into the air and travels miles, airborne, when he finally lands. I can hear his bones crunch from where I stand.

It's silent for a second. His ghost army starts to trail after him, but before they can, a hole opens up in the ground where they stand. They begin to fall, screeching, and Ameer stumbles away from the hole as he's the closest to it.

Now that their master is gone, they must go to where they rightfully belong: the underworld, the voice tells us with finality in its voice. The figure seems to notice my confused expression, because it says, *You shall not worry about the return of the entity. He is well gone by now. It has been his time, and we as a people had been looking for him centuries before you came along. Thank you for leading us to him. And as for the relationship between him and me, I am afraid there are parts of my past that I would like to forget. Now, what other way shall we assist you?*

"Arielle," I say, hoping that's this figure's name. "During all the destruction and panic Merrik caused, our camps, Serenity and Havoc, were damaged drastically. I was hoping, after all that you have done for us, you could find a way to return the camps to the way they were."

The white figure seems to consider it. *Very well. You* did *find Merrik for us, after all,* it says. *We will repair your camps and transport you to them.*

I let out an awed breath of happiness. "Thank you so much," I breathe.

Arielle is quiet for a moment. Finally, it—she?—says, *Your camps are returned to the way they were previously, and it is time for us to return back to the dungeons. Goodbye, Elysian Viggo, daughter of Aeolus. Goodbye, Ashlyn Kave, daughter of Adar.*

This, I believe, is one of the first and only times I've seen Ash stay silent when someone uses her full name. The white figures disappear as soon as they appeared. I glance at Ash, and then suddenly we're back on the grounds of Camp Serenity, campers working, belongings returned. Everything looks the way it did before.

Then everyone, *everything*, stops. They all stare at us. And then they're out the doors of their cabins, hugging and surrounding us and questioning us, telling us stories of their adventure. Max Kheefe comes up to me and hugs me, smiling broadly, and I see Sage hugging Lylah Berkley as Lylah sobs.

I feel a weight being lifted from my shoulders, weight removing itself from my shoulders. I'm with my friends, my family, my campers.

My home.

CHAPTER 32

SAGE

Elysian decided, due to the fact that we aren't dead right now, that we should have a celebratory feast. So the cooks have been at work for hours, preparing all sorts of dishes. I've dressed in fancy-ish clothes that I borrowed from Lylah Berkley, who was so happy to be able to lend me clothes again, and yet I don't feel uncomfortable. I'm at home here, with the people that I love.

Speaking of people that I love, my eye catches Ben's. He's changed into a light blue T-shirt and jeans, and he looks beyond uncomfortable. I smile at his expression.

He jogs over to me. "This place is not like how I imagined it would be."

"You imagined Camp Serenity?" I ask him, raising an eyebrow skeptically.

"Well, only since you held it in such high esteem," Ben tells me. "I almost thought it had to be a figment of your imagination, or a joke that everyone but me was in on."

"I would never do that to you."

"How dare you lie."

I laugh. Ben eyes my forehead nervously. It's been a few days since we got back to Camp Serenity, and Healers have already cleaned up and mended the cut on my forehead, but every now and then, he looks at it like it's going to burst open.

Actually, he's been on edge since we got here. I assumed it was just first-day jitters, but now I'm starting to get nervous. "Hey, Ben, can we talk?"

He pales slightly at my words, but follows me into the woods. As soon as we find a closed-off spot, I turn to him and ask him, "Are you all right?"

He looks at me like *I'm* the one who's going crazy. "What do you mean?"

"You've been on edge for days, Ben, staring at me like I'm a monster—" I cut myself off. Talking about the way he looks at me, the way it breaks my heart, is not something that's very easy. "I just want to know if you're okay."

"I'm okay." He gulps. "I'm okay."

"Are you sure?"

I lean forward and kiss him. I pull away instantly, though. He tastes like metal and blood, even though I know he's taken showers twice a day, every day since we got here.

"Ben, what is that?" I grimace, wiping my lips off with the back of my hand.

I look up and I'm met with a devilish grin.

"Really, Sage?" he asks, and his voice sounds deeper somehow. "You didn't notice it earlier?"

I straighten. *What* is the matter with him? "What do you mean?"

"You never wondered how I brought back food after being gone for a day when there was no civilization in sight?" he says, his eyebrows raising in surprise. My heart sinks as I register his words. "You never thought about the fact that Ash wasn't able to use her power after she ate it? And the panic that I had on my face whenever I thought you discovered me back in Ruri? The way that I contradicted myself and told you that there was no way you could beat fear and yet still trained you anyway? The way Merrik somehow knew where we were at all times?"

He looks incredulous, like he doesn't understand me.

"The entire time, I was giving your information away. When Ameer discovered he could waterbend, when Milo got hurt, when Elysian caused a storm because she was upset. I've been watching you, all of you. *Especially* you."

"Traitor," I breathe. "You betrayed us to Merrik."

He chuckles. "I can't believe it took you this long. I thought you were smarter than that."

It stings. My entire life, my smarts have been my most valuable asset. If I had nothing else, I had my intelligence. I was certain of it.

Now, I'm not so sure.

"All of it was an act?" I say, hearing how fragile I sound to myself. I notice, though, that it's hard to hear myself over the sudden ringing in my ears. "Was any of it real?"

I remember the way he touched me like I was going to break, the way he let me borrow his shirts, the way he cradled me close while I sobbed.

His face twitches, and in the desperation in his eyes, I see *Ben*: the Ben who kissed me on top of that mountain; the Ben who sobbed because of a nightmare and thanked me when I comforted him; the Ben who loved me just as much as I love him. But then a mask covers that Ben, and in his place is this new Ben, this traitorous Ben. "None of it," he says coldly, and I exhale in disbelief.

"Leave," I say. "Get out of here, and never come back."

He flashes a grin at me—a grin that looks a little too much like Merrik's—and then he spins on his heel, leaving me in the middle of the woods alone.

And then I start to cry.

I don't know how long I cry for. I feel arms around me at one point, and I assume it's Lylah's, but I recognize the smell of strawberries that Elysian carries with her everywhere. Someone carries me to my cabin, and I'm vaguely aware that I ruined Lylah's dress, but I don't care enough.

I cry myself to sleep that night.

And I dream of Ben.

EPILOGUE

AMEER

The day of my crowning ceremony approaches faster than I expect it to. I wait impatiently for November twenty-third, when I am crowned in front of the entire kingdom. When I officially become King of Buit.

During the days that *aren't* November twenty-third, I play cards with a few campers and hang out with Elysian. I steal food from the kitchen and play truth or dare with more campers. I make friends and am known as Ameer and not 'Elysian's weird brother' or 'the strange prince'—not that anyone really talked about my royalty weeks ago before I shut them down.

But finally, the days get shorter and shorter, and it's November twenty-third and I'm standing in front of my wardrobe in the new cabin that they built just for me in a *suit*.

There's a knock at my door. I crack it open and see Elysian. Before I can protest against her coming in, she pushes the door open and her eyes widen at the sight of me in a suit.

"Gods, Ameer, you look amazing," she tells me. "I can't believe that I'll be the sister of a king *and* a hottie."

"Okay, please don't ever use that word again," I say, grimacing.

She shrugs. "I've already got my dress picked out," she says. "It's light blue, like the one I wore to the ball."

I smile faintly, immensely glad that Elysian Viggo is my sister. "You'll look great."

She sits on the edge of my bed. Her hair is done up in an intricate bun-braid type thing that I can't make sense of. "Look, I get that you're nervous, but everything will be fine. Remember Mr. Gloomy?" she says, referring to the butler we had when we were kids that looked after us, always with a frown on his face.

"I don't think that was his actual name."

"It doesn't matter," she snaps. "Pretend with me, will you? Mr. Gloomy is going to walk you down the aisle—or whatever you call it—and he's going to announce you. You're going to have a crown, and then you bring all your royal things here so you can do your work."

I send her a sad look. "That's one of the things I wanted to talk to you about. I don't think I'll be able to live here anymore after my crowning ceremony."

She gives me a hurt glance. "Of course you'll be able to live here," she says. "I'm the princess, and I say you're allowed to. Plus, if they want someone to live in the castle, we'll put a few campers in there. The gods know we're crowded enough as it is. That extra space may help us immeasurably."

"We'll see," I say.

"Yes, we will," Elysian says cheerfully. She stands from my bed.
"I'm going to get dressed. Oh, and, Ameer?"

"Yeah?" I turn around, so my back is to the mirror.

"Be proud. You're going to be the king, for the gods' sakes," she
tells me, and then she exits my cabin, slamming the door shut behind
her.

* * *

"I think I completely forgot what this place looks like," I say.

I can almost hear Milo shrug from behind me. "Well, no one can
blame you. You *were* in a dungeon for a year."

I gulp.

One of the guards who took us here steps out from the carriage.
He pushes the castle door open, and my mouth almost falls open.

The castle is almost completely black—floors, walls, accents,
furniture. The only illumination in the dark rooms are torches
hanging on the walls, and, naturally, a chandelier or two in each
room.

The guard steps inside and begins to lead us down a long,
twisting corridor. I glance around at the black brick, trying to see
mostly if I can catch one of my friends' reactions from the corner of
my eye, but no such luck.

Eventually, we reach a glass door with sunlight streaming in
through it. My eyes have to adjust to the sudden brightness, but

when they do, I see the massive crowd of people, all here for the ceremony, and my mouth dries.

Elysian walks up to me and stops. Her shoulder reaches the point just above my elbow bend, and she reaches for my hand and squeezes it reassuringly.

"I will be right next to you," she whispers to me. "If you get nervous, think about that. But you'll be fine. I promise. I swear it."

"*Swear* is a strong word, don't you think?"

Ash comes up on my other side. She's wearing jeans and a blood red long-sleeved T-shirt, which is very similar to what she wore on our quest. She still looks great, regardless of how fancy her outfit is.

"You'll be fine," she tells me. "Those people are just going to be looking at the crown. They're all greedy."

"How reassuring," I say, removing my hand from Elysian's grasp and wiping both of them on my dress pants.

"It's better than being on a death quest with no reinforcements," Elysian says.

"What happened to our reinforcements, anyway?"

"Merrik stopped them in Ruri. Apparently, a boy named Adam convinced them to turn around."

I swallow. "You don't say."

"My point is, this will all be over before you know it."

"I hope you're right."

*　*　*

Mr. Gloomy comes to collect me about an hour later. He looks exactly the same way I remember him—gray hair, bald spot in the middle of his scalp, traditional black and white suit every single day. He barely acknowledges me as he leads me and Elysian out onto the balcony.

Elysian squeezes my hand one last time before the glass doors open and I step out, trying to hide my shaking hands. I attempt to hold my chin as high as I can, looking regal and royal and hopefully not like something laughable. Everyone claps and cheers as I exit, and I feel a smile beginning to grace my lips, despite the way that my stomach dips at the amount of people in the crowd.

I stand inches away from the railing, but I don't notice it. By the time the cheers calm down, the pastor in front of me is already telling me to repeat after him, his voice incredibly loud in this tight space.

"'I swear to protect my kingdom in the best ways possible: with courage, love, compassion, hard work, and loyalty,'" the pastor says, and my eyes travel to Elysian before I repeat after him.

"I swear to protect my kingdom in the best ways possible: with courage, love, compassion, hard work, and loyalty," I echo.

"'I swear to remain dutiful and listen to my citizens, even in times of hardship and famine, war and battle.'"

"I swear to remain dutiful and listen to my citizens, even in times of hardship and famine, war and battle."

"'And I swear that I will do everything in my power to be the best leader to my subjects, no matter what challenges I face.'"

"And I swear that I will do everything in my power to be the best king to my subjects, no matter what challenges I face."

"Then I pronounce you King of Buit," the pastor says. "Kneel, and accept your crown with the pride of your kingdom."

There are a few shouts from the crowd, but it's nothing that isn't silenced immediately. I kneel before the pastor. He places the crown of Buit, inscribed with ravens and gold accents, on top of my head.

"Rise, King Ameer Domhnall, our new leader," the pastor says, and I rise.

The crowd erupts into cheers. Elysian's grip on my hand tightens as we leave the balcony.

"I did it," I say, lingering butterflies fluttering in my stomach.

"You did it," Elysian agrees, beaming at me.

There's a pause as we relish in my victory.

"Now," Elysian says finally, holding up my arm, "let's go raise a toast to Ameer Domhnall, the new King of Buit."

I sling my arm around her shoulder and we walk down the hall like that—together, as one, the way we've been since the start of our lives.

The way it will be until the end of them.

392

ABOUT THE AUTHOR

E.G. Keith is a young author that is thrilled to have successfully launched her first book, Havoc, and was determined to continue The Magics trilogy with Serenity. She is very into Greek mythology and spends a lot of her time looking for books on the old stories, and she is convinced that her story, no matter how unique, has already been told by an old Greek writer. She strives for perfection in everything she does, and the several annotations in the first draft of this novel can prove that. E.G. is an adamant reader, and you can find her mostly wherever books are read or sold.

Follow her at egkeith.com for all of her next steps,

including the completion of this trilogy... coming soon...

ACKNOWLEDGEMENTS

It is simply unbelievable that I have made it this far, but there is no way I could have done it without the help of so many amazing people.

Thank you to my family for always supporting my ambitions, even if, at the time, they seem absolutely ridiculous. You are one of the reasons why I even have an acknowledgements page (and an excuse to sign things) and for that I thank you sincerely.

Thank you to Damon Freeman for your beautiful work on the cover of this book and Havoc. I have enjoyed working with you as you use your amazing talent to bring my ideas to life.

To my writing coach, John Jamison, for your excellent tips on how to improve my writing and introducing me to the world of independently published authors.

To my beta readers: Alyssa Bishop, Clayten Manley, Gracelyn Keith, and Max Miller. You suggested new story lines and plots, found things I was blind to, and encouraged me to keep writing. Thank you.

To my close friends and other supporters for your enthusiasm for my books and writing career.

To *anyone* else who has supported me and my family through this journey that I am simply overwhelmed and have neglected to mention, please know I am so grateful for all the love, support, and pride felt by others. I could not have done this without that.

To *my readers*, I hope this book makes you *feel* something and possibly something different from my first book. I hope we meet again.

PRAISE FOR **HAVOC** *AND* **E.G. KEITH**

I really have never found one (fantasy novel) written so well

by someone so young. I'm really kind of amazed.

ACCOMPLISHED WRITER JOHN B. JAMISON

A well-crafted and irresistible page-turner throughout,

it's an impressive contribution to the genre,

which I'm sure will be well received.

BOOK CRITIC/EDITOR LOUISE CROSS

Havoc was a phenomenal read.

I loved it so very much.

It's the perfect mix of romance and action. E.G. has a gift.

BETA READER ALYSSA BISHOP